DIRTY SECRETS

A brilliantly gripping crime mystery

JANICE FROST

JOFFE BOOKS

Published 2018 by Joffe Books, London.

www.joffebooks.com

This book is a work of fiction. Names, characters, businesses, organizations, places and events are either the product of the author's imagination or are used fictitiously. Any resemblance to actual persons, living or dead, events or locales is entirely coincidental. The spelling is British English.

ISBN-13: 978-1-78931-023-8

Prologue

At last, the spires of Stromford Cathedral appeared on the distant horizon. Valerie Marsh had seldom been so glad to see them. She'd left her daughter's house in Cambridge at five in the morning, hoping to beat the morning rush hour, but an overturned lorry on the A14 near Huntingdon had led to a delay of several hours, along with a thumping headache.

At least she'd left Ruth and Fin in better spirits than she'd found them a week ago. Her daughter, Ruth, and her partner, Fin O'Shea, had come down with a flu-like virus and were struggling to cope with their eighteen-month-old baby, Cam. Val hadn't had the heart to refuse to go down, even though relations between her and Ruth had been a bit strained of late because of Ruth's quarrel with her father.

A week of caring for her daughter and her family had left Val feeling exhausted. Things had been much worse than Ruth had led her to expect. As soon as she arrived, Val took one look at the pale, strained faces of her daughter and Fin and ordered them off to bed. They were happy to comply.

It was the first time Val had set foot in the terraced house that Ruth and Fin were renting, and she wasn't impressed. Two-up, two-down was an exaggeration. The two-down had been knocked into one to create a single kitchen and living area, but the open-plan effect failed miserably. Ruth had described it as 'cosy.' It was merely cramped.

Val suspected that Ruth's washed-out appearance wasn't wholly attributable to the virus. Was her daughter suffering from post-natal depression? She didn't like to ask. Lizzie hadn't mentioned it, and Ruth would have confided in her aunt. Val felt a twinge of jealousy.

Now her daughter was on the mend, Val began to worry about Russ, her husband. He hadn't been in touch for a couple of days, even though she'd left several messages on his mobile. She'd even called the landline and left a message on the answerphone. Not that Russ would see. She was the only one who ever checked. And when he was very busy, Russ had been known to shut himself away for days. Still, it was unusual, being out of touch for so long.

Russ had seemed anxious and preoccupied before her departure for Cambridge. After much probing, he admitted that there was some problem with the business, and had finally agreed to sit down and talk it over with her when she returned.

No doubt he'd be apologetic about forgetting to phone, and claim he hadn't noticed the time passing. She'd find him in his study with two or three days' growth on his face, most likely dressed in his lounge pants and that awful old T-shirt, the Star Wars one with Obe Wan Kenobe brandishing a sabre. The thought made her smile.

Val was right about one thing. She did find Russ in his study. Slumped over his writing desk, with a bullet through his head.

Chapter One

"Sir?"

Inspector Jim Neal had his hand on the door of the men's washroom. He stopped, annoyed, and glared at DC Polly Jenkins. *Can't this wait?* his look said, but PJ, as she was known, was on a mission.

"I've just taken a call from the desk. There's a report coming in about a possible shooting incident at Stainham."

Neal froze, and PJ was quick to reassure him that there wasn't a sniper or a lone gunman roaming the streets of one of Stromfordshire's prettiest villages.

"Single victim. White male. At his home. There's a patrol car on its way over. Probably a suicide. Just thought you'd like to know." Neal gave a perfunctory nod. He pressed on the door handle. "Would you like me to . . . ?"

Neal grunted, and pointed at the door. PJ made apologetic noises and scurried away.

A few minutes later, he walked back into the office that PJ shared with DS Ava Merry, and now also DS Tom Knight. Tom had joined Neal's team after the departure of his own DI in 'unfortunate' circumstances.

"Any news?" Neal asked.

Ava put down the phone and gave him a nod. "Uniform are there now. The victim's name is Russell Marsh. His wife discovered him about an hour ago in his study, shot in the head. She'd been staying at their daughter's in Cambridge and drove back early this morning. Apparently it looks messy."

"Right. Ava, you and I will head on over there now." He turned to the others. "Tom, PJ, inform forensics and find out if Ashley's available." Ashley Hunt was Neal's pathologist of choice. "Then see what you can find out about the victim. Desk will have the contact details."

Neal left them to get organised while he collected his things from his office. He'd driven to work in a cheerful mood. His sister, Maggie, had recently become engaged to his lifelong friend, Jock Dodds. This would bring about changes in his domestic life, because Maggie lived with Neal and his eleven-year-old son, Archie, and helped look after the boy. But Neal was delighted — for them, and for himself. Jock, who lived in Edinburgh, had hinted that he might relocate to Stromford.

The prospect of a 'messy' shooting brought things back into perspective. Neal joined Ava in the kitchen, where she was screwing down the lid on a plastic travel mug. He smelled coffee.

"Want one?" Ava asked.

Neal shook his head. "I'll drive. You drink."

Outside, it was a bright, clear morning. Autumn loomed. The leaves on the sprawling beech outside the station were tinged with orange and yellow. Soon it would be shorter days and trick or treating and fireworks, and then Christmas. Was it just him or did time seem to be passing at an alarming rate? He could hardly believe he'd been working with Ava Merry for over a year.

They made good time. Neal looked in his rear-view mirror and marvelled, as he always did, at how quickly town ceded to countryside in this part of the world. Now they were driving along quiet lanes lined with hedgerows.

"This is it," Ava said. Neal saw the sign for Stainham on the left, but Ava was pointing right. He looked both ways, seeing nothing.

"Indicate right now," Ava said, gesticulating. And then he saw it, an opening in the hedge, and the gravelly outline of a private road. "It's set within the walled grounds of an old hall that was knocked down years ago," Ava explained. She was looking the property up on her phone. She gave a low whistle. "According to Zoopla, it sold for five hundred grand."

That was a lot for Stromfordshire, where house prices tended to be well below the national average.

Neal turned in and followed the road for about a quarter of a mile, swerving repeatedly to avoid the potholes. Clearly there hadn't been any money left over to spend on road maintenance. The rooftops of the house rose into view over a high red-brick wall that was obviously much older than the house.

"It's an executive dwelling," Ava read off her phone. "Modern build. 'Stunning reception hall with sweeping oak staircase, five bedrooms, landscaped gardens.'" Finally they left the potholes and turned into a circular drive. "The victim's wife's name is Valerie Marsh." She shrugged. "I guess grief is grief, however much money you've got."

There was no arguing with that.

A patrol officer was standing in the arched porch over the front door. He showed Neal and Ava into a reception hall. The impressive oak staircase lay ahead.

A second uniformed officer met them in the hall. "Mrs Marsh is in here, sir. She's in a bit of a state, as you'd expect. Nice woman, as it happens."

Neal caught the subtext. Mrs Marsh lived in a big house, and that conjured up a certain image, one of arrogance born of right and privilege. It was often hard to believe that someone in that position could also be a kind or good person.

The officer showed them into a sitting room painted in calm sage. More polished wooden flooring, and tasteful furnishings. Dual-aspect windows and glazed doors guaranteed not just ample light, but also views of the landscaped garden alluded to in the estate agent's blurb. It featured a marble statue of a naked Greek goddess, water cascading over her from an urn held high on her shoulder.

Valerie Marsh sat, hunched on a sofa, looking as white as the goddess, wrapped in a velvety purple throw. She was shivering, despite the throw and the warm room. Shock.

"Mrs Marsh?" Neal said gently. "My name is Jim Neal. I'm a detective inspector, and this is Detective Sergeant Ava Merry. Firstly, I'm very sorry for your loss."

Val Marsh looked nervously at the door. Maybe she was seeing afresh her husband, dead at his desk. What must it be like to come home to a scene like that? Neal understood all too well. Not long ago, he had held his seriously wounded sister in his arms. Maggie had survived, but even now the memory of that near-tragedy haunted his dreams. It had changed him, he realised. Empathy is easier to access when it arises from personal experience.

Val Marsh picked at the fringed border of the throw. "Russ didn't kill himself." Her voice was steady, despite her distress.

"That's what Sergeant Merry and I are here to investigate," Neal said. "No one will make assumptions."

"Well, I can tell you now. Russ wasn't depressed. He's not the sort of person to run away from his problems. He wouldn't do that to Ruth and me." She waved, dismissively. "Go ahead. Look all you like, Inspector, but don't come back and tell me Russ did this to himself." Val Marsh was putting up a strong front.

Neal gave a nod. "Please excuse us."

Val pulled the purple velvet throw around her in a gesture that seemed at once regal and defiant. But it was neither. Beneath the velvet, her body was still shaking.

Leaving her with the uniformed officer, Neal and Ava crossed the hall to the crime scene. Neal braced himself. Beside him, Ava seemed composed, but he knew that she too was psyching herself up for what awaited them behind that door.

"It's a bit gruesome, this one," the first PC informed them unhelpfully. He pushed open the door.

Russell Marsh, slumped across his desk with his back to them, looked like he was sneaking a quick nap. His desk faced out toward the garden, and a beautiful cedar of Lebanon tree that must once have graced the old hall.

From where Neal was standing, it looked as though Marsh was wearing pyjama trousers and one of those old-fashioned quilted dressing gowns, drawn in at the waist with a cord. The tassel dangled at the side of the chair, stirring slightly in the draught from the open door.

Any illusion that he was merely sleeping was dispelled as soon as they neared the desk and took a closer look. Now they saw the blood, spilled out in front of him. And a substance that looked like tapioca. Brain matter. Neal thought of the porridge he'd had for breakfast and his stomach heaved. He swallowed.

"Where's the gun?" Ava asked, briskly. The PC pointed to Marsh's lap, where a sliver of something silver nestled in the folds of the dressing gown. Neal walked around the dead man, and bent over to get a better look. It was difficult to make any judgements without moving or touching him. They'd have to wait for forensics. And for Ashley Hunt, the pathologist.

"What do you think, sir?" Ava asked. Neal was conscious of the PC, waiting, no doubt, to hear his senior officer's assessment of the situation.

"Impossible to say. Could be suicide. I can't tell if there's any residue on his fingers."

"His missus will take some convincing that it's suicide," the PC remarked. Neal hoped he hadn't offered her any opinions. Speculation about cause of death wasn't something the deceased's loved ones needed to hear. They needed facts and certainties, not the ramblings of amateurs. Neal counted himself in that category. Ashley Hunt and the forensics team were the only ones who could offer certainties here.

"That's an old World War Two revolver," the PC commented. "My grandad had one just like it, God rest his soul." Neal wondered who had inherited the weapon upon the old man's demise.

Neal and Ava returned to the sitting room. Someone had placed a tray of mugs on the coffee table. The PC was standing looking out at the view, and Val Marsh was sitting where they had left her, still wrapped in her throw.

She must have seen Neal's eyebrow rise at the sight of the tea tray for she said, "My sister's here. PC Solway here was kind enough to call her when he arrived. Lizzie's good in a crisis. She makes tea." At the mention of her name, a woman bearing a strong resemblance to Val appeared in the doorway, holding another tray. On it was a large tea infuser and a cafetière, a milk jug and sugar bowl and a plate of biscuits.

Lizzie smiled at the assembled group. "Someone has to." PC Solway stepped forward to take the tray but she shook her head.

"Actually, it helps to be busy at times like this," she said. Her smile became replaced by a worried frown at her sister. "You sure you don't want me to call your GP, Val? You look terribly pale."

Val dismissed the suggestion with a wave of her hand. Lizzie pulled a small bottle of brandy from her pocket. "Will you at least have a drop of this in your tea?" A nod. "It was in the kitchen, by the way. I'm not in the habit of carrying alcohol around in my pocket."

Lizzie took everyone's orders, including PC Burns who was still on guard duty in the hall. While she busied herself distributing the drinks, Ava passed the biscuits round. Neal knew that she was studying the sisters every bit as attentively as he was.

They were close in age, perhaps as little as a couple of years apart. Lizzie looked to be the older of the two, but not by much. She was probably around fifty, Val a year or two younger, but any similarity ended there.

Val was elegant, well-groomed. Underneath the throw, she was wearing tailored trousers and a crisp, white shirt. Neal understood that she'd driven from Cambridge at first light, but she was remarkably unrumpled.

Lizzie's fashion sense was a world away from her sister's. She was wearing the sort of billowy trousers Neal's sister, Maggie, favoured — harem pants, she called them. As Lizzie moved about the room, the black-and-white zigzagging pattern caused Neal to blink. Her top was cherry red, in some sort of crinkly material — or maybe she just hadn't bothered to iron it. Neal wondered if the sisters' personalities were as far apart as their appearances. At a guess, he'd say Lizzie was the outgoing one, but Val's tasteful, understated look communicated poise and quiet confidence.

How to begin, when suicide was a possibility and murder not yet ruled out? Few relatives of suicides saw it coming, more so when the victim was male. Men are more likely to conceal their state of mind from their loved ones.

Neal wondered whether Val's sister would agree that suicide was unlikely. He was keen to talk to Lizzie out of Val's earshot.

"Mrs Marsh. You've told us how unlikely you think it is that your husband would take his own life . . ."

"That's right, Inspector," Val said. Lizzie had come to rest on the sofa beside her sister, and now placed a hand on her shoulder. "Russ believed in confronting his demons. He wasn't a quitter."

"Did your husband have demons?" Ava asked.

Val took the question head on. "We all have demons, Sergeant."

"Do we?" Ava asked.

"Are you always so literal, Sergeant Merry? I was just stressing the point that it wasn't Russ's way to run away from his problems."

"Problems, then. Did your husband have problems?" Ava said.

Lizzie's grip on her shoulder visibly tightened.

Val gave a thin-lipped smile, shrugged off the throw and covered her sister's hand with her own. The gesture seemed to reverse their roles of comforter and comforted. "Russ was a successful businessman. He had plenty of problems." She sighed. "But, yes. The whole week before I left he'd been brooding, and he finally admitted to me that it was something to do with the business. We'd arranged to sit down and talk it over, and then Ruth called me asking for help, so we had to put our talk on hold."

Permanently, as it turned out, Neal thought.

"I . . . He was definitely distracted, I'll say that much. And I know he'd been spending a lot of time looking over the accounts. I'm sorry I can't provide you with more information. I'm afraid I didn't take much interest in the business."

"What exactly was your husband's business, Mrs Marsh?" Neal asked.

"Russ and his business partner, Paul Cornish, are financial advisers. They're also investors. They give money to young entrepreneurs and struggling businesses. They invest in them and turn them around, make them profitable."

So-called 'angel investors.' The investors became shareholders in the businesses they supported. Val made it sound as if they were doing the small business owners a favour, but you only had to take a look around the house to see who was making the profit. Instinctively, Neal's thoughts turned to money as a motive for murder.

"Were your husband and his business partner on good terms?"

"On the whole," Val said.

"Meaning?"

Val sighed. "They've had their differences. But Russ and Paul go back a long way. They met at university and then they both worked in the City. They're friends as well as business partners. We often used to socialise with Paul and his wife, Gail."

Used to. Did that mean the socialising stopped before Russ's death, or that Val didn't see it continuing afterwards? Neal let it go for now.

From somewhere on Val's person came the sound of Led Zeppelin's 'Whole Lotta Love.' Neal was a fan. The sisters exchanged worried looks.

"Ruthie," Lizzie said.

"Ruth," Val added.

"Do you want me to tell her?" Lizzie said.

"Of course not. *I'm* her mother, for God's sake." There was a hint of acrimony in Val's tone. Neal heard the slight emphasis on the word 'I'm.' He exchanged a glance with Ava. She hadn't missed it. Val shrugged off the throw and stood up. "Excuse me," she said. "I'd like some privacy to speak with my daughter."

"Of course," Neal said. Ava stood up immediately. Lizzie sat where she was. Val glared at her. There was an awkward moment, and then Lizzie led Neal and Ava from the room. In the hall, her eyes darted to the door of the study, then quickly away.

"We can wait in the other reception room," she said, and led them to the other side of the sweeping staircase. She opened a door leading to another large, tastefully furnished room with more views of the landscaped garden. The spires of Stromford Cathedral were just visible in the far distance.

"Are you okay?" Neal asked. All at once, Lizzie seemed at a loss.

"I . . . It's Ruthie. She's had enough upset recently, and now this."

"Ruth is Val's daughter? The one she was visiting in Cambridge?" A nod. "What kind of upset?"

"She and her partner, Fin, have been unwell. Val went down to look after them and their son, Cam. Cam's eighteen months old."

Neal suspected that the word 'upset' meant more than a bout of illness. He was right.

"Ruth's going to take it badly. She adores her father. Despite . . ."

"Despite what?" Neal felt no guilt at being intrusive. Family stresses often lay at the heart of a murder enquiry — and its resolution.

"Oh dear. I suppose it'll come out anyway, I just wish I hadn't been the first to mention it." A sigh. "Ruth and her father haven't spoken since before Cam was born. Russ never saw his grandson."

"Go on."

"Russ didn't approve of Fin, Ruth's partner. He had him checked out by a private investigator, who found out that Fin had served some sort of sentence when he was a teenager. It was something to do with drugs."

The word *drugs* was uttered in a hushed tone. "Russ was overprotective. He wanted Ruth to leave Fin and move back home, especially when he found out she was pregnant. But Ruth was just as stubborn as him. She was furious when she found out her father had had Fin investigated. She refused to take another penny from Russ, and moved out of the flat he'd rented for her while she was at Cambridge."

This Fin would certainly need to be checked out. Still, it was the money and the business angles that interested Neal more at this point.

"Are you and your husband involved in your brother-in-law's business in any way, Ms . . . er?"

"Hamilton. My husband's name is Stephen. And to answer your question, no. Stephen's an electrical contractor. I'm a yoga instructor."

"What about Ruth Marsh? Is she involved in the business?"

"No. It's really not a family business."

"Your niece went to Cambridge?" Neal asked.

"Yes. Ruthie got her father's brains."

Neal tried not to think of his recent sighting of Russ Marsh's brains.

"But apart from the brains, Ruthie's like me. We're very close. It's me she comes to when she's got a problem. Val hates that Ruthie and I are so alike."

Neal remained silent. Interesting family dynamics.

"Do you have children, Mrs Hamilton?" Ava said. A shadow passed over Lizzie's face.

"I had a son. Will. He died in a fire when he was fourteen."

"I'm so sorry," Ava said. Neal nodded, thinking, inevitably, of Archie. How do you cope with losing a child? How do you come back from that?

"You and Mr Hamilton must have been devastated," Ava said.

"Will wasn't Stephen's. I was married before. My first husband, Craig, never got over our son's death. He took his own life six months later."

Neal and Ava exchanged glances. This woman had been dealt more than her share of tragedy. And now fate had dealt her sister a blow too.

PC Solway gave a polite cough. "Mrs Marsh has finished on the phone." They followed him back to the first reception room.

"How is Ruthie? How did she take the news?" Lizzie asked anxiously. Val, hunched on the sofa, throw around her shoulders, seemed to have aged in their absence. The flash of steeliness she'd shown earlier seemed imaginary now.

"Badly," she said, dully. "She wants to come here straight away, with Cam. I told her to wait until . . . until the police were finished and Russ's body's been . . . taken away." Val glanced nervously at her watch. "You know what Ruth's like. She's packing right now, and she could be here in three or four hours. I . . . I don't want her seeing her father like that."

"She shouldn't get in a car and drive when she's upset. Not with Cam." Neal nodded. Lizzie was right. No one should drive after a shock like that.

"Forensics are here," PC Solway said.

Neal turned to Lizzie Hamilton. "Would it be possible for your sister and your niece to stay with you for a couple of days?"

"Of course." She turned to her sister. "Val?"

"You'll love that, won't you, Lizzie? Having Ruth under your wing." A bitter sigh. "Oh, go on then. Ring her and tell her to go to your place. Tell her the police have forbidden her to come here. I'm not going anywhere, though."

"Mrs Marsh. It's not a good idea for you to stay here tonight," Ava said. She didn't add that if Russell Marsh hadn't taken his own life, the house would become a murder scene and would need to be processed as such.

Val relented. "Oh, alright. But I'm not leaving until you people accept that my husband was murdered."

They did. Within one hour of the arrival of the forensics team and Dr Ashley Hunt.

Chapter Two

Ruth Marsh's mobile phone clattered onto the tiles of her kitchen floor. Immediately, a tiny hand shot out and picked it up. Tears in her eyes, Ruth prised her phone out of Cam's chubby fist before he could damage it the way he had damaged so many of her things. The resulting screams of protest brought tears of another kind to Ruth's eyes. Why was he always so difficult?

Ruth felt a pang of guilt. Motherhood wasn't coming easily to her. She had done everything by the book, but whereas other people's babies seemed to sleep and gurgle and smile and steal their mother's hearts, Cam cried all night, vomited up her milk, and screamed and wriggled when she tried to comfort him. Bonding had become a game of nerves. She was convinced at one point that there'd been a mix-up at the hospital, and she'd brought home the wrong child.

And now this. Her father. Dead. And she hadn't spoken a word to him in over a year. Had he died thinking she hated him?

Loudly, Ruth hummed a tune trying to block out the image that had begun forming in her head. Her father, face down on his desk. Did a person have a face after they'd been shot in the head? "La la la . . ." At least the humming shut Cam up for a moment. He stared at her, wide-eyed.

Fragments of skull and brain matter and . . . "La la la."

Cam was imitating the sound, grinning all over his dirty, tear-stained face. Ruth gathered him up in her arms and hugged him to her. For once, he offered no resistance.

Aunt Lizzie. Why couldn't Val have let Aunt Lizzie break the news to her? Auntie Lizzie would have known the right words. She wouldn't have just blurted out, "Your father's dead. Someone shot him." Actually, Val had been quite tactful. "I'm sorry, Ruth. I have some bad news . . ."

"La la la." Cam had taken over the tuneless tune.

"My daddy's dead," she told him. "Not your daddy, Cam. Mummy's daddy. Grandpa Marsh." Cam gave her a quizzical look. He had never met his grandfather. Now he never would, Ruth realised, tearing up.

Ruth had been furious when she learned that her father had hired a PI to check Fin out. He had confronted her with the PI's report on one of her trips home. Fin, thankfully, hadn't accompanied her. Her father really believed that she would walk out on Fin, just like that. He refused to listen when she tried to tell him that Fin wasn't that person any more. But worst of all had been her father's cold insistence that she get rid of the baby.

"You arrogant, controlling bastard!" she shouted at him, and slammed the door of his study. She left the family home, never to return. The words he'd called after her still echoed in Ruth's head.

He opened the door to his study and stood in the hall. "He's no good, Ruth, dammit. He has a past. People don't change."

"I have a past too. Or had you forgotten our little secret, Dad?"

That had shut him up.

If she had known her father would be dead before Cam's second birthday, would she have done things differently? Would he? Would they have reconciled? How could he be dead?

Suicide.

If it were suicide, was it her fault? And if it wasn't? Had the last minutes of his life been filled with despair and regret, or had they been lived in terror? Had he thought of her at all? Or of the grandson he'd never seen? Had he thought of their secret? Worse, had he somehow died because of it?

So many questions. Ruth's head buzzed with anxiety and grief. Where were her pills? She was suffering from post-natal depression, as almost everyone who knew her said she would. Ruth's mental state was fragile at the best of times. She'd lurched along for years now, only half functioning, a tiny boat tossed about in a hostile sea. Ever since . . . "La la la."

"La la la," Cam echoed. His voice sounded glorious and funny and grating and Ruth wanted to both hug and scream at him.

She needed to pull herself together before Fin got home. He'd never let her drive if he saw her in this state. She'd called him after her mother rang with the news, and he'd said he was coming straight home. She'd go upstairs and pack now. Doing something practical would focus her thoughts.

Halfway up the stairs, she broke down. She was going home. Cam stared at her in confusion, and she smiled at him through her tears. Her father was dead, but she was going home. To Stromford. To the house she grew up in and where she felt safe. But her father had died a violent death within its walls. Would it now be the sanctuary it had been in the past? Still, she was going home.

Somehow Ruth managed to drag herself up the last few steps and stumble into her bedroom. There, she let go of Cam and began pulling clothes out of the drawers. Cam got hold of a hairbrush and began banging it against the wardrobe, yelling, "La la la!" at the top of his voice.

* * *

Ava and Neal were waiting for DS Tom Knight and DC Polly Jenkins to arrive for the morning briefing. Not having seen Maggie since her engagement meal some weeks ago, Ava risked a question.

"How are the lovebirds?"

"Never better. It's grand to see the people I care about so happy."

Ava was slightly taken aback. She wasn't used to her boss displaying so much enthusiasm. Was he beginning to let his guard down?

At the family meal, Ava had been embarrassed whenever Neal's friend or sister teased him, addressed him as 'Jimmy,' or told some anecdote that showed a different side to him than the stern image he'd always presented.

Neal had been easier-going too, laughing and chatting with his family. He'd made a big effort to include Ava, particularly when he and the others reminisced about their lives back in Scotland.

"Let me just explain that one to Ava," he'd said. As the meal went on, Ava began to wonder if she'd ever known this man at all.

But the minute he walked into the office, it was business as usual. Back to the brusque, somewhat dour demeanour she'd come to expect of him. Just then, he'd permitted her a glimpse of that other Neal.

Ava wanted to ask him whether he was happy — or had that ceased to matter to him? A father at nineteen, Neal had given up his place at university to join the police, so that he could support his son as a single parent. It had proved to be a shrewd move. Neal had made Detective Inspector at an impressively early age. He must derive satisfaction from knowing that he excelled at his job. But did it make him happy?

"They're going to be a great couple," Ava said. "Have they set a date for the wedding?"

"January," Neal answered. "In Edinburgh."

Ava shivered. "You'll all freeze! Are they going to live up there?" She hoped Neal wouldn't think her too nosey.

"Not sure," Neal said, apparently unfazed by the approaching disruption to his personal life. "By the way, you're invited. To the wedding."

"Oh." Ava had no time to respond before Neal abruptly brought the conversation back to the case.

"What did you make of Val Marsh?"

Ava frowned. "Bit hard to read, wasn't she? Seemed really upset when we first arrived. Her sister seemed like the strong one then, but after that they sort of reversed roles. She was pretty adamant her husband wouldn't commit suicide, but most people would say that, wouldn't they? And I couldn't get a handle on the relationship between the two of them. Felt a bit like one of those love–hate things. Then there's Ruth. Lot of undercurrents in this family, I reckon."

"Hmm. I agree."

PJ and Tom arrived. Ava noticed Neal glance at his watch, and then at the door, as if expecting someone else to arrive.

"Let's just give it five before we make a start," he said. "Given that Russ Marsh is a businessman with substantial assets, we need to consider that there might be a financial angle to this case. So I've asked Lesley Curran to give us a hand with that side of things. She's an experienced financial investigations officer."

Lesley arrived a couple of minutes later, sounding like she'd taken the stairs three at a time. Neal gave her a moment to get her breath before introducing her to the team. Lesley's eyes lingered a little longer on Tom than on the rest of them. Interesting. She was one of those impeccably groomed people whose age is difficult to determine. Early to mid-forties, at a guess. There were no deep-set wrinkles, only laughter lines. She had very short, dyed blonde hair and elfin features. Her darting, amber eyes gleamed with intelligence.

Neal gave her a brief smile. "Thanks for joining us, Lesley. A bit of financial nous could well be useful on this case. We spoke on the phone, but just to bring you up to speed, Val Marsh hinted that her husband was concerned about some aspect of his business. They were going to discuss it, but unfortunately he died before they got the opportunity. When wealthy people are killed, it's automatic to assume that money is at the root of it, and it's not a big leap to see how Russ Marsh's line of work could make him enemies. A money motive is a possibility but it's by no means the only avenue we need to explore."

He paused. "As Ava and I were just discussing before your arrival, there are tensions in this family that also need to be delved into, but, Lesley, I'd be grateful if you'd scrutinise Russ Marsh's financial affairs. Business and personal. Check whether Cornish and Marsh or any of the business ventures their partnership is associated with have been suspected of any suspicious activity. Or whether Russ Marsh or his business partner have been involved, even peripherally, in any allegations of corruption."

As an FIO, Ava knew, Lesley would have access to specialist databases holding sensitive financial information. She would also have had training on the morass of legislation pertaining to obtaining information on business and personal finances. She was potentially a real asset, if Neal's hunch about a money motive proved to be right.

"It'll take time," Lesley pointed out. "As you know, I'll need to go through the appropriate legal channels to obtain the information I need. Otherwise, anything I do come up with could be inadmissible as evidence in court."

"I appreciate that," Neal said.

At the end of the meeting, Lesley agreed to compile a full report on the state of Russ Marsh's financial affairs, and on Cornish and Marsh as individuals, and present it to them as soon as possible. In the meantime, she would make herself available to discuss the case as and when the need arose.

"Okay if I liaise with DS Knight, as a point of contact?" she asked, before Neal could assign the role to anyone else.

"That okay with you, Tom?" Neal asked. After a moment's hesitation, Tom nodded.

"Catch you all later, then," Lesley said breezily, addressing Tom more than the others. Their eyes followed her as she sashayed off. Lesley was shaped like an engorged pear. Tiny waist, round bottom and full hips. She wore tight black trousers and a leather bomber jacket. It was sort of mesmerising watching her exit.

"Ava, you're with me this morning. We're going out to Crystal Lakes to see Gail Cornish. She contacted me earlier and asked if she could speak with us. Grab a coffee, I have some urgent emails to attend to first." Neal retreated to his office.

Ava and PJ exchanged grins.

"So, Tom. You interested?" Ava said.

"What?" Tom was all innocence.

"Come on, her eyes were all over you," PJ said.

"You think so?"

"You know so."

"Bet you're looking forward to *liaising* with her," Ava said.

"Now you're embarrassing me," Tom protested. Ava thought of all the times she'd been on the receiving end of lewd comments from male colleagues, and felt no pity. She picked up her empty coffee cup and disappeared into the kitchen.

Neal was ready within twenty minutes, and they drove out to the Cornishes' place. Crystal Lakes was a new development of homes, retail outlets and leisure facilities arranged around a purpose-built marina and a series of artificial lakes, which led to a canal that ran through the centre of Stromford, two miles away. Set in acres of countryside, it represented the ultimate in luxury living for well-to-do professionals and retirees looking for prestigious accommodation with recreational facilities a stone's throw from the city. Or so went the blurb that Ava had read on the property developer's website.

Crystal Lakes boasted award-winning designer homes — luxury apartments with balconies overlooking the marina, and luxury houses with their own private jetty. The residential area was gated, providing twenty-four-hour security.

"How the other half live." Ava looked around her as they drove in.

"Wouldn't be my cup of tea," remarked Neal. "Wealth and privilege barricading itself in a fortress against the masses."

Ava chuckled. "Come the revolution, eh, sir?"

Neal scowled, but not at Ava's remark. He'd spotted the security post.

"Police," Neal said, and then smiled. The guard was one of the workers, after all.

"Thank you, sir." His accent was Eastern European. He was in his twenties, and probably on minimum wage.

"Can you direct us to the Cornishes' house?" Ava asked.

"Right at junction and follow curve of road to leisure club. Right again past club, then second left and is fourth house along."

"Thanks."

The houses seemed to get bigger and more elaborate the further they proceeded. Ava whistled softly. "It's like Hollywood without the sunshine."

"This seems to be the most exclusive part," Neal said with distaste.

"They go for more than half a million," Ava observed. "This is it," she said, and they pulled up at a tall security gate, the only chink in a formidable brick wall. "A fortress within a fortress."

Ava jumped out of the car and pressed the buzzer on the intercom. The gates slid open and they drove up a blue-gravelled drive and round a circular island landscaped with shrubs and low-hanging trees.

"Wow. Makes the Marshes' place look like a slum, doesn't it?"

A woman stood waiting in the porch.

"Mrs Cornish?" Neal asked. The woman shook her head, smiling.

"Dana Schell. I'm the Cornishes' domestic help." Neal and Ava exchanged looks as she led them inside. She showed them into a large sitting room with a view of the lake. "Please wait in here."

"Bit showy, isn't it?" Ava said, running her hand along the back of a sumptuous, black leather sofa. Everything in the room was black, grey or bright pink — an oblong zebra-striped rug, furry grey cushions, two very small, very pink chairs. One whole wall looked to be made of slate, though closer inspection revealed that it was in fact wallpaper. Another wall, made entirely of glass, looked out over a manicured lawn to the marina. True to its name, Crystal Lakes sparkled in the autumn sunshine.

Neal looked around at the décor. "Tasteless."

"*Designer* tasteless."

A polite cough alerted them to Mrs Cornish's presence. Ava coloured.

"Gail Cornish. Thanks for coming. I might have some information for you, or I might not. Either way, I thought I should tell you what I know." Neal nodded and introduced himself and Ava.

Gail indicated for them to sit down. "I was shocked to hear about Russ," she began, "but I'm not going to lie. Of late there's been no love lost between my husband and him."

Ava smiled inwardly. Nothing like being direct, is there? Saves everybody time.

"I knew it would get back to you sooner or later, so I thought it best to get it out in the open straightaway. You might as well know the truth from the outset. Last week,

Russ and Paul had a fight. Here, in this very house, Russ Marsh threatened my husband's life." Gail's eyes flashed in anger. "Russ actually told Paul he'd better, and I quote, 'watch his back.'"

Her voice shook. She took a moment to regain her composure. "Dana heard it too. You can ask her. I'm telling you, because I know that if the news got out and you thought we'd been keeping it from you, you'd look upon Paul as your prime suspect. That's right, isn't it? Paul would move right to the top of your list?"

Ava assumed the question was rhetorical. "What was the disagreement between your husband and Russell Marsh about, Mrs Cornish?"

"I don't know," she said.

This was a little surprising. "You just said you witnessed their argument," Ava said.

"Only the end of it. They were in the study. They started shouting, and I went to see what was going on. Dana must have heard them too, because she'd already come out of the kitchen."

"Did you discuss it with your husband afterwards?" Neal said.

"Paul refused to talk about it. He said it was a stupid difference of opinion over something. It escalated quickly because they were both a bit drunk."

"Did they often fall out? Over the business? Or other things?" Neal asked.

Gail reddened. After a moment's hesitation, she said, "I expect this will come out with the rest of the dirty washing, so I'll say it now. Russ and I slept together. Once. Two years ago. We were both drunk and, well, you know. It happened. I'm not proud of it. Paul found out. He forgave me, marched straight round to the Marshes' place and punched Russ in the face." A grimace.

"Thank you for telling us about this, Mrs Cornish," Neal said.

"Are you involved with the business, Mrs Cornish?" Ava asked.

Gail shook her head. "I used to be a physiotherapist but I gave it up when the business took off. We have four children, Sergeant. I've been kept busy." She nodded at a poster-size photograph showing the Cornish family, all six of them, posed in their show home.

"Oh. Yes. Nice. Is that a recent picture?" Ava asked.

"It was taken six months ago. The twins, Rupert and Quentin, are at the Cathedral School studying for their A levels. Very clever boys." Gail's voice was full of pride.

"Our daughter, Kitty, is at the same school. She's fifteen. Very talented musically."

Her eyes came to rest on the final Cornish child, a dark-eyed boy. Ava wondered why he'd been left to last.

"Our other son is Hector. He's the eldest. Twenty-three next month," Gail said briskly.

"Is he brainy too?" Ava asked. Her gaze lingered on the picture. The informal family portrait was clearly taken by a photographer who had artistic pretensions. It reminded her of the kind of portraits you see in glossy magazines.

The twins looked bemused. Kitty, smoky-eyed, tousle-haired, pouted. Standing next to her rather bullish husband, Gail seemed diminished in stature. Hector stood behind his parents, looking like he belonged to an entirely different family. Of them all, he was the only one smiling, albeit ironically. All six were framed by the wide French windows overlooking the marina. Behind them, the sky was an ominous, muted grey, signifying an approaching storm.

Gail bristled at Ava's question. Was Hector the odd one out in the family? Ava wondered. After a moment's pause, Gail said, "Hector has just graduated from Cambridge."

"Cambridge?" Gail mistook Neal's exclamation for admiration, but Ava suspected that, like her, he was struck by the coincidence of the Cornishes' son studying at the same university as the Marshes' daughter.

"Ruth Marsh went to Cambridge too, didn't she?" Ava said.

"Yes."

"So what's Hector going to do next, then? Follow in his dad's footsteps and become a financial wiz?" she asked.

"Actually, yes. He's starting a job soon. In the City."

Of course he is.

"You must be very proud of him."

There was just the slightest delay before Gail said, "Yes, I am."

"And your husband? He must be proud of Hector too, I imagine."

"Er . . . yes. I suppose he is." A sigh. "Paul and Hector aren't on the best of terms at the moment."

So there were undercurrents in this family too. "Why's that, Mrs Cornish?" Ava said.

Gail looked irritated. No doubt at herself for revealing more than she'd needed to. "That's a private family matter, Sergeant. It has nothing whatsoever to do with Russ Marsh's death. I shouldn't have even mentioned it."

Ava was about to say that in a murder investigation, nothing was private, but she bit back her words. Gail would learn this soon enough if the information proved to be relevant.

Gail glared at Neal. "You and your sergeant seem to have sidetracked things. All I really wanted was to put you in the picture about certain matters, not indulge in family gossip." She stood up, signalling that the visit was over. But Neal wasn't finished.

"We'll need to interview your husband, Mrs Cornish."

Gail gave a curt nod. "Obviously. Paul's a very busy man, Inspector Neal, but I appreciate you'll need to talk to him about . . . things. Given that my husband and Russ Marsh were business partners, it's pretty obvious really that . . . that Paul and the business will come under scrutiny."

Gail seemed to be falling apart in front of them. Her initial haughty demeanour had given way to uncertainty.

"Are you okay, Mrs Cornish? Is there something else you want to tell us?" Ava asked.

"No. It's just . . . you know. All the upset." Gail looked close to tears.

"We'd like to question the young woman who let us in," Neal said, "Dana, is it? You said she was present when your husband and Russ Marsh had their disagreement."

Gail called Dana, who arrived a little too promptly, as though she'd been listening at the door.

"The officers would like to speak with you now, Dana," Gail said.

"In private," added Neal. Gail hesitated, then left the room making a show of closing the door behind her.

"Please, sit down," Neal said to Dana.

Ava looked at her. She seemed to be around her own age, or a bit younger. Dana had described herself as the Cornish family's domestic help, but there had been a hint of irony in her tone. Ava wondered about her relationship with the various members of the household.

"This won't take long, Dana," Neal said. "Perhaps you could begin by telling us how long you've worked for the Cornish family?"

"Too long," Dana said. Her voice had none of the affect of her employer. "I've been here about two years. I'm saving up to go travelling. They don't pay much, but I get a nice room and all my meals provided, plus Gail — Mrs Cornish — has paid for me to join the gym and the other leisure facilities here."

"Wow," Ava said. "Lucky you." Ava was a fitness enthusiast. "Yet you're counting down the days?"

"The work's dead boring and," Dana lowered her voice, "you know the term 'dysfunctional family?' Doesn't begin to describe this lot."

It seemed as though Dana wouldn't take much prodding to spill all the Cornish family's secrets.

"Must be a bit weird when the Cornish kids are not much younger than you," Ava commented. "Do they boss you about?"

Dana snorted. "I'd like to see 'em try. Kitty's a stuck-up cow, the twins are so clever it's like they're from another planet, and Hector . . ." A glance at the door. "Well, Hector's okay sometimes, I suppose."

"And Mr and Mrs Cornish?"

"Gail can be a bit . . . you know . . . can't think of the word, sort of up and down: alright one minute, all wrong the next. You never know what mood she's going to be in. She can be a real bitch when she's got a mardy on. And between you and me, I don't think her and Paul are all that . . . if you know what I mean?" Dana paused, possibly regretting having said too much. "Didn't you say you wanted to ask me about that argument between Paul and that Russ Marsh?"

Actually, they hadn't. Not while Dana was in the room, at any rate. Ava noted that Dana had left Paul Cornish out of her appraisal of the family members. Why was that?

"Did you witness the argument?" she asked.

"Only the end of it, when they was shouting." Dana had lowered her voice again. "Paul and Russ Marsh were in the study. I were in the kitchen, clearing up. I could hear their voices getting louder, so I came through into the hall to see what was going on. I could see the pair of them sort of puffing their chests out the way men do when they're about to have a fight. Squaring up to each other. Russ's face were bright red. He were sort of stabbing his finger at Paul's chest. Not actually touching him, but, you know, being pretty aggressive."

They let Dana run on. She'd clearly found the whole incident exciting. Ava asked, "Were you able to make out anything that was said between them?"

"No," Dana said. A little too decisively? The men had been shouting, after all.

"Nothing at all?" Ava said.

"Something about money, maybe? Sorry, but I couldn't catch what they was saying, really."

"Did you witness Mr Marsh making a threat against Mr Cornish?"

Dana thought for a moment. "Yeah, he said something like, 'You better watch your back, mate.' It's the sort of thing people say, in't it, when they're angry? I don't think he really meant it." A pause. "To be honest, it were more like a warning than a threat."

"Were any of the Cornish children in the house at the time?" Neal asked. Dana shook her head.

"Do you know why Hector Cornish fell out with his dad?" he said.

Dana looked slightly fazed by the abrupt change of subject. "No. No one tells me anything around here."

"Did Mrs Cornish and her husband socialise much with the Marsh family?" Ava asked, suddenly recalling Val's assertion that they 'used to socialise,' and her hint that the families were no longer particularly close.

"No."

"What do you think of the Marsh family? Did you ever meet their daughter, Ruth?"

"I only met Mrs Marsh once. She seemed kind of . . . aloof? Is that the right word? Not chatty. Ruth lives in Cambridge. She's my age but she's got a kid. Mr Marsh came here occasionally. To talk business with Paul, I suppose."

There was a knock at the door. Gail Cornish asked if they were nearly finished. Neal gave a nod. Gail looked at Dana. "I'd like you to drive into Stromford and pick up some things for me, Dana. When you're ready." In other words, *now*.

Gail Cornish saw them to the door.

"Thanks for the information," Neal said. "We'll be in touch. Just one more thing," he added, sounding like

Columbo. "Did Russ Marsh contact the police after your husband assaulted him that time over the affair?"

"Assault is a bit over the top, Inspector. Paul gave him a black eye, that's all. No, Russ didn't report it. Maybe he felt he had it coming."

Gail closed the door almost as soon as Neal and Ava turned their backs.

"If Paul had given *her* a black eye instead of Russ, I doubt she'd have felt she had it coming," Ava remarked. "What a lot. Funny, isn't it? Ruth Marsh didn't speak to her father, Hector and his dad had a falling out. Makes you wonder, doesn't it? About the parents, I mean."

Neal was quiet. Maybe he was worrying about Archie falling out with him.

"And did you notice the way Dana avoided saying what she thought of Paul Cornish? She was a bit evasive about Hector too. What was that all about?" Ava said.

"Are you saying you think Dana might have been having an affair with Paul or Hector?" Neal gave a grimace of distaste.

"Or both," Ava answered, ignoring the look.

Dana was certainly pretty enough. Gail Marsh must have been aware that the presence of a pretty young woman might lead to some sexual tension in a predominantly male household. Ava's mind strayed to the bawdy comedy sketches on TV from years ago, involving au pairs and their employers. Her grandfather laughing at old *Benny Hill* videos . . . Paul Cornish chasing Dana around the kitchen table.

"Dana's probably right in describing the Cornish lot as dysfunctional, though I reckon the Marshes could give them a good run for their money. Come to think of it, most families would fit that description, mine included," Ava said.

"Interesting what Dana said about Russ telling Paul to watch his back, wasn't it?"

“What was it she said exactly?” Ava searched her memory. “She said it sounded more like a warning than a threat.”

“Which begs the question, who did Russ feel Paul needed to watch out for?”

Chapter Three

The morning after her arrival at her aunt's house, Ruth woke feeling refreshed after a good night's sleep. She was full of trepidation about the days ahead, but hopeful that with her Aunt Lizzie — and possibly her mother — taking care of Cam when he woke in the night, just maybe she'd manage to hold it together.

The previous day had passed in a blur. In a trance, she'd packed two suitcases of clothes, most of which belonged to Cam.

She had no idea how long she'd be staying. Aunt Lizzie had called her back to confirm that her father had been murdered. That meant a delay before his body could be released for burial. Ruth planned to stay with her mother until after the funeral. She hoped that by then the police would have some answers.

She lay in bed, luxuriating in the lie-in, thinking back over the past twenty-four hours.

She had been almost ready to leave by the time Fin showed up. Cam was having his usual reaction to being forced into his car seat — kicking and screaming and making his body go rigid so she couldn't do up the straps.

Ruth was nearing the end of her tether. Blinking back tears, she pleaded, "Please, please, please, Cam, just give me a break.

"You're doing it all wrong."

"Oh, Fin! I'm so glad you're here."

At the sight of his father, Cam stopped struggling and held out his arms, gurgling, "Dada." Fin took his son and Ruth in his arms, and for a moment their little family unit was at peace. Thank goodness for Fin! Everything about him was reassuring. She breathed in his familiar scent.

She told him the bleak news. "My dad was murdered." A beat. "You don't think . . . ?"

Fin's grip on her tightened. "No," he said fiercely. "It's nothing to do with that." Ruth gave a nod. It was what she'd wanted him to say. "I'm so sorry, Ruth. What happened?"

"I don't know the details yet. Mum phoned me as soon as she knew. He was shot in the head. At first they thought it might be suicide, but the police are saying murder."

"And you're driving home? In this state? Let me drive you."

"No!" Ruth said, sharply. "You've got seminars to supervise and work to do. I can manage."

"Anything you need, Ruth, any time, just call and I'll be there." Ruth gave him a desperate kiss. Then she strapped a strangely compliant Cam into his seat, got behind the wheel and drove off, watching in the rear-view mirror the forlorn figure of Fin growing smaller, until she turned off at the junction.

Cam fought sleep for the first hour, then, perhaps realising that oblivion was preferable to boredom, he dropped off and didn't stir again until Ruth parked the car outside her aunt's house in Stromford.

"Ruthie!" Aunt Lizzie hadn't been able to restrain her sheer delight at seeing her niece and her great-nephew. As soon as Ruth got out of the car, though, Lizzie drew her to her, and held her as they both wept.

"Aunt Lizzie . . ."

"Oh, Ruthie, I'm so, so sorry."

"I didn't speak to him for all that time and now he's dead."

"I know, sweetie. I know." Lizzie understood tragedy. She'd had her share of it, losing Will and then Craig.

"Is Mum here?"

Lizzie shook her head. "She's gone out for a walk. You know your mum. Even grieving, she's restless. Now, let's get you both inside." A weight seemed to lift from Ruth's shoulders as she watched her capable aunt take control of Cam.

"Is Stephen here?" she asked.

"He's at work. You'll see him this evening."

"How is Mum?"

"Still in shock, I think. A bit better now that the police have accepted the fact that your father didn't take his own life."

"He would never do a stupid thing like that." Ruth coloured. "I'm sorry. Uncle Craig . . . I didn't mean . . ."

"It's alright, sweetheart. I'm not one to take offence, you should know that by now." Ruth bit her lip. She really hadn't meant to make it sound like her Uncle Craig had been weak. He'd just been unable to get over the death of his son.

Ruth followed her aunt indoors. This wasn't the house she had been used to visiting and staying in when she was younger and had come to play with her cousin when Will was still alive. Aunt Lizzie had moved to a new place closer to the centre of town. Ruth didn't think she'd have been able to go inside the old house.

Even so, when she walked into the room that her aunt had prepared for her and Cam, she couldn't help thinking of Will.

"You look exhausted, Ruth. Why don't you take a nap? I'll see to Cam."

"I'd like a cup of tea first, if that's alright. And Cam should have something to eat."

"Come on, then. Let's sort you both out. I know I shouldn't say it under the circumstances, but it's lovely to have you here."

Ruth knew she shouldn't think it, but it was lovely to know she'd be looked after for a while. It had been so restful when she and Fin had been ill and her mother had taken care of them. Ruth had sometimes regarded her as a disengaged sort of mother, more interested in her own life than in Ruth's, but the visit had made her think again.

Now that she had a child of her own, Ruth was beginning to realise that the selfless mother was a bit of a myth. Even the most dedicated and loving mothers must harbour some resentment about the compromises and sacrifices involved in bringing up a child.

Aunt Lizzie was easier to talk to than Val. She never tired of telling Ruth that the two of them were alike, and that's why they were so close. The implication being that Ruth and her mother were too different to get along. But Ruth alone knew that the truth about her relationship with her aunt was far more complicated than either Lizzie or her mother could guess at.

At her aunt's insistence, Ruth had her cup of tea and put her head down, intending to rest for half an hour or so. She'd been astonished to wake up and discover that two hours had passed. Downstairs, her mother and her aunt were talking. Ruth splashed some water on her face and went to join them.

They were sitting on the floor. Cam was lying nearby, fast asleep on the rug, surrounded by the toys that Ruth had packed for him.

"He lasted a lot longer than you, but he's out for the count now," Aunt Lizzie said cheerfully. Ruth was mildly surprised to see her mother on the floor. Now she'd become a grandmother, Val was showing a different side to her character. She got to her feet and embraced her daughter. So much had happened that morning, yet Val seemed remarkably calm.

"Can I see him?" Ruth asked. Val shook her head.

"Not yet. They're going to do an autopsy. It'll be a while before we can claim his body."

"When can we go home?"

"In a couple of days. The police forensics people are crawling all over the place at the moment." Val gave a shudder of revulsion.

"Who do you think did it?" Ruth said, hotly. "Who would hate Dad enough to kill him?"

"Hate probably had very little to do with it, darling. I'd be very surprised if it wasn't all about money."

"Money?"

Her mother stared at her for a moment. "I sometimes forget you were born into wealth. I wasn't always well-off, you know, Ruth. Lizzie and I grew up in a house where money was scarce. I was just a humble secretary when I met your dad. A lot of people will do bad things, if it means they don't have to face the despair of a lifetime trying to make ends meet."

Ruth rolled her eyes. She'd heard it all before.

Val droned on. "I know you've had a little experience of what it's like to be hard up in the past couple of months, but you always knew you had a safety net in the family's wealth. Your inheritance."

"Stop it! You sound just like Fin," Ruth said.

"You need to stop being so naïve," Val said. "Greed is one of the oldest motives in the world for murder. What's that phrase? 'Follow the money.' If the police want to find out who killed your father, they'd be wise to heed that advice."

"But what do you mean by that exactly? No one stands to benefit from Dad's death but us."

Val rambled on about disgruntled shareholders and jealous rivals, and Ruth quickly grasped that her mother knew as little as she did about her father's business affairs. Or the reason for his death. Still, there was no denying that money and wrongdoing often did go hand in hand.

Her mother changed tack. "Of course, money won't be an issue for you in the future. I have more money than I know what to do with now, and I plan to ensure that you and your family are well provided for."

Ruth bit her lip. Val had included Fin! She'd said 'you and your family.' Of late, she and Fin had experienced considerable anxiety over money. It had seemed exciting at first, but the debts were mounting up, and the bills were being left unpaid. Fin's postgraduate funding wasn't enough for a family to live on, and her part-time job didn't pay much. Ruth could see how a person could be ground down by the prospect of life continuing like that forever.

She'd told herself she could bear it. For love. For Fin. But there was no doubt that she wanted more for Cam. Much as she hated to admit it, her mother was right. Money mattered.

Lizzie hadn't said much. Ruth looked around. Her aunt and Stephen Hamilton had a nice home, but it wasn't a pricey executive one. Lizzie and Stephen were comfortably off, but not wealthy. Val sometimes forgot that her sister probably still had to be careful about money.

"Anyone like a drink?" Lizzie asked breezily. She disappeared for a few moments, returning with three gins and a bottle of tonic. Ruth had been expecting more tea.

Then Stephen came home. He seemed shaken by the news of Russ's death. A couple of years ago, he'd expanded his business with the help of a loan from his brother-in-law. Cynically, Ruth wondered how much of his apparent grief was actually worry about his own financial security. She noticed Lizzie pour him an extra-stiff drink.

Val was downing the gin faster than any of them. Not long after dinner she announced she was going to bed.

Ruth too, was exhausted, despite her unaccustomed afternoon nap. She yawned.

"Off to bed with you, and don't worry about Cam. I'll get up if he wakes in the night," Lizzie said.

Twice. He always wakes up at least twice. Ruth hugged her aunt, her relief quickly superseded by guilt when it occurred to her that it had taken a death in the family to get her a decent night's sleep.

* * *

Ruth got out of bed and tiptoed into the bathroom, hoping she'd have time to take a rare morning shower before Cam started to miss her. Aunt Lizzie was so good with him. Ruth suddenly wondered if her aunt had expected her to name her son after Will. The thought was like a blow, and reminded her of the enormity of Lizzie's loss.

Ruth sank to the floor in the shower cubicle. She sat, watching the water disappear down the plughole, until she began to shiver. It was the thought of anything bad happening to Cam that did it. All of a sudden she felt as tired as if she hadn't slept a wink.

* * *

Neal and Ava met Paul Cornish in the office he had shared with his deceased business partner. It was the day after they'd spoken with his wife. Paul accepted their condolences, and said, "I've been expecting you since Gail told me about your visit yesterday."

Neal got straight to the point. "Tell us about your relationship with Russ Marsh."

"You want to know about the fight, don't you? Gail thinks it was to do with business, and I only wish she could continue to believe it." He gave a weary sigh. "I suppose there's not much chance of that happening now, is there?"

They remained silent.

"I thought not. It was about our eldest son, Hector. Russ loaned Hector a considerable sum of money without first consulting Gail and me. When I found out, I was furious." Paul leaned forward in his chair, his legs spread beneath his polished desk, asserting his virility.

"Look. Russ and I were friends as well as partners, you know. But we had our tiffs. No one can get along all the time."

"You fell out once before, didn't you? Over your wife's affair with Russ Marsh?" Ava said.

Cornish turned his chilly grey gaze on Ava as if noticing her for the first time. It wasn't something she was used to.

"Yes, Sergeant."

"Not a lot of friendships would survive a betrayal like that." Neal almost smiled. Typical Ava. Straight for the jugular.

"We all moved on. Gail was distraught about what she'd done. Russ apologised. We didn't want to destroy everything we all had going for us in terms of business and friendship because of a stupid mistake that would never be repeated. Gail had no feelings for Russ, or Russ for her."

"What did Val think?" Ava said.

He shrugged. "You'd have to ask her. I suppose, like me, she decided to be pragmatic about it."

"What did Hector need the money for?" Neal asked.

"To pay off a debt."

"I take it we're not talking about a student loan?"

"This has nothing at all to do with your investigation into Russ's death, Inspector."

"That's not for you to judge, Mr Cornish," Neal said politely.

Cornish sighed. "Look, the lad got himself in with a bad crowd. Started gambling."

"How much did he owe?" Neal asked.

"Ten k. Not so much in the scheme of things."

"Drop in the ocean, really," Ava said. "Why do you think he went to Russ instead of you and Gail?"

"Isn't that obvious, Sergeant?"

"Not at all."

"*Obviously* he didn't want Gail and me to know he'd got into trouble."

"How did you find out?" she asked.

"Russ accidentally sent me a message about it instead of Hector."

"Oops," Ava said. "Who did you confront first, Russ or Hector?"

"Hector. The other reason he didn't come to Gail and me was that we'd bailed him out once already, and I'd cut his allowance as a deterrent to further gambling."

"You must have been doubly pissed off at Russ. First, he sleeps with your wife, then your son turns to him instead of you when he's in trouble." Ava was embracing her inner bad cop today. Neal almost felt sorry for Paul Cornish.

"I didn't kill Russ if that's where you're headed." Cornish's face and neck were red and blotchy. He fiddled with the collar of his shirt, and loosened it with a finger. "Gail was right when she said you'd make a big deal about the fight. That's why she told you about it up front. Things sometimes got a bit frosty between Russ and me, I'd be the first to admit that. But at the end of the day, we were still mates. We go back a long way, Russ and I. That's not something you sacrifice over a stupid error of judgement. The bad feeling would've blown over eventually."

"You seem to have a very forgiving nature, Mr Cornish," Neal observed.

Cornish shrugged. "Yeah, well. Power of positivity and all that jazz. Look, I was angry and I lost my temper. That's all."

"Lose your temper a lot, do you?" Ava asked.

"No more than the next person." Cornish looked at her with active dislike.

"Right. Obviously we'll need to talk to Hector. He'll be able to confirm your story about Russ lending him money?"

"Of course, Sergeant. And it's not a story. It's a fact."

"Concerning your business, Mr Cornish. You and Mr Marsh made a lot of money back in the eighties so I'm told," Neal said.

"It was a case of right place, right time. We made our money and had enough foresight to get out before everything went tits up."

"You came back to Stromford and founded Cornish and Marsh. What exactly do you do, Mr Cornish?" Neal said.

"We're financial advisers."

"You also lend money to help struggling businesses?"

"We help young entrepreneurs get on the ladder, yes. That's what we do . . . er, did." He frowned. There was no longer a 'we.' "When potential clients approach us, we assess their business capabilities, take a look at their plan. We calculate the risks and if we like what we see, we invest in the business."

"You then have a share in the pie?" Neal said.

"Crudely speaking, yes. There's always an element of risk when you invest so much money in an individual. Bit of a leap of faith in some cases, but Russ and I are . . . were . . ." Confusion again. "Good at what we do. Of course sometimes it can take years before we see our investment making good returns. What's that saying? 'Good things come to those who wait?'" He gave a self-satisfied smile.

"Have there been issues with any of your clients lately?"

Cornish was silent for a couple of moments, and then he shook his head. "I . . . er . . . not exactly an issue but we did disagree over a client. I thought it was a lost cause, but Russ was dead set on going ahead with the investment. In the end, I acquiesced. Against my better judgement. In fact, Russ and I sometimes have our own projects. This became one of Russ's."

"And the client's name?"

"Stephen Hamilton."

Neal and Ava exchanged a glance. "Russ Marsh's brother-in-law?"

"The same." Cornish shook his head. "I understood Russ's desire to help his wife's sister out. God knows that woman's had enough tragedy in her life." He gave them a questioning look. "You know about her son, Will, and her first husband?" Neal and Ava nodded. "Stephen Hamilton's a good enough man, but he's no businessman."

"What sum of money was involved?" Neal asked.

"Twenty k." A look of regret crossed Cornish's face. "It was the first time I've felt truly angelic lending money. I never expected Cornish and Marsh to get a pennyworth of profit from that venture." His eyes widened. "You don't think . . . ? You're not suggesting Stephen . . . ?"

"Should we?" Neal asked. The mere fact that Stephen Hamilton had received a sum of money from his brother-in-law didn't make him a potential murderer. Cornish was the one making suggestions.

"Oh no, no, no. Never in a million years. Stephen Hamilton may be a total disaster as a businessman, but the man doesn't have a bad bone in his body."

"Couldn't Russell have just given Stephen the money as a gift or a personal loan?" Ava asked.

"Stephen would never have accepted it on that basis. He's a proud man."

"You have a generous as well as a forgiving nature, Mr Cornish." Neal commented.

"Actually, not as generous as you might think. Russ gave me his word that if Stephen's business went pear-shaped, he'd shoulder the loss himself."

"I see. We'll be needing a list of your clients, Mr Cornish. And you'll be hearing from one of our financial investigators, Lesley Curran."

Cornish gave a curt nod, as if to say he'd expected nothing less. He glanced at the clock. "Are we nearly finished, officers? I have an important meeting in twenty minutes."

Back outside, Ava said, "He was rattled when we mentioned the FIO, but he managed to hide it well."

"I noticed."

"Probably fiddling his taxes. They're all at it, aren't they?"

Neal didn't comment. Ava was probably right. People like Cornish knew all about how to operate just within the law, with the help of an unscrupulous accountant.

"Did you hear him boasting about 'foresight?'" Ava said. "Bloody lucky, more like. He and Russ have been making money since the eighties. You'd think they'd slow down a bit. How much money is enough?"

"Actually, I think Russ Marsh has stopped."

Ava stared at him. "Did you just make a joke, sir?"

"I'm not completely devoid of humour, Sergeant."

"Okaaay." Ava didn't sound entirely convinced.

Chapter Four

Stephen Hamilton was having a hard time coming to terms with the news of his brother-in-law's death. He hadn't been particularly fond of Russell, but the fact that his modest electrician's business was doing well was all down to a generous investment from Russ and his partner, Paul Cornish.

He'd listened to Lizzie's account of Russ's murder with mounting unease. Lizzie hadn't been a big fan of Russ either — she'd hardly spoken to him since the tragic fire that had led to her son's death and her first husband's suicide.

"Val wouldn't entertain the idea that it might be suicide. You should have heard her, Stephen. Anyway, before I left the house, it was confirmed. They're treating his death as suspicious. Can you believe Russ is even dead, never mind murdered?"

She must have wished it often enough after the fire. All Stephen could manage was to keep nodding in agreement with his wife. He didn't trust his voice to be steady. When she told him the news, his heart had pounded alarmingly, and his palms prickled with sweat. Fortunately, Lizzie was too excited to notice his distress.

"I mean, why would he commit suicide? I know the business over Ruth upset him but it made him angry, not depressed. Did you think he seemed suicidal at Val's birthday party last month?"

Stephen shook his head. At least he could agree with that. Why was Lizzie banging on about suicide anyway? She'd just said the police had already established it was murder. That hadn't taken them long either.

Stephen was worried about the fallout from Russ's death. Would he be questioned by the police? He was Russ's brother-in-law. Close family members always came under scrutiny, didn't they? The police coming here, asking questions, poking their noses in . . . It didn't bear thinking about.

He wished he hadn't accepted that money from Russ. Stephen was a grafter. He'd puttered along steadily for years as a self-employed electrician. He'd never been ambitious, and as long as he made enough to live on he was content. Then he'd met Lizzie.

At the time, he'd been overwhelmed by her fortitude, when his own strength was sadly depleted. Like Lizzie, he'd had his share of tragedy in his life. He'd lost his wife, and then his beloved twin sister within a month of each other. But Lizzie had lost a child. A child!

They'd met in a pub in Stromford. Both had been dragged out, reluctantly, by well-intentioned friends anxious to keep them in circulation, stop them brooding. Neither of them had been out much since their bereavements, and both had become socially isolated. By some twist of fate, they had ended up talking at the bar. For three hours, they'd told each other how much they missed their loved ones and then, in the heat of the moment, arranged to meet again.

It had taken many months and many meetings — neither of them had regarded these get-togethers as dates

— for them to begin talking, occasionally, about other things.

"Do you realise, I haven't mentioned Will or Craig once this evening!" Lizzie exclaimed one night. They were in their usual haunt, a pub on the Long Hill, the one where they'd met that fateful evening.

"And I haven't even thought about Kim. Or Rosie," Stephen said, in equal wonderment.

"Is that bad?" Lizzie had asked. "Or does it mean we're coping better?" She put a hand to her breast. "I can still feel it, right here. A heaviness. But sometimes now it sort of fades into the background. Like my back pain did when I was taking those strong painkillers." A sob. He'd covered her hand with his.

"I feel it too, Lizzie, that heaviness. It will never go away. The most we can hope for is that sometimes it will weigh less . . . heavily." Stephen wished he was a more eloquent man.

After that evening, Stephen, at least, had felt lighter. Something incredible had happened. It was as though his wife, Kim, and his sister, Rosie, had given him permission to go on without them. At least, that's what he'd told Lizzie. Deep down, Stephen suspected it was himself who'd granted that permission.

It took a bit longer for Lizzie to reach a similar place, but when she did, their relationship blossomed into love. It hadn't been what either of them expected, or even wanted. It would almost have been easier for each of them to deny love's existence than to risk losing it again. Funny the way life took you by surprise.

It was for Lizzie's sake that Stephen had expanded his business. One of the qualities he admired in her was that she never envied her sister's wealth. The first time Stephen visited Val and Russ in their house, he'd felt inadequate. He wanted Lizzie to have some of the luxuries her sister enjoyed. He'd found himself saying as much to Val as they did a tour of the garden, after he'd had a few too many glasses of Russ's excellent Scotch. Next thing he knew, Russ was offering him a loan, or an 'investment' as he termed it, to scale up, take on a couple of employees, an apprentice. Faced with a beaming Lizzie, Stephen didn't have the heart to refuse.

That had been five years ago. Stephen had used the money to update and buy more equipment, rent a small premises to work from and take on a couple of young lads. During that time a number of good opportunities had come his way, and he'd been awarded a couple of contracts. But he was under no illusions. He was never going to amount to anything more than a small businessman.

Money still wasn't plentiful, but there was no doubt that his and Lizzie's life had become more comfortable. There were the occasional holidays abroad and the conservatory Lizzie had always wanted. And a planned extension to the house. Not that they really needed it. Having money, Stephen was learning, created needs and desires you never knew you had.

Whatever the outcome of the police investigation, things were bound to change at Cornish and Marsh. The death of a partner was a momentous event. Paul Cornish was in his mid-fifties. One way or another, he was bound to look at Russ's death as a turning point. What would he do? Carry on solo or with a new partner? Retire? Any of these scenarios would entail change.

But the possibility of change wasn't what was at the root of Stephen's anxiety. His unease was rooted in a discovery he'd made some time ago, and which he now regretted never telling Russ about.

"Stephen! Are you even listening to me?"

"Sorry, love. I think I'm in shock. Russ dead. Murdered. I don't have the words." That, at least, was the truth.

"Bless you," Lizzie said, giving him a hug. "Don't look so worried. Nobody's going to think it was you."

That's not what I'm worried about, thought Stephen. He drew Lizzie towards him and held her as if his life depended upon it.

* * *

Lesley Curran was hungry. The evening before, she'd consulted a carefully selected list of eating establishments and was now standing outside one of them, bracing herself to go in. It was Wednesday evening. Not the busiest night of the week, but she'd expected to see at least a couple of other customers when she walked in the door.

"I take it I can sit anywhere?" she asked the waiter. He was a thin, wiry-looking lad, who seemed to be skulking in the shadows, as if hiding from potential customers.

"Is it always this quiet?" she asked.

His accent was indeterminate. "Is early. Busy later." Lesley wasn't convinced. She ordered a steak, and washed it down with a glass of red wine. The restaurant remained eerily empty.

In the next day or two, she intended to eat at different times at another couple of restaurants in Stromford and Nottingham. She was expecting a similar absence of customers. Maybe she'd invite that good-looking Tom Knight sometime, so she didn't look like such a saddo eating alone.

The restaurants she planned to visit were all located in the less fashionable areas. They all had some potential, yet none of them seemed to be trying very hard to attract customers. Some clever marketing and a bit of a facelift would surely help draw the punters in.

Lesley wasn't choosing these seemingly unpopular restaurants at random. She knew that when she eventually got her hands on their financial records, they'd probably tell a different story. One that showed up to fifty per cent profit margins in a trade where that sort of achievement relied on a footfall far higher than these restaurants had.

Successful restaurants served exceptional food, or were well-established and popular. That certainly wasn't the case with this place. The food was mediocre, the service grudging, the décor unremarkable. She guessed the experience would be replicated over the coming evenings.

Lesley already knew that other restaurants in this area had fared quite badly of late. Two well-established family restaurants had gone out of business in the past six months. Yet this place was still open.

Lesley couldn't wait to get her hands on those accounts.

* * *

While Lesley chewed on her steak, Ava was drinking coffee with Maggie Neal. Maggie had asked if they could meet, so Ava guessed there was something she wanted to talk about.

"What's Jim been like at work in the past few days?" Maggie asked.

Ava thought about this. He'd been fine at the beginning of the week, but yesterday he'd seemed a bit off. "Bit distracted. Why? Is something up at home?"

Maggie looked around as though expecting her brother to be hiding under a table. "It's Myrna."

"His ex?" Ava was all ears.

"She contacted him the night before last and asked if she could come and see him."

Ava's heart missed a beat. "Oh? What does she want?"

Maggie hissed. "I don't care what she wants. All I know is that Jimmy and Archie are doing just fine without her."

"Has she asked to see Archie?"

"I don't think so. I asked, but Jimmy was evasive."

"When's she coming?" Ava asked.

"Tomorrow."

"Oh."

"Yeah." Maggie scowled. "He's agreed to meet her."

"What's she like?" Ava asked.

She had looked Myrna up, of course. Myrna was fairly well known in the world of musical theatre but she wasn't yet a household name. Apparently she'd once wanted to be an opera singer. Maybe that was still on the cards. Ava had a vague notion that opera singers' voices needed time to mature.

Maggie grimaced. "She's clever. Manipulative." Maggie sighed, and began counting on her fingers. "Attractive, talented, beguiling, voice of an angel . . ."

"Yup. I've heard it," Ava blurted out.

Maggie gave an amused smile. "You've looked her up? On YouTube?"

"Out of curiosity. I swear I haven't told anyone else that the DI's got a famous ex."

"She's not that famous."

Ava leaned forward. "Why now?"

"Exactly."

"I'm sure it'll be okay." Ava meant to reassure, but she didn't even manage to convince herself. "Well, it's going to be difficult for the DI to take time off. We're in the middle of a murder investigation."

Maggie shrugged. "Good. The less he sees of her the better."

Ava hesitated, then came out with it anyway. "Do you think she wants to get back together with your brother? Is that what you're worried about?"

Maggie frowned. She gave Ava a searching look, followed by a long sigh. "Och, I don't know. It's just, well, he was always such an idiot when it came to Myrna. She could twist him round her little finger. To tell the truth, what's really buggin' me is that I don't know what she wants."

You and me both, Ava said to herself.

* * *

Val Marsh was surprised they'd allowed her to move back home so soon. On the surface, the forensics team had left her house as they'd found it, but everywhere she looked, she could see their traces.

Despite the fairly recent addition of a conservatory, Lizzie's house had seemed poky in comparison, but that wasn't why Val was impatient to leave. Whenever the two of them were together, unresolved tensions from their past welled up to the surface.

When they were children, she and Lizzie had been inseparable. She'd looked up to Lizzie, and followed her around like a little dog. Only a year apart at primary school, they were often mistaken for twins. Later, though, they'd grown distant from each other.

Lizzie liked to say that she didn't envy Val her wealth, but she brought the millionaire thing up at every opportunity. It was pointless for Val to remind Lizzie that she'd left school at sixteen, and worked hard for ten years before she married her millionaire. Lizzie stayed on at school, got good A levels and went to university. At twenty-one, she'd never had so much as a Saturday job. Val could still remember her first one, working in a fruit-and-veg shop at the bottom end of Stromford High Street. She'd been paid three pounds a day. Not a lot, even then, but it had kept her out of the house.

Val left home, and never saw her parents again. She went to London, enrolled on a secretarial course and landed a job in the City. She made good money and her looks served her well in the clubs and bars where the City boys partied and threw their money around. Val and Lizzie often compared their eighties' lives. It was as if they'd been on two different planets.

Lizzie had only stayed with her once, and Val had been glad to see the back of her. She hadn't stopped going on about how depressing everything was 'back home.' Their dad was out of work, their mum was out at bingo every night, and Lizzie, a year out of university and living back at home, still hadn't managed to find a decent job.

Val had encouraged her to move to London, but for all her supposed cleverness, Lizzie seemed to lack initiative. And she'd been so tediously left wing. She supported the miners, she bemoaned the hedonistic lifestyle that the haves were leading at the expense of the have-nots, she criticised Val for lacking a social conscience, and so it went on.

Their father drank himself to an early death, and their mother died from a brain haemorrhage within six months of his funeral. The suddenness of it all came as a shock to Val, but she wasn't saddened. All her parents had ever given her was an inferiority complex. They never seemed to stop asking her why she couldn't be more like her sister. Val could never understand what they meant. Was she so different from Lizzie? And if so, what was it about Lizzie that they loved so much and failed to see in her?

Val wondered what her parents would have made of Ruth. Probably the only thing they'd have found to praise was her resemblance to Lizzie. Not that Val would ever have allowed Ruth anywhere near her father.

Leaving Lizzie's place that morning seemed to take for ever. Val almost cried with relief when she heard her sister declare, "That's the last one." She felt a bit guilty for sitting in the car, keeping Cam company while Lizzie helped Ruth with the suitcases and all the baby paraphernalia.

"How are you feeling?" Lizzie asked, her face full of pained concern.

"I'm fine. Can't wait to get home, that's all," Val answered.

"Of course, but I meant how are you *really* feeling?" Lizzie persisted, the intensity of her stare making Val uncomfortable.

Not for the first time, Val wished she could summon up tears at will. She ignored her sister and turned to Ruth. "Ready, darling?"

Val started up the car and they waved to Lizzie until she was a tiny speck in the distance. "Did you mind staying with Lizzie and Stephen?" she asked her daughter.

"It was nice to get some sleep. Aunt Lizzie was great about getting up in the night."

Val bristled. She'd spent a whole week in Cambridge getting up in the night. Had Ruth forgotten already?

"So, do you think the police will question Stephen?" Ruth asked.

"Stephen? You don't think . . . ?"

"No, Mum, I don't think Stephen killed Dad. It's just that Aunt Lizzie said she was surprised how upset it made him, much more than she expected."

"Well, your aunt was more upset than I expected *her* to be."

Ruth didn't comment. Predictably. Any reference to Lizzie's dislike of Russ brought on a stubborn silence.

"I suppose she was upset on my behalf more than anything," Val said.

"The police will probably need to talk to you and Aunt Lizzie again. And me, I expect."

"They've already spoken to Lizzie and me, the morning I found your father."

"Yes, but that was immediately afterwards. You were upset. I imagine other questions have arisen since then."

"Such as?"

"I don't know, Mum. I'm not a bloody cop. Family always fall under suspicion, don't they? They say most murders are committed by someone close to home." Ruth sounded bitter.

Val glanced in the rear-view mirror. Cam was fast asleep. Lizzie had played with him since the crack of dawn and tired him out.

Ruth added, in what seemed like an afterthought, "I didn't mean you'd fall under suspicion, Mum. Apart from anything else, you were with me in Cambridge when . . . when it happened."

Yes. The perfect alibi.

If anyone thought she needed one.

Chapter Five

Ava and Neal stood on the doorstep of the Hamiltons' nineteen thirties semi. "Bit modest compared to her sister's place, isn't it?" Ava remarked.

She knocked, and Lizzie Hamilton soon appeared. Today her zigzag harem pants had been replaced with a tunic-style ethnic-print dress, a pair of black leggings, and furry bootie slippers. The aroma of freshly brewed coffee spilled out into the hallway. Ava was happy to accept a cup.

In contrast to her sister's elegant, tidy home, Lizzie's house felt lived-in. It wasn't untidy, but it was filled with cushions and scattered magazines, and photographs and pictures crowded the walls. One in particular caught Ava's eye. It showed a smiling dark-haired boy of around fourteen with his arm around a fat Labrador. With a pang, she realised that this must be Will.

Lizzie brought their coffee. "Stephen will be here in a minute. He's just texted to say he's on his way. He's doing a big rewiring job on an old house in Herriot Street."

"Is that your son?" Ava pointed at the photograph.

"Yes, that's my Will," Lizzie answered softly.

"He's lovely. Your eyes, I'd say."

Lizzie smiled. "When he was a baby he was often mistaken for a girl because of his lovely big eyes and long lashes. I didn't mind." A faraway look came into her eyes, and then passed. "That's Flossie with him. She was a lovely dog. Will loved her to bits. Broke his heart when she died. Are you an animal lover, Sergeant Merry?"

"I'm more of a cat person really. I have a fat moggie called Camden."

The sound of a van drawing up outside heralded the arrival of Stephen Hamilton. He seemed nervous at finding two detectives in his sitting room, even though they were the reason he'd come home from work at this hour of the day. Still, there was nothing strange in that. The mere presence of the police can make perfectly innocent people feel guilty.

Lizzie brought coffee for her husband, and then tactfully withdrew.

Stephen's anxiety seemed to escalate following his wife's departure. He was a tall, gangly man, and sat folded up on the sofa like a giant stick insect, all twitchy arms and legs.

"Relax, Mr Hamilton," Neal said kindly. "It's routine for us to interview members of the immediate family when someone dies in suspicious circumstances."

"I still can't believe it," Stephen said. "We were round at Val's only a few weeks back, and Russ looked as strong as an ox."

Ava tried not to roll her eyes. Well, he hadn't died of a wasting disease, had he? Up until the moment his brains parted company with his skull, he would have been perfectly healthy.

"What was your relationship with your brother-in-law, Mr Hamilton?" she asked. "Were you on good terms?"

"I . . . I suppose so. I didn't see all that much of him really, just on family occasions, like birthdays, and Lizzie and I were sometimes invited to parties at his and Val's house. I wouldn't say we were mates, as such. We don't — didn't — have much in common. He was a businessman."

"You're a businessman too, aren't you, Mr Hamilton?" Ava said.

"I'm not in Russ's league, Sergeant," Stephen said. "Russ used to work in the City. He were a very successful man as I'm sure you know. I'm an electrician by trade. I employ between two and five sparkies at any given time, and I have someone who comes in part-time to do the books. All very modest. And it's still more than I can cope with."

"You received a loan from Cornish and Marsh to expand your business," Neal stated.

"Yes. It were Val's idea. She spoke to Russ. He and his partner don't usually touch people like me. Not much of a return in it for them. I think Paul Cornish took some persuading."

"So the investment was more of a favour for a family member."

Stephen looked offended. "It were an investment, not a gift, Inspector Neal."

"And is your business doing well?"

"It's . . . ticking over." He lowered his voice, perhaps afraid that Lizzie might be listening. "To tell the truth, I'm a bit worried now that Russ is gone. I'm not getting as much work as I'd like at the moment. I might have to let some of my employees go. Being a businessman's just not in my blood. I were happy enough working by myself, getting my work where I found it. Trouble is, I saw that big house of Val's and happened to say to her that I wished I could earn a bit more for Lizzie's sake, you know? Next thing I know, I'm a contractor. I tell you, the extra money's not worth the stress. I'm worried the profits aren't enough. I were going to talk to Russ about it."

"Can't you talk to Paul Cornish instead? Wouldn't he be sympathetic?" Neal asked.

Stephen's eyes darted around the room. The mention of Paul Cornish's name seemed to make him uneasy, almost fearful.

"Mr Hamilton?" Neal prompted. "Is something worrying you?"

"What? No. I were just thinking. Like you said, I'll probably have to make an appointment to speak to Cornish about my financial situation. I'm not looking forward to it, that's all."

"Why not speak to Val?" Ava asked.

"Why would I do that? Val doesn't know anything about finance."

Ava shrugged. "Maybe she could put your case to Paul Cornish. She must have some influence. After all, her husband was Cornish's business partner."

"If Val's got any sense, she'll steer well clear of that man." Stephen's voice shook, the fear in his eyes replaced by anger.

"You don't like Paul Cornish?" Ava asked.

"What? I didn't say that. He's just not my sort of person, that's all." Ava let it go. For now.

"And what about Lizzie?" she asked. "What was her relationship with Russ?"

Stephen looked startled. "Surely you don't think . . . ?"

"Just answer the question, please, Mr Hamilton," Neal said.

"Lizzie liked him well enough."

"We've heard differently. I get the feeling there's something you're not telling us, Mr Hamilton," Ava said.

Stephen raised his hand. He wasn't an intimidating figure, but at the mention of his wife, he seemed to grow in stature. He pulled himself upright in his chair and for the first time made eye contact. "Don't go upsetting Lizzie with all this, please." He gave a sigh, and shook his head. "People are going to tell you that Lizzie hated Russ, but that's not true. She just couldn't forgive him for what happened to her son, Will. Over the years, she's made a big effort to hide her feelings about him, for her sister's sake."

"Will died in a fire at his home," Ava said. "Does Lizzie think Russ was responsible in some way?"

"Not directly. I mean, she knows he didn't start the fire. It's just . . ." He sighed. "Lizzie and Val were going on a shopping expedition and staying overnight. Craig, Lizzie's first husband, was working away. Will were fourteen, old enough to be left on his own, but Lizzie didn't like leaving him in the house by himself at night, even at that age. Russ said he'd pick Will up from school, take him for a burger and then to a football match, and then on to his and Val's house for the night. The thing is, Russ got delayed. Something to do with business. The fire was reported at nine o'clock. They found Will in the living room, overcome by the smoke."

A silence followed. Ava guessed Neal would be thinking of his own son, Archie, and the horror of losing a child in such a terrible manner. She cleared her throat. "So Lizzie blamed Russ for Will's death because he put business first?"

"Yes." Stephen's eyes shone with tenderness and regret.

Ava couldn't blame Lizzie for feeling the way she did.

"Is there anything else you'd like to tell us, Mr Hamilton?" Neal asked.

"No. I hope you find out who killed Russ, I really do. Do you have any . . . any leads?" There was something like hopefulness in his voice, or was it despair? Ava couldn't work out which.

Neal provided the usual cliché. "We're exploring various avenues of investigation." He paused. "Were you aware that Russ had a World War Two revolver in the drawer of his desk, Mr Hamilton?"

"Yes. It were a beauty. Hard to believe Russ were shot with his own grandfather's gun. Ironical, in't it?" He shook his head, looked down, opened his mouth to speak, and then collapsed back into the sofa. His eyes were guarded again. What was up with him? Was it merely reaction to Russ's death?

Neal stood up. "Thanks for your time, Mr Hamilton. Be sure to call if you have any more to tell us."

As if on cue, Lizzie Hamilton came back into the room. She gave her husband a look of concern, Ava and Neal one of reproach. They left her to bring her husband back from whatever pit of self-torment he'd fallen into.

Ava started the car. "Did you see his reaction when Paul Cornish's name came up? Like a frightened bunny. I can't believe it's just because he's scared Paul will hassle him over his poor profits."

"I'm inclined to agree."

"Well, you offered him the chance to speak out if he knew something, but he just shut down. Pity we didn't get Lizzie on her own. I'd like to ask if he's always so nervy and anxious. Makes you wonder what he's not saying, doesn't it? Or whether he might have something to hide himself?"

Neal said nothing. He seemed deep in thought. Myrna, Ava guessed. Had she charmed her way right back into his life? Oh, why couldn't she just come right out and ask him? Neal's face, as always, gave nothing away.

* * *

Dana Schell had just been to the spa to get her nails done. Gail had made the appointment for herself, forgetting it was parents' evening at the twins' school, and rather than cancel, she'd decided to give Dana a treat. Now, admiring her neatly manicured fingernails, Dana was feeling a bit treacherous about slagging off almost every member of the Cornish family to the two detectives. Well, she did dislike them, with the possible exception of Hector. Paul had been good to her, though. Good? Was that the right word? She'd caught him eyeing her up almost from the moment she walked through the door of

Kingfisher Lodge. He'd only needed a nudge from her to cheat on his wife.

Still, Dana had to admit that her behaviour towards Gail was shabby. She blamed boredom. Her duties at Kingfisher Lodge weren't demanding, and having illicit sex with Paul whenever the opportunity arose provided a distraction. If it hadn't been for the excitement of the affair, and the 'tips' — Paul didn't like to think he was paying for sex — Dana would probably have quit her job at Kingfisher Lodge a long time ago.

She had to admit that she particularly enjoyed having sex right under the noses of the other family members. They'd done it practically all over the house. Once they'd even done it on the boat while Gail was sunbathing in the garden. It hadn't taken more than ten minutes. Gail thought Paul was 'showing Dana the ropes.' Anyway, Gail was no angel herself, sleeping with that dead man, Russ Marsh!

It had seriously creeped Dana out when the police spoke to her after interviewing Gail. The things she could have told them! Slagging everyone off hadn't been particularly clever, though. It only occurred to her later that she hadn't included Paul in her rant about the Cornishes. What would the police make of that?

She'd almost spilled everything when they asked what she'd overheard that time when Paul and Russ Marsh were slugging it out in the study. She hoped she'd managed to convince them that she hadn't heard a thing. She'd sweated it a bit at that point. Surely, they must be able to read people pretty well in their line of work. Still, they'd seemed satisfied with what she'd told them.

DI Neal had seemed a bit stern. Not really her type. He was pretty hot, though. She wouldn't say no, given the opportunity. His assistant, sergeant or whatever she was, seemed okay. Dana was sure she'd seen her in the clubs in town. She probably knew how to have a good time, unlike her anally retentive boss.

All in all, it was time she got right away from this rotten family. Russ's death had spooked her big time. Suddenly she realised she was in way above her head. With Gail out and Paul at work, she planned to make her escape this evening. She'd already booked her flight to Oz. No harm in having her nails done first, was there? For free. Her taxi wasn't coming until eight.

There was a shortcut back to Kingfisher Lodge, a path that cut through a wooded area beside one of the lakes. Dana hesitated a moment. It was already getting dark and the path wasn't well lit. *Come on, Dana, this place is gated. It's as safe as houses.*

Halfway along the path, she began to feel uneasy. It's just the trees, she told herself, and all those creepy fairy tales where bad things happen in woods.

Dana quickened her pace. The feeling intensified. She imagined she could hear rustling in the bushes lining the left-hand side of the path. Twigs snapping. A shadow moving in the trees.

But it wasn't her imagination. Her fears materialised suddenly, ahead of her on the path. A man, hurtling towards her.

His eyes glittered. There was no mistaking his intent.

Chapter Six

Ava was at Stromford hospital. A little while ago, she'd been surprised to receive a text message from Dr Joel Agard, an A&E doctor at Stromford County Hospital. She and Joel had had a fling a few months back, but he'd been looking for more commitment than Ava was ready to make, so they'd parted — on friendly terms. Joel had been dating someone else for a while now, and when she saw the text, Ava wondered whether this relationship too had ended in disappointment. Perhaps he was in need of a shoulder to cry on.

Happily for Joel, his message wasn't about a break-up. When she called him back, he explained that he had a patient with possible concussion, who'd been blathering about finding a dead body. She was confused, and Joel hadn't been able to elicit any coherent details from her.

Now Ava was on her way to the Emergency Assessment Unit, or EAU. Joel's patient, whose name was Tara Spears, had been transferred from the A&E for observation.

Maybe Tara was simply rambling, or else she'd been reading or watching a murder mystery recently and was confusing real memories with fiction.

Ava found Tara sitting up in a chair by her bed, fully clothed. She certainly didn't look delusional. A copy of *The Times* newspaper lay across her lap and she was studying the crossword, which was half filled in.

"Hi," Ava said. She showed Tara her ID. "I'm Detective Sergeant Ava Merry. I understand you think you might have found a body?"

"Oh, thank goodness. That doctor said he'd contact the police, but I wasn't sure if you'd get the message. Everyone's so busy here. And I wasn't sure if they believed me because of the bump." Tara tapped the side of her forehead where a rectangle of gauze was secured with tape.

"Tell me what you saw," Ava said, drawing up an orange plastic chair.

"I was out running. I left the house at around seven like I do every morning. It normally takes me about eight minutes to reach the woods."

"What woods?" Ava asked.

"At Crystal Lakes. That's where I live."

Oh, Ava thought. *Now what?*

"I think it must have been around seven fifteen when I came across this woman's body." Tara looked embarrassed. "I went off the path a bit because I needed to pee. I think she'd been lying there all night."

"What made you think that?"

"Her clothes looked damp. It rained during the night, didn't it?"

Ava nodded, remembering her leaking gutter. "Did you get a look at her face?"

"Yes. Her eyes were sort of staring and empty."

"Uh-huh. Did you touch her?"

Tara gulped. "Yes. First, I asked her if she was okay, even though I knew she wasn't. She didn't answer, so I knelt beside her and gave her a shake. She . . . she felt stiff.

It really scared me. I decided to run back home and call the police. I was almost at my house when I tripped and struck my head on a wall. Next thing I know, I'm in an ambulance with a king-sized headache. I think the paramedic thought I was concussed when I started telling him about the body."

"It's alright," Ava soothed. "We'll check it out."

"Will you let me know what happens?"

"Of course." Ava turned to go. Feeling like a hypocrite, for she did it herself, she said, "It's not such a great idea running through the woods alone." Tara nodded. Ava had the feeling that it would be a long time before she ventured into those woods again. "You take care of yourself. I'll be in touch."

She left Tara with her crossword and walked over to the nurses' station where she interrupted a couple of staff nurses deep in conversation. She showed them her ID.

"Can you tell me how Tara Spears is getting on now? Dr Agard said she was a bit confused when she came in earlier."

"Is she still going on about finding a body in the woods?" one of the nurses asked.

"That's kind of why I'm here."

"Well, she lost consciousness for a while, so we're keeping her in for observation. She did seem a bit confused earlier, but she's doing really well now. We thought maybe she'd stumbled across a vagrant sleeping rough in the woods?" They looked at her expectantly. "So, are you taking it seriously?"

"We'll check it out. Probably a false alarm, like you said, but best not to mention it to anyone until we know for sure." The last thing she wanted was a crowd of nosey onlookers at the site. Ava put in a call to the station and explained the situation. In her opinion, Tara was credible, and so she instructed uniform to dispatch a patrol car to the area immediately.

As Ava made her way back to A&E, the nurse she'd been speaking with on the ward appeared behind her. "I . . . er . . . don't suppose you've got time for a coffee? Or a drink some other time, when it's convenient?"

Ava smiled politely. "I'm sorry, I'm with someone."

"Oh, right. Of course you are. Oh well, it was worth a try. See you around, Detective."

"Still pulling I see, Ava." It was Joel Agard. They kissed each other on the cheek.

"He was cute, but . . ." But what? Joel was cute too, good in bed, attentive and sexy, and they'd got on well together. Since Joel, there'd been no one.

"You've been talking to my concussed patient, I take it? Or are you just here to see me?" Joel smiled.

"Actually, I came by to say thanks for contacting me."

"No problem." Joel's pager beeped. "Sorry, got to go." He gave her an apologetic smile.

With a pang of regret, Ava watched him disappear through the doors to A&E. She hadn't thought about him that much since they broke up, but all of a sudden she missed him. It was wrong, she knew, but if he suggested a night together for old times' sake, she'd accept without hesitation.

* * *

When Ava got to the station, PJ greeted her with the words, "Your jogger wasn't hallucinating. It looks like we've got another murder."

"Right." Ava said. Why did murders always seem to come in twos?

"You're going out to the scene, aren't you?" PJ asked.

"Yeah. Fancy a walk in the woods?"

"Okay. Just . . . give me five, can you?"

Ava was leaning on the bonnet of her car checking her emails on her phone when PJ finally joined her, having changed into jeans and a pair of trainers. Unlike Ava, who tended to dress down for work, PJ, freshly out of uniform, favoured smart dresses and tailored trousers. Evidently she'd considered the red A-line dress she'd been wearing to be unsuitable attire for a country ramble.

"Always keep a change of clothing in my locker for times like this," she said, breezily. Then, as they both belted up, "So, how did your dinner with the DI and his family go?"

Ava had been anticipating the question since PJ returned to work. She'd been away on a week's holiday with her partner, DC Steve Bryce. She wondered why it had taken her friend so long to ask. Come to think of it, PJ had been a bit quiet of late.

"It was . . . nice. I'm still surprised they invited me to a family occasion. I think it was Maggie's way of thanking me for saving her brother's life."

Ava couldn't believe it was only a few weeks ago that she'd rescued Jim Neal from a deranged killer who'd been trying to choke him to death with a plank of wood. She'd grabbed the first weapon to hand — an old-fashioned flat iron — and belted the killer over the head with it.

The invitation to a family dinner celebrating Maggie's engagement to Neal's best friend, Jock Dodds, had indeed come from Maggie, but Ava had left out a crucial nugget of information. Maggie's exact words were, "Jimmy would like you to come to dinner . . ." It would only have fed into PJ's fantasy about a romance between Ava and the DI.

The evening had been more than just nice. Ava had been welcomed as part of the family. She and Neal — somehow she couldn't think of him having any other name — had been completely at ease in each other's company. She'd have to content herself with that for now. Maybe friendship and a good working relationship was the best they could manage when they worked so closely together. Still, her encounter with Joel Agard had reminded Ava that something was missing from her life. And it wasn't just sex.

To her surprise, PJ didn't ask her to elaborate. This seemed out of character to say the least. PJ wasn't known for holding back. Ava glanced sideways at her friend and saw that she was staring straight ahead. She looked miserable.

"Is everything okay between you and Steve?" Ava asked.

PJ burst into tears. "No. Oh, Ava. Steve might have cancer."

Taken aback, Ava stalled at the traffic lights. She'd been imagining a lovers' tiff, or even a major bust-up. Not this.

"*Might* have cancer? What does that mean? Has he seen a doctor? Had tests done?" The gears grated and they moved away.

"He found a lump when we were on holiday. On his left testicle. The doctor thinks it could be a tumour. He's got to see a specialist and have an ultrasound scan."

"I'm so sorry, Peej. You must be worried sick." Ava never knew what to say at such times. She didn't want to offer platitudes, didn't want to play down the risk or PJ's worries. She pulled over.

"Whatever happens, I'm here for you Peej. You know that, don't you?" PJ nodded, tearfully. Ava took her hand. "Does he have an appointment?"

"The twenty-fifth, unless a cancellation comes through. His GP prioritised it but he's still got to wait ages to see someone. Lucky it's not longer, I suppose, but it's going to be an endless wait." Ava could only agree.

"Does Neal know?" she asked. PJ shook her head.

"You need to tell him as soon as possible," Ava advised.

"I won't let it affect my work." PJ's promotion to detective constable was recent and she was keen to prove her worth.

"I know, but you should still tell him."

"I'll tell him this afternoon."

PJ's news cast a cloud over the morning. Instead of hearing about her friend's trip to Alicante, Ava listened instead to her worries about diagnosis, treatment and all the longer-term things, like whether they would be able to have children. Ava let PJ get it all off her chest. By the time they reached Crystal Lakes, she seemed to be in a more positive frame of mind.

They parked the car at the marina beside a police patrol car. A uniformed officer, who introduced himself as PC Patrick Doyle, met them and led the way into the woods.

"Creepy place to go running alone," PJ remarked, as they entered the wood and the light dwindled under the canopy of trees. "You don't go anywhere this off the beaten track, do you, Ava?"

Ava was a keen runner and she hated to think that any routes were off limits to her simply because of her gender. She wasn't easily intimidated, but then again she was a cop. "This isn't really off the beaten track. We're inside a gated community, remember?"

"Yeah, but there's a body in the woods," PJ reminded her.

"I can remember when this was all woodland and countryside," PC Doyle said, waving an arm at the Crystal Lakes ghetto.

"Me too," said PJ, who was Stromfordshire born and bred. "My grandad used to bring me and my brothers here to play."

It was still a sizeable wood, Ava thought, pleased that the developers had left some of the mature trees.

"Not much further," Doyle said. The flattened vegetation on either side of the path showed that Doyle and his colleague had searched the undergrowth.

"Find anything?" Ava asked him.

"Just the sort of stuff you'd expect to find in a patch of woodland. Ava nodded. Parks and wooded areas were often littered with empty drinks cans and torn Rizla packets. Sometimes there would be evidence that someone had been sleeping rough — old clothes or traces of a campfire.

"Any obvious cause of death?"

"Oh yes. Very obvious. Looks like her head was bashed in with a shillelagh."

"A what?" Ava asked.

"A club," PJ said. "Are you Irish?" The PC didn't have an accent.

"My parents are. Clue's in the name." PC Doyle winked at her. "Here we are." He pointed off the path into the trees. Ava and PJ followed him through a tangle of bushes, until they almost stumbled over a middle-aged PC sitting on a wide tree stump.

"Ah, at last," he said. "Still, don't reckon she's in a hurry to go anywhere." His eyes sought out a spot amid the undergrowth, where a discarded ballerina pump was the only sign of what they had come to see.

Ava saw PJ steel herself. The grumpy PC struggled to his feet and took them to the body.

They stood in silence, staring down at the victim. She lay amid a clump of flattened bracken, grass springing up between her legs and arms, her wide-open eyes staring up at the underside of a blazing, autumnal awning, as if astonished at its splendour. Blood had dried in grainy streaks of purplish brown and red ochre, painted across her face like camouflage.

All of a sudden Ava felt cold. It was as though, in seconds, the season had slipped, unnoticed, into winter. Every bird, every creature in their radius had fallen silent.

"I know her," Ava said, at last. "That's Dana Schell, the Cornishes' help."

"I found a phone," the older PC said. "Could be hers. Bit careless of the killer to leave it near the scene. But they're not always thinking straight right after the act, are they?"

Ava knelt to take a closer look at the body. Her eyes were drawn to Dana's hands. At first she couldn't work out why, and then she realised it was the nails.

"Look at her nails," she said to PJ. "Looks like she'd had them done recently, but see how they're torn."

"She tried to fight her attacker off." PJ shuddered. "Let's hope she got some of the fucker's DNA on those nails." It was unusual for PJ to swear. Ava found it strangely worrying.

Ava remained at the scene as the senior presiding officer. PJ waited with her until the CSIs arrived and evidence collection was underway. It was late afternoon by the time they drove back to the station, with the phone in the glove compartment, tucked securely in an evidence bag.

As soon as they walked into the office, Ava crossed to her desk and rummaged in her drawer. She extracted a charging lead and plugged in the phone. "Don't know if it'll work after lying in the woods all night, especially after all that rain. Here's hoping the case protected it a bit."

They waited. The phone flickered back to life. A selfie of Dana's smiling face filled the screen.

It wasn't password protected, so Ava checked through the more recent text messages. One immediately caught her attention.

It was from Russ Marsh. *Go to hell.*

Chapter Seven

"So Dana Schell communicated with Russ Marsh shortly before his death?" Neal looked up from reading the string of text messages that had passed between Dana and Russ. "Who's been checking the phone Russ Marsh had on his desk when he was found?"

"Tom, sir," Ava replied. "He said it was mostly business stuff. He didn't mention this." She hoped Tom wasn't in trouble. "Maybe Russ Marsh deleted the messages?"

"What do you make of that question in her opening text?" Neal asked. He read it aloud. "'There are no secrets in a house that has servants. Do you agree?'"

Ava frowned. "The tone's obviously sarcastic. I doubt Dana thought of herself as a servant. But it's clearly a reference to her position in the Cornish household."

"What's she getting at? Is she telling him she's overheard something in the Cornish household that might be of interest to Russ Marsh?" Neal said.

"Do you think she was working up to blackmail?"

Neal shrugged. "Reading between the lines? Could be. Or, she could be offering him information in return for money."

Ava reread the conversation. Dana had texted Russell three times. First with her enigmatic teaser about no secrets in a house with servants, to which Russ had responded with a question mark. In her second text, Dana strongly hinted that she knew something and that Russ should meet with her to talk about it. This had elicited two question marks from Russ.

Her third text was more pressing. It read, *You can't afford to ignore my texts.* A thinly veiled threat? It was this message that had prompted Russ Marsh to respond with, 'Go to hell.' Would he still be alive if he'd responded differently?

"So what did Dana know? Or think she knew? Something about Paul and the business? Or something more personal, perhaps," Ava said. "Should we speak with Val Marsh? Maybe Russ told her about the texts, although the fact that he deleted the thread suggests he didn't want anyone knowing." She paused. "Could Dana have learned something that ended up getting her killed?" Ava said.

"As always, we make no assumptions," Neal said.

Ouch. Neal hadn't taken that tone with her for some time. What had got him riled?

"Sir," Ava said. "Are we going to visit the Cornishes now?"

Neal glanced at his watch. It was already quite late, but it was important for at least one of them to see how the Cornishes would receive the news of Dana's death. Neal rubbed his chin.

"Drive out there now. Take DS Knight with you. I have other matters to attend to, or I'd accompany you myself."

What other matters? Myrna? Ava nodded and left Neal to his thoughts. Outside his office, she broke the news to Tom.

"Where's PJ?" she asked, looking around.

"Had to go," Tom said. "Something about her partner." Ava frowned and took another minute to ping off a supportive text to PJ.

She left the station with Tom. Knowing that he liked everything to do with cars, she let him drive.

A queue of traffic on the road outside the car park held them up for a few minutes. Tom drummed impatiently on the steering wheel and looked in the rear-view mirror. "Hello, looks like the boss's got himself a date."

Ava swung round and saw a red-haired woman walk up to a waiting Neal, and kiss him on both cheeks.

"Myrna!" she exclaimed before she could stop herself.

"Myrna? Unusual name," Tom said.

"She's an ex-girlfriend."

"Doesn't look like it to me." Ava looked over her shoulder as discreetly as she could. Myrna had linked arms with Neal and was leaning in like a tender lover.

"Ouch." Tom had pulled suddenly out onto the road and she'd hit the window, but her exclamation wasn't solely a reaction to the pain.

"So, doing anything exciting at the weekend?" Ava asked Tom to distract herself.

"Going to a mate's stag do back home." Tom had grown up in the East End of London, and he returned every so often to catch up with family and friends.

"Paintballing. Semi-automatics. Fifteen of us running around like lunatics. Ratatatatatat . . . Wicked. Can't wait."

Ava laughed. "PJ loves paintballing. And laser tag."

"Yeah? Never would have guessed it," Tom said.

"What? You think she'd prefer to dress up as a princess and get her nails done?"

"No offence, Ava, but PJ just doesn't strike me as an action girl. Now if you'd told me you were into paintballing, I'd have no problem believing it."

"Huh." Ava was slightly put out at Tom's assessment of PJ. Just because she was on the small side, roundish and feminine, didn't mean she couldn't squirt paint at a target. You didn't have to be an Olympic athlete to do that. Aware that her annoyance with Tom was partly displaced irritation at seeing Jim Neal with Myrna, she said, "Yeah, well. Who doesn't love paintballing?"

Tom slowed down. "Is this the turnoff?"

"Next one," Ava said.

"Looks well posh. What's this? Flipping sentry post?" Tom drew to a halt at the security barrier. A burly guard was already approaching.

"It's a gated community. Just flash your ID."

Ava directed Tom to the Cornishes' house. "You could fit the whole estate that I lived on in Tower Hamlets into these grounds," he commented.

They parked and walked up to the imposing front door of Kingfisher Lodge. Ava couldn't help thinking of the last time she'd been here with Jim Neal. They'd been let in by Dana Schell. Ava wondered who would answer the door now she wasn't around.

Paul Cornish, it seemed.

Ava hadn't expected him to be home at this hour. He greeted Ava, and she introduced Tom. Paul showed them into the sitting room with a view of the lake and went off in search of Gail. Tom crossed to the French doors and gave a low whistle. "Is that . . . ?"

"The Cornishes' boat? Yep. Most of the residents here have got one."

"Do they have a daughter?"

Ava grinned. "Yes, but she's a bit young for you."

"Pity."

Gail Cornish appeared. "DS Merry. I've been in the garden." Paul Cornish hovered just inside the door.

"What can we do for you this time, Sergeant?" Gail's tone was as cool as her handshake.

"We wanted to speak with you about your help, Dana Schell." Ava watched the Cornishes. Gail looked puzzled. Paul raised his eyebrows, questioningly.

"Dana's not here. It's her day off," Gail said.

"When did you last see her?"

"Yesterday. Sixish. She was going to the spa for a nail appointment. Mine, actually. I'd forgotten it was parents' evening at the twins' school and it was too late to cancel the appointment."

"Did she sleep here last night?" Ava asked.

"No, but that's not unusual. Dana has friends in Stromford. She sometimes stays the night with them when she's got a day off the next day. I don't expect her to tell me what she does in her free time. What's all this about, Sergeant?" Either Gail had no idea that Dana was dead, or she was a very convincing liar. Ava turned to Paul, who'd remained silent. He gave no hint of what he was thinking.

"Either something has happened to Dana, or she's done something wrong. Which is it, officers?" His wife stared at him as though this had not occurred to her.

"I'm sorry to have to give you this news," Ava said. "Dana Schell's body was found in the woods, here at Crystal Lakes, early this morning. We believe she was murdered."

Gail and Paul exchanged looks. "Are you sure?" Paul asked.

"Yes. I met Dana. I was able to identify her body," Ava replied. Gail looked genuinely shocked.

"That's terrible news," Paul said. "What happened?"

"I don't know what to say," Gail said. "Did she suffer?" Ava told Gail that Dana's death would have been quick. She hoped this would satisfy her for now. It was not in the police's interest to reveal the probable cause of death at this stage. Besides, it had yet to be firmly established.

"Does this have anything to do with Russ Marsh's murder?" Gail asked.

"I'm sorry. I don't have any further information at the moment."

"But surely there must be a connection. I mean, it can't just be a coincidence that two people connected to us are murdered in one week? Unless this is some kind of random serial killer thing."

"I'm not able to speculate, Mrs Cornish, but I think I can reassure you that this is not the work of a serial killer."

"Then there *must* be a connection between the deaths," Gail insisted.

"That's not logical, sweetheart. The one doesn't follow from the other." Paul Cornish's tone was mildly patronising.

"We retrieved Dana's phone from the scene," Tom said. Ava had been looking at Paul, and now she thought she detected a tiny rift in his composure. If so, it was fleeting. "Dana had been in contact with Russell Marsh shortly before his death."

"Told you so," Gail said immediately. "A connection." No one contradicted her. In any case, she was probably right. Ava wasn't sure that it was wise of Tom to have brought up the phone at this point, but she was interested in studying Paul Cornish's reactions — or lack thereof.

"Dana sent Russ Marsh some cryptic texts. She seemed to suggest that she had some information that Mr Marsh might be willing to pay to obtain. Any ideas?" Tom asked. His tone was accusatory. Ava would have pitched the question differently.

"What?" Paul immediately adopted a defensive stance, arms folded across his chest, legs wide apart.

Gail looked uncomfortable. "My affair with Russ Marsh was over and done with, if that's what you're getting at. Whatever secret Dana thought she'd stumbled upon, it didn't involve Russ and me."

So why mention it?

Tom followed up with routine questions. Gail had been at the parents' evening until nine o'clock. She'd driven home with the twins afterwards, and they'd arrived home at around nine thirty. Paul claimed he'd got home just before them. Kitty Cornish had been at a friend's house, returning at around ten.

Time of death for Dana was most likely between seven forty-five and nine o'clock. Her nails had looked newly manicured, though several were broken off. She must have met her attacker on her way home from the salon, while taking a shortcut through the woods to Kingfisher Lodge. Obviously Gail knew about the nail appointment, but there was no way of ascertaining who else Dana might have told.

"We'd like to take a look at Dana's room," Ava said.

Ava and Tom followed Gail upstairs. Not unexpectedly, Dana's room was on the small side and was probably the only room in the house without a view of the lake. On the plus side, it was pleasantly furnished and had an en suite bathroom. There was a tray with some mugs and a stainless-steel kettle on a dressing table, which gave the room a hotel-like feel. Gail excused herself, saying that she had to 'sort out a meal.' Was that normally Dana's job?

Dana hadn't been particularly tidy. There were discarded items of clothing on the floor and a bath towel hanging loosely over a chair. The mugs were dirty and the bin was overflowing with empty crisp packets and biscuit wrappers. Ava ventured into the en suite and found it crammed with skincare and beauty products. Pricey stuff too. How did Dana afford this?

She put on some latex gloves and rummaged in the bin. Nothing of interest. Loads of cotton wool balls and discarded make-up products, much like the one in Ava's own bathroom. She returned to the bedroom.

Tom was looking pleased with himself. "Look what I found under the bed!" He held up a tartan tin with a picture of a stag on the lid.

"Petticoat tails?" Ava asked.

"Take a butcher's inside." He removed the lid and held it out. Ten or so plastic snap bags of white powder were tucked neatly inside.

Ava gave a low whistle. "Interesting."

Tom held up one of the bags. "Got to be a few k's worth in here."

"So, d'you reckon Dana's been doing a bit of dealing to supplement her income? Explains the upmarket cosmetics she's got all around the bathroom. Was she dealing herself, or just storing the stuff for someone, I wonder?"

"Friend? Member of the Cornish family?"

Ava nodded. Statistically, people were more likely to become involved in the drug trade through friends or family members who were already involved.

"Could this have got her killed?" Tom asked.

"Maybe. Find anything else?" Ava asked.

Tom laughed. "Five k's worth of coke isn't enough?"

Ava took a quick look in Dana's wardrobes and drawers, but she found nothing out of the ordinary.

They went downstairs and into the kitchen, Tom carrying the shortbread tin tucked under his arm.

"What's that?" Gail Cornish peered at the tin. Tom opened the lid and showed them. Gail gasped.

Paul frowned. "Dana was taking drugs?"

"Not necessarily," Tom said. "This is way too much coke for one person. Dealers aren't always users themselves."

"Dealers? Dana was a drug dealer?" Gail shrieked. "Oh, this just keeps getting better and better. Oh my god! The children. Has she been giving that shit to my kids? Is she mixed up with some big drugs cartel?"

"Calm down, Gail," Paul said. His voice could have cut steel.

"Fuck off, Paul. It's bad enough that you were shagging the little slut, but she's put my kids in danger. I won't have you defending her."

A profound silence followed her words. Paul's face turned puce, whether out of rage or embarrassment it was impossible to tell.

Now that she had started, there was no stopping Gail. "What? You thought I didn't know? How stupid do you think I am? I've seen the clothes she's got hanging in her wardrobe up there, and the expensive toiletries. She can't afford stuff like that on what we're paying her."

"She was dealing cocaine," Paul said coolly. "You don't think that would have helped her afford a few luxuries?"

Gail looked unconvinced.

"Besides, aren't you the one who indulges in extramarital affairs?"

Ava and Tom listened in silence, embarrassed for the pair of them.

"Once. One bloody time in twenty-five years of marriage. You just can never resist an opportunity to rub my nose in it, can you?"

Ignoring his wife's remark, Paul Cornish turned his icy gaze on Ava and Tom. "Enjoying this are you, officers? How the other half live, eh? Not as idyllic as it looks, is it?"

Ava risked a glance at Tom. You bet he was enjoying it.

"Come on," she said briskly, and grabbed Tom's arm. "Thank you for your cooperation, Mr and Mrs Cornish. You can expect a visit from our forensics people. DS Knight and I will see ourselves out."

Chapter Eight

Hector read Kitty's text in utter dismay. *Hi bro. WTF the police have just raided Dana's room and found a humungous stash of coke under her bed!!*

He had a burning urge to call Kitty back immediately and demand more information. But that would be foolish. Far better to play it down.

His fingerprints were all over those clip bags. That didn't matter, did it? He wasn't on a police database anywhere, was he? So they couldn't identify him, right? Hector relaxed a notch. Panicked again. What if they wanted to take fingerprints from everyone in the family, just to rule them out? Shit. Could they do that? He ran through the possibilities, his heart pounding.

At least the police weren't going to be pointing the finger at him. Not right away, anyway. With a sick feeling in his gut, he wondered just how much digging they were likely to do.

All because his parents had left him in near penury after that gambling business. The way he saw it, his father was partly responsible for his current predicament. He'd only got involved in dealing after Paul cut his allowance.

Not that he'd be stupid enough to say that to his face when the inevitable showdown took place.

Could he be certain of his father's help? When he found out about the gambling, Paul had refused to pay off any more of his debts. Hector had endured a long lecture about money and responsibility, about learning the hard way. Tough love, Paul had called it.

And it had been tough. Gambling was more than a distraction, it was a necessity. Everything about Cambridge bored Hector. He hadn't even wanted to go there in the first place. He wasn't an academic. If it hadn't been for all the extra tutoring his parents had paid for, he'd never have attained his A levels, or the grades that he'd needed to secure his place.

After Cambridge, there was a job lined up for him in the City with an old friend of his father's. But not if he were charged with possession with intent to deal. He could even be looking at a spell in prison. He'd end up with a criminal record, meaning he could kiss goodbye to any hopes of a career in banking.

The more he thought about it the more he realised that someone else needed to take the fall for him. And it might as well be Dana.

* * *

Ruth had been having a good day prior to Hector's phone call. Her mother had been making a big effort with her and Cam, and he was enjoying running about in the big house and its grounds. This afternoon, Val had taken him swimming, insisting that she could cope easily with a toddler splashing about in the pool. Everyone, it seemed, could manage Cam better than his own mother.

Ruth's homecoming hadn't been all good. Walking into the study and looking at her father's desk had been pretty upsetting. Someone — the police? Val? — had made an effort to clean up, but wherever she looked, Ruth could see tiny tell-tale dots that had been missed.

Ruth was in the study now. Despite the horror of what had happened there, it was still the place where she felt closest to her father. The room drew her like a magnet every time she passed the door.

She crossed to the bookcase and picked out the old volume of eighteenth-century verse that she'd given her father for his fiftieth birthday. She'd found it in a second-hand bookshop and knew at once that he'd like it. It was the last gift she'd given him, as it turned out. The foxing on the top edge looked like dried blood. Ruth shuddered. She returned it to the shelf before it set off a chain of associations in her mind.

Next, Ruth took a few tentative steps closer to Russ's desk and picked up his paperweight, a bronze replica of a flying horse of the Tan Dynasty that she had coveted for most of her life. She remembered playing with it on the floor of her father's study while he worked. "I'll leave it to you in my will," he had joked. If she asked her mother for it now, it would be hers at once. The thought made Ruth realise that her father was truly gone.

He'd taught her a lesson by not simply giving it to her all those years ago. Ruth had always known her parents were wealthy, but she'd also learned that she couldn't have everything she wanted.

What she wanted more than anything in the world right now was to see her father sitting there in his ergonomic leather chair, smiling at her and bouncing Cam on his knee. Ruth wiped away a tear, and replaced the paperweight.

Her phone rang. Hector Cornish. What did he want now? He'd promised to leave her and Fin alone. Perhaps she was wrong to assume his call meant more trouble. Perhaps Hector had heard the news of her father's death and was ringing to offer his condolences. But Hector tended to have some agenda of his own. She was right.

"I need a little favour, Ruth. Can we meet? This evening?"

"It's not a great time, Hector. In case you didn't hear, my dad died. He was murdered, actually."

"Yes, I heard. I'm sorry, Ruth. I wouldn't trouble you at such a time but it's kind of urgent. It affects Fin, maybe you and Cam too. Shall we say seven? I'll pick you up."

"What's this about, Hector? You said you'd leave us alone. Is this something to do with—?"

"Have you heard about Dana?"

Ruth caught her breath.

"I didn't kill her if that's what you're thinking. You always did have an overactive imagination, Ruthie."

"Why did you ask about Dana, then?"

"Because her death has complicated things. Look, I don't want to say any more on the phone. Can you meet me or not? I know what I said about our little secret, but needs must . . ."

Did she have a choice? Given what Hector knew about her past, Ruth didn't think so. He'd used that knowledge against her once and promised never to use it again. She and Fin had been stupid to trust him.

Ruth sighed. "I'll meet you." Hector named a bar that they'd spent a lot of time in as teenagers.

Ruth texted her mother and asked if she could look after Cam that evening, so she could go out with a friend. Val sent her back a picture of Cam looking cute in his tiny Nemo swimming trunks.

Later, Val offered to drop Ruth off in town so that she could 'have a drink and forget her worries for a bit.' She even offered to pick Ruth up afterwards, but Ruth said she'd take a taxi to save disturbing Cam.

"Who are you meeting, sweetheart?"

"A friend from Cambridge. Her name's Peri," Ruth said. She kissed Cam, surprised — and a little disappointed — that he didn't protest about being left with Val.

Hector was waiting for her outside the bar. Although they had both been at Cambridge at roughly the same time, their paths had seldom crossed there. Until, one afternoon, she and Fin had bumped into Hector and Dana Schell in the Grafton shopping centre, and Ruth had invited them round for a meal.

After they had been reminiscing for a while, Ruth had grown comfortable and trusting, and had stupidly told them why her father wouldn't accept Fin as a suitable partner for her. He had been involved with dealing drugs, years ago. If only she'd kept her mouth shut.

This evening, they greeted each other with mutual suspicion. Hector paid for their drinks and led Ruth upstairs. The pub was in a medieval building. It had a warren of connecting rooms spread over two different levels. All of the rooms had low, beamed ceilings and small, leaded light windows. To compensate for the dimness, and, presumably, to provide atmosphere, the owners of the bar had provided table lamps with colourful Tiffany-style shades. On any other occasion the room might have seemed cosy and intimate. This evening though, the building's great age and the dark room added to Ruth's sense of unease.

Hector chose a quiet room on the second floor, where they were the sole customers. As soon as they were settled at the table, she came straight to the point. "So what do you want, Hector?"

Hector got straight to the point too. "I need you to lie for me."

Ruth nodded, unsurprised. "What makes you think I still care about keeping what happened that night a secret? Now that my father's dead . . ."

Hector leaned across the table, and covered her hand with his. "Your father's death doesn't change a thing." He leaned in closer. The whites of his eyes were criss-crossed with thready red veins. "You know that, don't you, Ruth?"

Facetious bastard. Ruth scarcely knew herself, so how could Hector sit there and claim to know what made her tick? But he was right. Hector understood not only the source of her sadness, but also her need for silence. Still, she challenged him. "No, actually, I don't."

Hector's look said, *Oh, come on.* "Look at you," he said. "Twenty-two years old and saddled with a kid we both know you never wanted. You were a high flier, Ruth. With your privileged upbringing, you should be well on the way to a great career by now. You wanted to be a doctor when we were kids, didn't you? Before—"

"What's your point, Hector?"

"You're living the life you think you deserve."

"I like my life well enough." It was true. She loved Fin. Her feelings for Cam were complex, but there was love mixed in with all the other emotions. In time, perhaps, love would be uppermost. Wearily, she asked again. "What do you want?"

"Nothing much. The police found some coke under Dana's bed. I persuaded her to hide it there in case Gail or Kitty or the twins found it in my room. Dana at least had a lock on her door. Just in case the police point the finger at me, I need you to tell them that you saw Dana doing drugs in Cambridge. I'll tell them she was a cokehead and that's why we split up. Because I don't do drugs."

"What if they start asking questions in Cambridge? It won't take them long to discover what you've been up to."

"They won't get anything on me. I've been the soul of discretion," Hector said. "My clients are loyal to me and they know how to keep their mouths shut. Besides, like me, most of them are headed for lucrative careers when they leave Cambridge, and it wouldn't do for their future employers to know they had a drug habit."

"You'd blackmail them?"

"I've had practice." Hector smirked. Ruth wanted to punch him in the mouth. "You and your father."

"My father?" Ruth was shocked.

"I needed a little help with some gambling debts and *Pater* was being boring. He cut my allowance."

"You asked my dad for money? You bastard."

"Again, needs must. You'd be surprised how much he was prepared to cough up to protect his little darling's reputation."

Ruth felt sick. Her past was like the ripples from a whirlpool. Eventually it sucked everyone in.

"The pigs are already asking themselves how that poor working-class girl could afford to buy that amount of drugs from her wages as a skivvy. Was it, in fact, the rich kid she was screwing? Look, all you need to do is tell them Dana was doing a lot of drugs when she was in Cambridge. That your boyfriend, Fin, thought she might be dealing. With Fin's background, they'll believe him."

"But won't that make it seem like you were involved too?"

"Not if you tell them otherwise. Come on, Ruthie. It's no big deal. Dana *was* into drugs, that's no lie. She agreed to hide the stuff in her room for cash and a share of the coke."

Ruth considered this. It seemed like an ill-conceived plan to her. And she didn't want any part in sullying Dana's reputation. But Hector had power over her. "Alright, I'll do it. On one condition. You don't involve Fin."

"Can't think what you see in that nerdy intellectual, Ruthie. No, Fin has to be involved. Like I said, he can tell the police he recognised the signs in Dana because he used to deal himself. It will give a flavour of authenticity to the story."

Ruth pondered what to do.

"You can do this little favour for me, Ruthie." Hector leaned back in his chair. "Alternatively, I can have a little chat with—"

"Shut up!" Ruth's eyes darted around the empty room. As if in a dream, she found herself complying with Hector's request.

* * *

Ava put her head around the door to Neal's office. "Ruth Marsh just called to say she has some information about Dana Schell that might be useful. She's on her way now. Okay to put her in interview room one?"

Neal merely nodded. Then he smiled.

"Shall I take PJ?" Was he even listening? Another nod. And, miraculously, another smile. He seemed almost happy. Was it Myrna's influence? Ava wondered, surprised at how much this mattered to her.

"Okay." Ava risked a question. "Is everything okay, sir?"

"Fine, considering we have two murder investigations underway and we don't seem to making much progress," Neal said.

Not what she'd been after, but if Neal wanted to keep his affairs close to his chest, that was up to him.

Ava and PJ went to the interview room. Ruth arrived five minutes later, out of breath and flustered. She had Cam with her in his pushchair. "Sorry, no one to watch him at the moment," she explained.

"Family room?" PJ asked. Ava nodded.

They all trooped out. In the family room, Cam made for a big toy box and began strewing the contents over the floor.

"You have some information for us? About Dana Schell?" Ava asked.

Ruth nodded. "Yes. I don't know if it's relevant, but the more I think about it the more certain I am that it might be."

Ava gave her an encouraging nod.

"You know my father's business partner, Paul Cornish?" Ava said nothing. "You know he has a son called Hector?" She paused. "Well, Hector was in the same year as me at school."

Cam had found a tambourine and began banging it against the leg of the nearest chair. PJ slid to the floor beside the child and redirected his attention to some colourful plastic building bricks. Ruth looked surprised.

"You're probably wondering why I'm telling you about Hector." Ruth gave a nervous laugh. *Not really.* Ava had a hunch it was going to be something about the drugs found in Dana's room.

"Hector was sort of seeing Dana for a while. I mean, it wasn't anything serious. Just, well, just sex really."

Why else would a rich boy like Hector bother with a pretty but penniless girl like Dana? Sometimes Ava wondered if Jim Neal's political views were rubbing off on her.

"She came to stay with him in Cambridge sometimes. I saw them together a couple of times at the market, and around and about."

"Go on," Ava said.

"One day, my partner Fin and I bumped into them in the Grafton shopping centre." Ruth stared at Cam and PJ for a moment, as if gathering her thoughts. *She looks a bit like her father*, Ava thought. Or how he'd looked prior to having his head practically blown off. Ava had seen pictures. They had the same deep-set eyes.

"Fin and I, we don't know many other couples in Cambridge. Not socially, anyway. So I invited them round for dinner." Ruth looked down. "This is kind of embarrassing. Did my mum tell you that my dad and I weren't talking? Like for ages before . . . before . . . you know?"

"Your Aunt Lizzie told us about that. It was because your father disapproved of Cam's dad, wasn't it?" Ava said.

"Yes. Dad hired a private detective to look into Fin's background. I was furious. It seemed like such a big deal at the time. Now I . . ."

"You realise he was just looking out for you, being overprotective. Dads tend to do that. He would have forgiven you," PJ said from the floor.

Ava smiled inwardly. So like her friend to provide emotional support. PJ would probably have found some way of reconciling everyone without the whole family breaking up. *They would have talked it over.* Ava was sure she would have reacted exactly as Ruth had.

"Fin had already told me he had a past. Dad's PI didn't find out anything I didn't already know."

"The PI found out that Fin had been involved with drugs when he was a teenager? Your aunt told us that too."

"Oh, trust Aunt Lizzie. So you know already?"

"Yes."

"Well, Fin caught Dana doing drugs in our bathroom. He walked in on her doing a line of coke. He knew what she was doing because . . . because of his own experience. Anyway, he had a quiet word with Hector about it and Hector swore he didn't know that Dana was using. He . . . he was really angry with her for . . . for abusing our hospitality."

Ruth seemed to falter. She watched in a detached sort of way as PJ hugged a succession of soft toys handed to her by a giggling Cam.

"Later, Hector told me he'd found out Dana was doing a bit of dealing. He didn't want anything to do with her after that. And he threatened to tell his dad if she didn't stop." Ruth's words tumbled out as though she needed to get them said quickly, like a child repeating a lesson learned by heart.

"I . . . just thought you should know, in case . . . in case drugs had something to do with Dana's death?" She looked from Ava to PJ for reassurance and gave another nervous laugh.

Ava thought of the shortbread tin and what it contained. Could Ruth have heard about it from a member of the Cornish household? From Hector, to be precise? Highly likely.

"It was thoughtful of you to volunteer this information, Ms Marsh," Ava said. "We were already aware of a possible drug connection, but you did the right thing in coming forward."

Ruth stood up. "Th-that's okay." She looked own at PJ. "Thank you for playing with Cam. He can be a handful."

"My pleasure. He's a little sweetheart," PJ said, getting to her feet and brushing at her trousers.

"So people keep telling me," Ruth said. She sounded resentful.

They escorted Ruth back to the front door with Cam in his pushchair and watched her walk away. "What did you make of that?" Ava said. "Were you able to hear down there with all the noise that kid was making?"

"Cam. His name's Cam. And yes, I heard most of it. Strange, isn't it, how these two families keep getting intertangled."

"Think you've just invented a new word, Peej, but I know what you mean. It's exactly what I was thinking. One thing I did notice, though. Ruth didn't make eye contact with me much. Her eyes kept sliding to you and Cam."

"Not that odd, she is a mum. They're always watchful."

"You're probably right. Still, I thought there was something not quite right about that whole interview. She was way too nervous for one thing, and I had a feeling she didn't believe her own story."

"I agree," PJ said. "It was almost as if she didn't believe that we'd believe what she was saying. Do you think someone put her up to it? Hector Cornish perhaps?

"To deflect our attention from himself, maybe? I wouldn't be surprised. But maybe that's just my prejudice talking. You know, bored rich kid with more money than he knows what to do with. To tell the truth, we know very little about Dana or her background. For all we know, she could be Stromford's answer to Walter White. "

As they made their way back to the office, PJ blurted out, "Steve's ultrasound's the day after tomorrow. He got a cancellation."

Ava put a hand on her arm. "That's good. You did talk to the chief about having time off to go to the hospital, didn't you?"

"Yes, it's all sorted. Oh, Ava, I'm so worried I don't know what to do with myself."

Ava squeezed the arm. "I wish I could say everything's going to be alright."

"That's the worst thing about being a grown-up, isn't it?" PJ said, quietly. "No longer being able to believe someone when they tell you that."

"At least you'll know. For better or worse."

In the end, all Ava could offer was a cliché.

Chapter Nine

Gail Cornish stood at her jetty looking at their neat little river cruiser. She and Paul had bought it soon after they moved to Crystal Lakes. It had been their anniversary present to each other. It was a status symbol, like the house they lived in and their cars. An emblem of their wealth and success. But not their happiness. They'd bought the boat a month after Gail confessed to her fling with Russ Marsh, when their marriage was hanging by a thread.

Paul had been angrier about the affair than he let on, Gail knew. Angry at Russ's betrayal as much as hers. Gail would have bet her life that Paul and Russ's friendship, their partnership, everything, would have fallen apart, but somehow, against all the odds, the centre had held.

There had been the inevitable outburst of violence when Paul learned the truth. He'd broken Russ's nose. Afterwards, Paul had talked of building bridges, of not throwing away nearly thirty years of friendship. But Gail knew from experience that her husband was not a particularly forgiving man.

Paul had once told her that he'd agreed to go into business with Russ because Russ was good at assessing risk. As such, he was a useful business partner. Gail knew that Paul also found Russ easy to manipulate, as he did most people, and believed he could count on his loyalty. The affair had been a betrayal by those he trusted most.

Gail knew that her husband liked, no, *needed* to be the one in control. She'd long suspected him of being a sociopath. Paul hid it well under a patina of charisma, moving effortlessly through his life, attracting admiration and attention. He hid it so well, in fact, that even she had only slowly, over the course of many years, worked out what kind of man he really was.

Paul conducted himself impeccably in all aspects of his life, business, social and family. His clients liked him and were loyal, his friends considered themselves fortunate to be included in his circle. His children, with the possible exception of Hector, adored him. But in Hector's case, it was only because of the harsh penalties Paul had imposed to curb his son's gambling addiction.

Paul seldom revealed his true nature. There was just the odd occasion when she'd observed his smile die in his eyes before it left his lips. Or, the way he looked when he thought he wasn't being observed. Cold. Without a drop of empathy. But most of all it was because she never really sensed any emotional connection between them. It was like living with one of those lifelike robots you saw in science fiction films. Human in appearance but underneath, no beating heart. If it hadn't been for Russ, Gail would never have realised that a relationship could be otherwise. She hadn't been lonely when she was with Russ.

Gail went back indoors. She was alone at home. Not unusual these days, now that the kids were spreading their wings. Dana had been an almost continual presence but now she was gone too. Dead. It hardly seemed real.

She climbed the stairs to Dana's room and stripped the bed. The police forensics team had been in, turned everything upside down and put it back together again. Gail had watched them go about their work, wondering what else they might find. Surely there couldn't be anything more than what they'd already discovered in that tin under Dana's bed? But Gail knew that there was. Much more.

Hiring Dana had been a big mistake. Paul had denied it in front of those police officers but he'd been screwing Dana. Gail had known from the very first day it happened. She'd returned from town one afternoon to find Dana, feet up on the kitchen table, drinking coffee and reading a magazine instead of preparing the vegetables for dinner. The relationship between them had changed. Dana was no longer just the help.

And then there was Hector. So like his father. Was her son responsible for what was in that tin? It wouldn't take the police long to figure out that he'd been in some sort of relationship with Dana. Or that he'd needed a way to make money.

She and Paul had hoped that cutting Hector's allowance would curb their son's gambling excesses. Had Hector turned to drug dealing as a source of income? Gail bitterly regretted asking Russ to help Hector out with a loan that time.

After stripping Dana's bed, Gail began collecting her things together to pack into boxes. Her brother was travelling up to collect them sometime in the next week. As she worked, she thought of Val Marsh going through this same process with Russ's things. Deciding what to keep and what to throw away. She ought to go and see Val and offer her condolences, but the affair with Russ had soured their relationship.

There wasn't much to pack. At a loss for what to do next, Gail went back downstairs, and made some coffee. It tasted bitter.

Every time Gail looked at her husband, she felt more certain that he had killed Russ. Perhaps he'd killed Dana too. She'd given him an alibi, even though it was a lie. Paul had expected it of her, and she couldn't have refused without making him suspicious. He had no alibi either, for the evening Dana died.

Despite having guessed at Paul's true nature many years ago, it had never occurred to Gail until now that he might be capable of murder. She'd always believed that his sociopathic tendencies were satisfied by his success in business.

Gail tipped her coffee away, noticing that her hand was shaking. She felt an unaccustomed tightness in her chest, a thin pain in her jaw and across her shoulder. She stood completely still until it passed. *Anxiety*, she thought, not wishing to call it fear. Funny how we choose our words to disguise the truths we are unable to acknowledge.

* * *

Paul Cornish stepped out of the lift into a carpeted corridor leading to the penthouse flat where his son Hector had been staying since his return from Cambridge. The penthouse belonged to Paul. He'd invested in the development company that built the luxury block of flats, Marton Tower, and got himself a very good deal.

Paul knocked on the door to the flat. No answer. Paul knocked again, and after a delay of some minutes, he heard the key turn in the lock.

"Dad?" Hector stood before him, dressed in a Spiderman onesie that Kitty had given him last Christmas. It emphasised his gangly thinness, made him look boyish. The sight of Hector calmed Paul's fury. The years fell away. This was his son. His firstborn. Hector had worn Spiderman pyjamas just like this as a three-year-old.

"Can I come in?" Paul asked. As if Hector would dare refuse him. He looked around with approval at the open-plan apartment with its expanse of floor space. It would fetch a tidy sum when the market perked up. Then he turned to Hector.

"Did that little haul the police got from Dana's room have anything to do with you? Don't even think about lying to me, Hector."

"I'm not using," Hector said.

"So you're dealing?"

A shrug. "Not dealing. Selling to mates. A few select friends in Cambridge. People who'd have a lot to lose if word got around they were using, so they wouldn't rat me out. I've been careful, Dad. Discreet."

"Was Dana involved?"

"Dana was no angel, Dad. She was snorting coke at Kingfisher Lodge, under your very nose. Okay, the coke was mine. I hid it in my room and she must have stolen it from me and was intending to do a runner. The trouble is, Dad—"

Paul raised his hand, cutting Hector off. He turned his back on him and walked over to the glazed sliding door that opened onto a balcony with views of the river. He sensed his tightly controlled life unravelling, like the river below.

"Don't worry. I've made sure the police won't be looking at me." Hector had crept up behind him.

Paul turned to face his son. "What have you done? Tell me you haven't done anything stupid."

"I spoke with Ruth Marsh."

Paul stared at Hector in his ridiculous Spiderman onesie. The image of his sweet little three-year-old boy vanished.

"Why in hell would you involve Ruth Marsh in this mess?"

"Before you go off on one, Dad, hear me out. Dana stayed with me in Cambridge a couple of times. We were sort of seeing each other for a bit. Nothing serious."

"You and Dana?" Paul was unable to disguise his shock.

Hector caught on immediately. "What? You too? You were fucking Dana too?" Hector gave a sardonic laugh.

Not for the first time since Hector's toddler days, Paul felt an urge to slap his son. Now, as then, he restrained himself.

"You were telling me about Ruth Marsh."

"Her partner, Fin. You know about him, right? From Russ?" Paul nodded. Russ had told him about the private investigator he'd hired to vet Fin as a suitable partner for Ruth. Turned out Fin had been in trouble over drugs in his youth.

"I asked Ruth to go to the police and tell them Dana was doing drugs one evening when we were at Ruth's place in Cambridge. That Fin questioned her and figured out she was dealing, because of his own past experience with drugs. Dana's not in a position to tell them otherwise now, is she?"

It was worse than Paul thought. "And the police are just going to believe that you had nothing to do with it? That Dana saved enough money out of her minimum wage to buy a kilo of coke?"

Hector gave a shrug. "She could have stolen the money. Plenty of dealers do." His face brightened. "You could tell the police that Dana stole stuff from the house. Like some of Mum's jewellery that she thought she'd lost?"

Paul sat down. He needed to think. Items had disappeared from time to time. It wasn't inconceivable that Dana might have been stealing from them. And Gail was careless with her jewellery. He'd lost count of the number of times he'd had to unscrew the S bend on the sink in the en suite to retrieve an earring, or a ring that she'd left balanced on the edge of the bowl when she took off her make-up. Rings, gold chains had gone up the vacuum cleaner. He'd found Dana going through the contents of the dust cylinder one morning looking for a lost gold bracelet. But no. He shook his head. It wasn't believable.

"Why the hell would Ruth Marsh and her partner lie for you?" A chill ran through him. "You didn't threaten to harm—?"

"No, Dad! What do you take me for? Look, I know something about Ruth, that's all. She did something years ago. That's what could harm her, not me."

"So you blackmailed her?" What, Paul wondered, could Hector possibly have on Ruth Marsh that would induce her to lie for him on such a scale?

Paul sensed that he was no longer in control. It wasn't a familiar feeling and he didn't like it. He had come here to confront Hector over the drugs in Dana's room, to tell him how he intended to manage that fiasco. Instead, Hector was telling *him*.

He stared at his son. "I can't even begin to tell you how badly you've fucked everything up." He wasn't simply referring to this whole mess over Dana and the drugs. Now wasn't the time to take Hector into his confidence over Cornish's and Marsh's — or should that be Cornish's? — wider concerns. Hector had no idea of the potential mess he'd created for his father.

"This stupid story you've got Ruth feeding the police. Do you think they're going to believe a word of it?" He mimicked Ruth's voice. "*Oh, Detective. My boyfriend thinks Dana Schell's dealing drugs because he used to do that himself and he's got some sort of magic radar that tells him when he's near a fellow pusher.*" Paul slammed his fist against the wall. Rubbing his knuckles, he said. "Just . . . promise me you won't do another thing until I've had time to think?" Hector gave an uncertain nod. He looked at Paul almost shyly.

"You didn't have feelings for Dana, did you, Dad?"

"No. Did you?"

"No. Good fuck, though, wasn't she?" Their eyes met again. This time Paul felt a stab of recognition.

* * *

"Has PJ told you about Steve's, er, problem?" Tom asked.

Ava had just arrived at the station. She gave a sigh, dropped her handbag to the floor and began unwinding her scarf. "He's got to have an ultrasound scan," she said. "Apparently they can tell from that whether it needs to be investigated further." Tom grimaced. "If a tumour is indicated, he'll need to have a biopsy and blood tests to assess whether the cancer's spread."

"Shit. Poor bloke," Tom said. His voice was full of sympathy.

"Yeah, well, let's try to be positive for PJ's sake."

"Is she coming in?"

"She's going to be a bit late, but, yeah, she's coming in."

"Should I . . . you know . . . mention it to her?" Tom asked. Ava shrugged. "Is that yes? Or no? I'm confused, and I want to get it right."

"Bloody hell, Tom. Of course you should mention it to her. Just . . . don't go over the top. Or maybe you should just wait and see if she brings it up. She's gonna want to talk about it, but just maybe when she's ready."

Tom's mouth gaped. Muttering something like, "Mixed messages," he stood up and offered to make some coffee.

"Wrong mug," Ava growled at him when he returned after a couple of minutes. "And I don't take milk." She stood up and walked into the kitchen where she poured the weak, milky liquid down the sink. When she turned around, Neal was standing in the doorway.

"I've arranged for us to speak with Hector Cornish this morning at his father's penthouse in that poncy new development, Marton Tower. Can you be ready in five?" It wasn't really a question.

Ava's stomach growled. She'd been hoping to grab a sandwich. She'd skipped breakfast. Her younger brother, Ollie, had been running late and she'd spent her eating time proofreading an A-level history essay for him, which was due to be handed in that morning.

PJ was standing by Tom's desk when Ava emerged from the kitchen.

"Thanks, Tom," she heard PJ say. Evidently Tom had decided to speak to her about Steve's 'problem.'

Must have found the right words, then. If only he'd stopped there.

"Remember, Hitler only had one ball and he conquered half of Europe." Both women stared at him.

"Was that supposed to be a joke?" Ava asked, after a long silence.

"Actually, no . . . er, I was just saying to PJ that having only one testicle isn't necessarily a drawback in life. I've just googled it and apparently it doesn't affect your sex life and you can still have kids. And—"

"Tom?" Ava said, one eye on PJ who looked stupefied. Tom cocked an eyebrow. "Shut up." She turned to PJ. "Sorry, Peej, I've got to go. Speak to you later, okay?"

PJ looked injured. "You're not leaving me alone with him, are you?"

Ava glared at Tom. "Yeah, well, he can't really say anything worse, can he?"

"That's true," PJ said. "He's right about the kids though."

Ava squeezed her arm and hurried after Neal who was waiting by the door.

"Oh, we're walking, are we?" Ava muttered to herself on seeing him stride past the gap in the wall that led to the car park.

The hammering of a pneumatic drill as they turned onto the main road put paid to any conversation. Ava's stomach grumbled in tune with the din from the roadworks. She gazed wistfully at a workman biting down on a tasty-looking bacon butty. When he gave her a wink and held the butty out, she was almost tempted.

Neal was in a hurry. If Ava hadn't been so fit, she'd have been struggling to keep up. Come to think of it, since when had Jim Neal been so fit? He came to an abrupt halt, and Ava just stopped herself from walking into him.

They had arrived at Marton Tower. Another exclusive development. This case was certainly giving them a glimpse of luxury living. Ava had seen advertisements for Marton Tower in the *Stromford Courier* about six months ago, when the building works were nearing completion. Despite the exorbitant prices, every single apartment had been sold before the scaffolding came down.

The apartments weren't even in the most prestigious location in town. That honour belonged to the Uphill district, the older part of Stromford, near the cathedral. But they were within striking distance of the town centre, and pleasantly situated overlooking the river and Stromford marina, with its strip of fashionable bars and restaurants. They were also a stone's throw from the university, and provided an alternative to university accommodation for those staff and students who could afford a bit of luxury.

Out of interest, Ava had looked at some of the flats online. The fixtures and fittings looked bespoke and high end. She'd liked the open-plan living space and the floor-to-ceiling windows with their cityscape views. Still, even if she could afford it, she wasn't tempted to swap the charm of her rented country cottage for the advantages of living in town.

The doors leading to the reception desk were glazed, giving a view of a spacious, carpeted entrance area. Ava followed Neal through the swooshing doors. A bored-looking concierge sat behind a polished desk, staring at a screen. Neal approached him, while Ava wandered over to look at a series of photographs on the wall near the lift. The pictures showed the transitional phases in the construction of the building from foundations to finished product. One picture showed a group of men and women in suits and hard hats. They were holding trowels and smiling awkwardly for the camera. One woman was laying a brick in a foundation wall.

One of the male members of the group looked familiar. It was Paul Cornish, she realised. Presumably Cornish and Marsh had been involved in the financing of the development. On the way up in the lift to Hector's sixth-floor penthouse, Ava told Neal what she had seen.

"Well, we knew Paul Cornish owns the penthouse flat where Hector's staying. I didn't know he'd had a hand in the project itself."

The lift doors slid open into a wide, bright corridor. A familiar figure stood before them. "Good morning, Mr Cornish," Neal said.

"Good morning, Inspector Neal. Sergeant Merry."

"Have you and your son resolved your differences?" Neal asked.

Paul Cornish shrugged. "Russ's death has put things in perspective somewhat. What's your business with Hector?"

"We need to ask him a few questions about his relationship with Dana Schell," Neal said.

"What relationship? Hector hardly knew Dana."

"Dana visited Hector in Cambridge," Neal said. "Perhaps he knew her better than you thought."

"Fine. Question him all you like. Then stop wasting everyone's time and start looking for the real killer."

Paul made to brush past, but Neal and Ava were blocking his way. He shifted from foot to foot, looking over their shoulders towards the lift. His whole demeanour suggested that he had better things to do than talk to them.

"I see Cornish and Marsh have links with this building," Ava said chattily, as she and Neal finally stood aside to let him pass. Paul's eyes narrowed. "The photos, downstairs?"

"We invested some money in the construction company, Ballgreen Construction, yes," Paul said.

She smiled. "Well, you must have made your money back on that one. Every flat was sold ahead of the completion date, so I read in the *Courier*."

"It was a successful venture for Cornish and Walsh, yes."

"Must be great to have your talent for spotting a lucrative investment," Ava said. "Hector's a lucky lad to live in a place like this."

"Yes, well, it's temporary. Hector won't be needing it much longer. He'll soon be moving to London to start his career."

"In the City, is it?" Ava said.

"Yes, as a matter of fact. Look, I have to be in a meeting in half an hour . . ."

"Oh. Sorry to keep you, Mr Cornish. You have a nice day," Ava said.

"Sergeant. Inspector." Paul Cornish stepped into the lift without a backward glance.

"Now for junior," Ava said. The concierge had contacted Hector and obtained permission for Neal and Ava to have access to the narrow corridor leading to his flat. Neal used a fob to open the door.

"They take their security seriously," Ava observed, thinking of Kingfisher Lodge.

The sight of a grown man dressed as Spiderman didn't faze Ava, but Neal wasn't quick enough to suppress an exclamation.

"What the—?"

"Yeah?" Hector said. His gaze flickered from Neal to Ava, and stayed there. "Can I help you?"

"Police, remember? You just spoke with the concierge?" Ava reminded him politely, flashing her ID. "Can we come in?"

"What's this about?"

"We'd like to ask you some questions about Dana Schell."

"Oh, yeah. Shit. Poor Dana." Hector ran long fingers through his floppy hair. He repeated her name, shaking his head.

"So, okay if we come in?" Ava asked again.

"What? Sure." He drew in a whistling breath through his teeth. "Place's a mess."

"Don't worry, we're not here to judge how you live. Hey, we just met your dad out in the corridor," Ava said.

"What? Really? No shit. Do you want to sit down or something?"

Ava sat on the sofa, Neal at a table.

Ava looked around. "Nice place."

"Yeah, not bad, is it?"

Neal evidently considered the small talk had gone on long enough. "Tell us about your relationship with Dana."

A guarded look entered Hector's eyes. "She was my parents' live-in help."

"She was a bit more to you than that, wasn't she? We know you were seeing her," Neal said.

"Okaaay," Hector admitted, "Yeah, we were together for a bit, but it was nothing serious. Dana wasn't really interested in a proper relationship. She was planning on going off travelling. We enjoyed each other's company, but we both knew it wasn't going anywhere."

"When we searched Ms Schell's room at your parent's home, we found a kilo of cocaine in a tin under her bed. That's a sizeable quantity. More than someone would normally keep for personal use. It suggests that she was either looking after the drugs for someone or involved in dealing. Did Dana ever use cocaine when she was with you?"

Hector's eyes had widened when Neal mentioned the quantity of drugs involved. "Jeez, yeah, my father told me about it. I'm pretty sure he would have killed her if he'd known she was hiding drugs in his house . . . Oh shit. I didn't mean that the way it sounded. I didn't mean he'd *literally* kill her. Oh, man . . ."

Cut the act. Ava knew Hector Cornish wasn't stupid. Despite the performance, there was no disguising the flash of intelligence in his eyes.

She said, "Ruth Marsh came to the station yesterday with a story about her partner, Fin, catching Dana doing a line of coke in their bathroom. Ruth also told us you knew that Dana was dealing."

"Okay. So, I wasn't going to dump Dana in it but she's dead and I'm not, so I'll be straight with you."

I doubt that.

"Yes, I knew Dana was doing drugs . . . dealing drugs. We bumped into Ruth and her partner in Cambridge. We chatted for a while, and at one point it was kind of like me and Ruth talking to each other about the old days. Dana was chatting with Fin, and later on Fin apparently told Ruth that Dana'd asked him where she could score. Then, like you said, he caught her doing a line in their bathroom. I was furious when I found out. I told her to give my parents notice or I'd tell them about her nasty little habit. I swear I had no idea she was hiding the stuff in their home."

Hector ran the zipper of his onesie up and down, revealing a tuft of chest hair. He rolled his neck from side to side as if relieving some tension. "Are you thinking that Dana got herself mixed up in something and got in over her head, officers?"

"You mean, was Dana killed over her involvement with drugs?" Ava threw his question back at him.

He shrugged. "Isn't that why you brought the drugs up in the first place?"

"We don't even know if the drugs found at Kingfisher Lodge belonged to Dana. We're having a hard time working out how she could afford to buy that quantity of coke on the minimum wage."

"*Seriously?* Oh, I get it. You think I'm the one who could afford to have a habit." A hurt look. "Dad's right.

Just because you have money, people make all sorts of assumptions."

"With great wealth comes great responsibility," Ava said, paraphrasing Spiderman's uncle.

Hector didn't appreciate the joke. "I don't do drugs. I mean, yeah, maybe I did the odd line at a party in my first year at uni, but who doesn't? It's just everywhere. Dana probably got the money the way most girls like her do — prostitution, stealing. Come to think of it, my mum's lost a few bits of expensive jewellery since Dana came to stay at Kingfisher Lodge."

Most girls like her. Hector's comment disgusted Ava.

Neal intervened. "The first time we spoke with your father, he mentioned that you'd 'got yourself in with a bad crowd,' and run up gambling debts. That you'd gone to Russ Marsh for a loan."

"I know what you're trying to say. That I was dealing to pay off my debts, but that's bullshit. My father cut off my allowance. Why would I need to ask Russ Marsh for money if I were dealing?"

"Hector," Neal said, "it would be easy enough for us to look into your affairs at Cambridge. Believe me, it wouldn't take us long to establish what you've been up to. Unless you'd like to talk to us first?"

"Go ahead. I've got nothing to hide."

"How did you persuade Russ Marsh to help you out? That was a sizeable amount of money he gave you. Why would he do that and risk upsetting his business partner? Were you able to give him something in exchange?" Ava said.

"Like what?"

"You tell us."

"I've no idea what you're getting at."

Ava was stabbing in the dark, but she sensed that her question had hit a nerve. *Interesting*.

Hector shrugged. "Russ is a friend of the family."

"More your father's friend, surely?" Ava said.

"I asked. He was happy to help me out."

She frowned. "Hmm . . . He must have known it would piss your dad off."

"Why can't you just accept that Russ helped me out because he genuinely liked me and wanted to help? You know, it's not easy being well-off, even at Cambridge, where a lot of people are from affluent backgrounds. People take advantage. They take the piss because they know you've got money. It's not easy to tell who likes you for what you are and who likes you because of what you can give them."

Neal felt no sympathy for the poor rich boy. "That's life, son."

"Yeah, well, I knew I could go to Russ and he'd help me without wanting anything in return. I offered to pay him back, by the way. I'm going to be working in the City soon."

Ava doodled in her notebook. Did Hector really think they'd feel sorry for him? She knew it wasn't always a good idea to have hunches about people in a murder investigation. Nearly everyone lied, or at the very least omitted certain things. But Hector was behaving like a person who had something to hide.

"So, returning to your friends. 'Bad lot' was just your dad's way of describing the type of people who are after a free ride?"

"Yeah, that's right."

Ava nodded. "I get it. We've all had friends like that. The ones who expect you to run them around without contributing to the cost of fuel, or stand them drinks without ever buying you one back." Hector was nodding enthusiastically. Never mind that he'd run up his debts playing poker with his wealthy friends.

She smiled. "They must have really been taking you to the cleaners. Mind you, I can see your dad's point, docking your allowance. He was probably just concerned. How *do* you get through that much money anyway, Hector? I mean, your friends must have been partying hard at your expense. As well as thrashing you at poker." Hector looked surly.

"What were you doing on Monday evening?" Neal asked.

"The night Dana was killed, right? I was here, alone, unfortunately, so no alibi. That's bad, right?"

Ava made a face. "Well, it's not the best, to be frank. Especially as you were involved with Dana." She paused. "But we'll hold off arresting you for now." She flashed him a beatific, blatantly insincere smile.

Chapter Ten

Fin was alone in the little terraced house he shared with Ruth and their son. He sat in the kitchen, missing his family and thinking about the past.

He remembered the day he first met Ruth. Fin didn't go for the lookers. He liked character in a woman, or a sense of mystery. So he noticed plain Jane Ruth immediately, and walked across the smoke-filled student bar to chat her up. She seemed wary for someone so young — nineteen, he found out later. She looked like she had a past, and Fin was curious.

So he'd asked her outright. What was the terrible secret she was harbouring that made her look so haunted? Probably not the best opening gambit, but it certainly made Ruth notice him. After her initial surprise, she seemed interested in her turn. They spent the rest of the evening talking and dancing. Fin had walked her back to her college, and she agreed to meet him for coffee the following day.

Their relationship blossomed. It hadn't taken long for Fin to realise that Ruth was 'the one.' To his perpetual astonishment, she felt the same way about him.

The next big shock had been Ruth's pregnancy. When she made her declaration, Fin had been speechless, incapable of forming a single coherent thought. The only part of him that still seemed to function was his legs. He walked away.

Then he came back. One hour later, bearing a huge bouquet of flowers and a bottle of champagne that he'd had to drink himself. Ruth refused to touch a drop for fear of harming the baby. Though he didn't say as much to Ruth, Fin was worried about how they'd cope, money-wise. Ruth hadn't yet graduated and he was embarking on a full-time PhD. He'd received funding, but it wasn't enough to keep all three of them. Ruth did have money, of course. Plenty. A big fat bank account that she refused to touch, following her row with her father. Fin didn't blame her father for having him checked out. Wealthy people had to be wary of gold-diggers.

Russ Marsh's PI hadn't discovered anything about Fin's past that Fin hadn't already revealed to Ruth. She'd accepted that he wasn't that person any more. Actually, he never had been that person. Nothing about his life as a runner for Liam Sharp had been of his choosing. He'd been trapped by circumstance. And fear, of course.

There was no disputing that he knew the drugs trade. For a fraction of a second, it had crossed his mind that he could do well at Cambridge as a drug dealer. He'd lost count of the number of times he'd been approached for tips on where to buy, or been offered the stuff himself. The market was buoyant. Fin knew that a gram of coke in Cambridge sold for around double the asking price in London. Finding clients would be a piece of cake. His profit margin would be phenomenal. Within six months, he'd have more money than he knew what to do with.

But Fin had a conscience, and an appreciation of the drug trade that he'd been ignorant of in his days as Liam's lackey. He was aware that every drug dealer — and every user — was at the end of a chain of violence and misery that reached all the way to the backstreets of Columbia, where people were dying on a daily basis thanks to the activities of the greedy drug cartels. Fin wanted nothing more to do with it.

But life threw him one of its curveballs.

Fin and Ruth had collided with Hector Cornish and Dana Schell in the Grafton shopping centre. Ruth had already mentioned that her ex-classmate, son of her father's business partner, was at Cambridge. She hadn't seemed interested in socialising with him, until their chance meeting resulted in Ruth inviting Hector and Dana for dinner. Fin was less than enthusiastic.

Ruth assumed he was jealous. She patted her stomach. "Did you hear that, little baby? Daddy's jealous of Mummy's friend."

It wasn't that. It was Hector's air of entitlement, of privilege. Ruth came from a similar background, but she had none of that arrogance so characteristic of her socioeconomic peers. Instead, there was sadness at her core, that aura of mystery.

Once she'd asked Fin, "Do you ever wonder how your whole life can change in an instant because of one stupid act?" When he asked her to explain, she laughed it off. Fin was a romantic at heart, but he was realistic enough to know that the source of her sadness might turn out to be something quite mundane.

Something else bothered Fin about Hector. A look in Hector's eyes that reminded him of Liam Sharp.

Maybe Ruth's pregnancy was making her feel unattractive? So he played along with the jealousy thing because it seemed to cheer her up, make her feel more desirable.

Hector and Dana duly turned up on their doorstep on a chilly January evening bearing a six pack of lager, and a bunch of pink peonies for Ruth. Earlier in the day, Fin had cooked a big pot of chilli, and he served this up on a bed of rice with some crusty bread that Ruth had bought from what she called an 'artisanal' bakers.

Ruth and Hector talked a lot about their shared past. Fin was glad to be able to just listen, and nod occasionally without having to contribute much to the conversation. He found Hector's presence in their home unsettling. It had nothing to do with sexual jealousy.

Excluded from the conversation, Fin began to drink steadily. Tongue loosened, he told them about the night he and Ruth met. Hector seemed particularly interested in Fin's reference to Ruth's 'air of mystery.'

"Like she has some secret in her past?" He'd been teasing, but Ruth didn't seem amused. Suddenly the atmosphere became charged with things unsaid. Dangerous things.

Ruth, her face drained of colour, excused herself, saying she felt nauseous. She laughed it off. "Morning sickness in the evening." Dana accompanied her upstairs.

Left alone at the table with Hector, Fin had looked him in the eye, and asked, "What was that all about?"

Hector's gaze was like a searchlight, forcing Fin to look away. And then he said, "I know Ruth's secret."

* * *

"So, talk to me about Dana Schell," Neal said, his eyes roving across the faces of Ava, PJ and Tom, who were his key officers in the Russ Marsh and Dana Schell inquiries. For now, they were treating these murders as discrete cases, but keeping an open mind on how the investigations might develop.

"Twenty-four years old. Not from Stromford, She met a Stromford lad, Nathan Brewer, at a music festival and came back here with him. They were together for a while afterwards. Dana lived at his house share. Originally she's from somewhere down south, er . . ." Tom floundered.

"Braintree, in Essex," PJ chipped in.

"That's the one. Left school at sixteen and attended her local FE college where she upgraded her GCSEs and then did an accounting qualification."

". . . Got a job with Colchester City Council and stayed there for a couple of years," PJ added.

"Her line manager at the council said she was a competent worker, but she took a lot of time off sick . . ." Tom said.

". . . In inverted commas," PJ chorused.

Neal felt he was watching a tennis match.

"Actually, she was disciplined over the amount of time she took off. She was on a final warning." Advantage PJ.

"Not the most dependable character, then. How did she end up working for the Cornish family?" Neal asked.

But Tom wasn't done yet. "She answered an ad in the *Courier* after doing a series of temping jobs in Stromford."

"What do we know about this Nathan Brewer, the boyfriend, if that's what he was?" Neal now felt like a referee.

Ball in PJ's court. "He works in Tesco's. Actually, I think I know him." This was unsurprising. Unlike the rest of them, PJ had lived all her life in Stromford and seemed to know everyone. She turned to Ava. "Bet you do too, Ava. Young bloke on chilled foods? With the ginger coif?"

Ava looked blank.

"Anyway, according to Dana's mum, the relationship didn't last long. But Dana decided to stay on in Stromford and save money to go travelling."

"How long since they split up?" Neal asked.

"Don't know exactly, but more than a year, boss." Tom said. "Want us to question him?"

"Yes. He's a potential suspect."

"On it, boss."

Neal ran his fingers through his hair. It felt like there was more to tug through than usual. Time for a trip to the barber's. When he got entrenched in a case, there never seemed time for that sort of thing.

"Hector Cornish was reluctant to admit to a relationship, if you can call it that, with Dana. We know she visited him in Cambridge and according to Ruth Marsh — and Hector — she was dealing."

"More intertangling," remarked PJ. "Sorry for interrupting, sir."

"Given the internecine affairs of these two families, the word is curiously . . . apt," Neal said. He thought for a moment. "Dana was transferring a couple of hundred pounds a month into her savings account from her salary, presumably to save for her travels. She would have had very little left to live on, certainly not enough to purchase that amount of cocaine."

"Hector could easily have stashed the coke in Dana's room after her death. He would have been expecting a police visit," Tom said.

"Why bother hiding it in Dana's room, instead of just getting rid of it?" Ava said. "There's always the possibility that Paul Cornish was paying Dana for sex. His wife was pretty convinced he and Dana were at it, wasn't she, sir?"

Neal nodded. "Not sure he'd be paying her enough to buy a kilo of coke though."

He recalled Hector's suggestion that Dana could have been paid for sex. He'd practically accused her of prostitution. Surely, he couldn't have meant his father was the one paying her?

"Tomorrow morning, I'd like you to accompany me on a trip to Cambridge, Ava. I want to see what this Fin O'Shea has to say for himself. Background in drugs or not, I'm having a hard time believing he sussed out Dana's drug credentials like a bloody sniffer dog."

"Yes, sir."

"Now," Neal said. "Let's discuss where we are with Russ Marsh's murder."

"If you ask me, it's all connected," Tom said. "I've seen this before in Hertfordshire. Drugs at the root of everything." He looked around the room expectantly, as if he'd just made an earth-shattering pronouncement. No one seemed impressed. "Just putting it out there."

"Yes, well, we've all considered that the deaths might be linked," Neal pointed out impatiently. There was a lengthy silence.

"My money's on Paul Cornish," Ava said. "His alibi is weak. Admittedly, we don't have much evidence against him. And not a lot in the way of motive, despite his row with Russ. It's got to be something to do with the business."

"Maybe Paul had been bottling up his resentment over Gail's affair with Russ Marsh and it just exploded," PJ said. "Maybe Russ lending Hector that money was the last straw."

"Yeah, seems like that really pissed Paul off," Tom said. "Though Russ was the one who warned Paul to 'watch his back.'"

"It seems likely that Russell Marsh knew his killer and let him or her in. The burglar alarm wasn't triggered. We're still checking into non-residents admitted to Crystal Lakes from the day before Russ's murder. There were plenty of tradespeople of course, visitors calling on friends and relatives, employees of the various recreational facilities and shops at Crystal Lakes. It's a gated community, which means it has enhanced security measures, but it's not impregnable. Obviously," Neal said. "And there might be some forensic evidence when we get the results back. I'm interested in why Russell Marsh agreed to bail Hector Cornish out." Neal was thinking of something Ava had hinted at during their interview with Hector. "When we interviewed Hector, Ava, you asked him something along the lines of, was there something he could offer Russell in return for his generosity. He was rattled by the question even though he made light of it."

"I was stabbing in the dark," Ava admitted. "But if Dana overheard stuff in the Cornish household, why not Hector too? Something to do with the business, perhaps? He might have been listening in when Paul and Russ were discussing something confidential with a client."

Neal frowned. "Hmm." All of these were possibilities.

"Yeah, or what if Hector found out that Russ was cheating on his father with Gail again, and was blackmailing him?" Tom's words tumbled out in his excitement.

Neal raised an eyebrow. "Not bad, Tom." He thought for a moment, interested by the comment. "Coming back to that argument between Russ and Paul, I'm not convinced it was simply over Russ bailing Hector out of his gambling debts. If Ava's right and Russ died because of something to do with the business, that row they had might have been because Russ had his suspicions and decided to confront Paul."

They were all silent for a moment as they contemplated the possibilities that spun out from that.

"Val Marsh did say that Russ was worried about some aspect of the business," Ava said. "They were going to talk about it when she got home from Ruth's."

"We need more information," Neal said. "Tom, contact Lesley Curran directly after the briefing and see if she's got anything useful for us yet."

"Yes, sir."

"Coming back to Hector again, maybe there's some personal element involved," PJ suggested quietly. They all looked at her. "Hector was at Cambridge with Ruth, right? Maybe he was blackmailing Russ Marsh over something to do with Ruth. It seemed so odd Ruth coming to us with that story about Dana being a drug dealer. Almost as though Hector put her up to it."

"What are you thinking, PJ?" Ava asked.

PJ coloured. "It's just . . . well . . . I was just thinking, fathers will go to great lengths to protect their daughters, won't they? I didn't really have something specific in mind. Sorry, I should have given it a bit more thought."

"No need to apologise," Ava reassured her quickly. "It's always good to get ideas on the table."

Neal noticed how supportive of PJ Ava was. She always made PJ feel like a valued member of the team. He was aware that PJ had some personal issues at the moment concerning her boyfriend, Steve. Probably her confidence was in need of a boost.

"That's an interesting angle, PJ. See what you can find out," he said, though he doubted it would throw up any lead.

"Ava, I propose we make an early start tomorrow. Tom, PJ, I'd like you two to interview this Nathan Brewer, Dana Schell's ex, as soon as possible."

"A couple of PCs have taken a statement from him already," Tom said. "He has an alibi for the approximate time of Dana's death."

Neal was aware of this. He gave a brief nod. "Everyone clear on what they're doing?"

Neal returned to his office and closed the door. Through the glass partition he could see Ava, PJ and Tom talking together. Ava touched PJ on the arm, and he guessed they were discussing Steve. He should probably say something. He would ask Ava in the morning if there was any support he could offer PJ. She was a good officer. His present team gelled well, unlike other teams he'd worked with, where petty jealousies and rivalries got in the way of their work. If people just basically didn't get along, it made his job impossible.

Ava and Tom were driven individuals. Both were leaders, and they'd go far. Tom, who was of mixed race, had endured racial prejudice in Hertfordshire. It was admirable that he'd chosen to move to largely white Stromfordshire, where people with his skin colour still attracted the wrong sort of looks.

PJ was no less dedicated, but Neal sensed that she was less ambitious. She derived her satisfaction from dealing with people and doing her job well, not from any burning ambition to move up through the ranks. Of them all, she was the most skilled at communicating with others. They responded to her warmth and sympathy. Neal realised that he was actually becoming fond of this team.

Since he'd entered the force, he'd kept colleagues at a distance, saving the warmer side of his nature for his family, and his close childhood friend, Jock Dodds, whom he'd always regarded as a brother, and who was about to become his brother-in-law.

He shook himself. If he carried on like this he was in danger of becoming sentimental.

Chapter Eleven

Come on, Ollie. Ava drummed her fingers on the steering wheel. It was six thirty, earlier than they usually set off, and Ollie didn't take kindly to being rushed. He had his routines in the morning, and these took an allotted amount of time. Last night, Ava's suggestion that he get up half an hour earlier had been met with stony disapproval.

Sure enough, he emerged from the cottage looking dishevelled, jacket half on, bag slung over his shoulder with the straps gaping open, books just waiting to spill out all over the path. He slumped into the seat next to her, hand on the door, ready to slam it shut.

"Did you lock up?" Ava asked. Ollie scowled at her and threw his bag into the backseat. He got out of the car and stomped back to the front door. He returned, dangling the door keys in front of him.

"Sandwiches?" Ava asked, closing her eyes. Ollie pointed to the back seat. Knowing the journey was likely to be passed in silence, Ava turned the radio on and listened to the news.

Ollie's mood still hadn't brightened by the time Ava dropped him off at the school gates. She hoped the disruption to his morning wouldn't throw him off kilter for the entire day. To her relief, he thanked her for the lift and said, "You too," when she wished him a good day.

Neal was waiting in the kitchen when she arrived at the station. To her surprise, he pointed to a takeaway coffee on the worktop near the kettle. "I'll drive," he said. If he'd been anyone else but Neal, Ava would have hugged him.

It was about a two-hour drive to Cambridge. Just getting out of Stromfordshire could take ages in the rush hour, hence the early start. Stromfordshire wasn't connected to any main arterial routes. It was also in a predominantly rural and agricultural area and at some point this morning, Ava knew, they'd be stuck behind a tractor for miles.

"How's Archie getting along?" Ava asked, as they chuntered along at fifteen miles an hour behind said tractor, with Neal sighing loudly. "He's in his last year at primary school now, isn't he? Have you thought about which secondary school he'll go to?"

"I think he'll probably go to the Crossgate Academy," Neal answered. "It's the nearest to us and he seemed to like it when we visited."

"It has a good reputation."

Neal agreed. He craned his neck to see if the road beyond the tractor was clear. Mentioning Archie was a clumsy lead into what Ava really wanted to ask of him. "So, Maggie told me that Archie's mother's been in touch."

There was a pause while Neal pulled out and overtook the tractor. "Er . . . yes," he answered, his eyes fixed on the road ahead. Not keen to talk about it, then. And really, it was none of her business.

Still unsure of how to be with Neal, Ava didn't press. Maybe she'd misinterpreted the look that had passed between them when she'd saved his life that time. Maybe it had been gratitude, plain and simple.

But then, there'd been the meal. Again, perhaps she had misinterpreted Neal's easy manner as meaning something more. She had left Neal's house that evening feeling almost like one of the family. Neal had even pecked her on the cheek when she got into her taxi. She sighed. She wished he would tell her what Myrna wanted. *Him, no doubt.* Time to give Maggie a call.

She gave up and steered the conversation to the case at hand, and how they would handle the interview with Fin O'Shea.

"I'm still kind of puzzled about Ruth volunteering that info. PJ and I both got the impression there was something off about it. I still think Hector Cornish might have put her up to it to deflect suspicion from himself. When we interviewed him, he sort of kept bringing drugs up as though he expected we would if he didn't, if you see what I mean."

"Dana's prints weren't the only ones on the clip bags," Neal pointed out. "But even if Hector's or Paul's — or anyone else in the family's prints were on there, all that would prove was that they'd touched the bags at some point, not that they'd had the drugs in their possession. The bags might have come from a kitchen cupboard. Thinking about what PJ said yesterday about Ruth and Hector being at Cambridge together, it would make sense that if Hector had something on Ruth that would compel Russ Marsh to lend him money, that same thing would potentially give him control over Ruth herself." Neal beeped the horn at a van driver overtaking on the inside.

The rest of the journey passed in dreary motorway monotony. Ava, though sustained by the coffee, only just managed to stay awake. On arriving in Cambridge, they parked up and walked a short way to Ruth and Fin's terraced house.

A young man with a bushy beard answered their knock and invited them inside. A laptop lay on the floor next to a two-seater sofa, papers and books strewn around it. Fin had evidently been working.

There wasn't a lot of space. Ava couldn't help thinking that it was a modest home for a millionaire's daughter to be living in. She remembered that Ruth and her father hadn't been on speaking terms for some time before Russ Marsh's death. She and Fin had been fending for themselves. Ruth was working part-time teaching English to foreign students. Ava wasn't sure if Fin worked as well as pursuing his studies.

"I can't believe what happened to Ruth's father," Fin said, shaking his head. "I never met the man, and I know he didn't approve of me, but no one deserves to die like that. And poor Val, finding him. Have you got any leads?"

"One or two," Neal said evasively. "We're here to talk to you about Dana Schell. A shadow descended over Fin's face at the mention of Dana's name.

"Yes, poor Dana."

"How would you describe your relationship with Ms Schell, Mr O'Shea?"

"Non-existent. I only met her twice. The first time was when Ruth and I bumped into her and Ruth's school friend Hector Cornish, in the Grafton shopping centre in Cambridge. I chatted with her for a bit while Ruth and Hector had a catch up. Ruth invited them for dinner."

"What did you chat about?" Ava asked.

"It was small talk, mostly. I asked Dana if it was her first visit to Cambridge, whether she'd done much sightseeing. She told me she'd been once before, as a child, and couldn't remember anything much except seeing the punts on the river."

"Did the topic of drugs come up in your conversation? Cocaine, in particular. Did Dana ask you where she could get some in Cambridge, or offer to sell you some?" Ava asked.

"Er . . . yes. She asked me where she could score. I told her I didn't know. That I wasn't interested." All at once, Fin's manner seemed guarded.

"You were arrested for drug offences, weren't you, Mr O'Shea?" Ava said.

"That was a long time ago, Sergeant. I've moved on since those days. And I was never a user." His tone was polite, even deferential. Ava had expected her comment to provoke him. He was telling the truth. About his own metamorphosis, at any rate.

"Your partner, Ruth Marsh, claims that you caught Dana doing a line of coke in your bathroom one evening, when Hector and Dana came to dinner," she said.

"Yes. That's right." Fin's lips were a thin, puckered line set in a taut face.

"Did Hector indulge?" Ava said.

"No."

She frowned. "You seem very sure of that."

"I know the signs. As you pointed out, I have experience."

"Did Hector know Dana was using?" she asked.

"I'm not sure, but he wasn't aware she was dealing. He was pretty mad when I told him that's what I suspected."

"And what exactly made you suspect Dana was dealing coke?" Ava watched him carefully.

"She, er, said as much. Said it was good stuff she was taking and if I wanted she could sell me some."

His story seemed to chime more or less with Ruth's. Nevertheless, Ava had the feeling, as she had when Ruth came to the station, that this story had a false ring to it.

"What was your impression of Hector Cornish, Mr O'Shea?" Neal asked.

"I'll be honest. He's not my sort of person. Too full of himself. I tolerated him for Ruth's sake, but I was glad when the evening was over, not least because of catching

Dana at her habit. It made me nervous. I'd closed that chapter of my life and didn't want to be reminded of it."

"How did Hector seem with Dana, before you told him about the incident in the bathroom?" Ava said.

"How do you mean?"

"Did he treat her with respect, for example?" Her question seemed to throw Fin. There was a prolonged silence.

He cleared his throat. "I suppose so."

"You suppose?" Ava waited.

"He was a bit — you know — condescending. Kept correcting her grammar, mimicking her accent."

"Belittling her?"

"Maybe, yes, probably. Wait, is Hector a suspect?"

"He was Dana's boyfriend, so we have to ask questions. It doesn't mean he's a suspect as such." Ava changed tack. "How well did you know the rest of Ruth's family?"

Fin frowned. "As I said, I never met her father. Val's okay, we get on alright. She didn't agree with her husband's prejudices about me. I'm assuming you know already that Ruth's father didn't approve of me?"

"Yes, but we'd like to hear your side of the story."

Fin gave sigh. "Look. When I first met Ruth, I was a penniless student living in a house share from which I was about to be evicted. Ruth was staying in her college, but later she moved into a nice flat that her dad was paying for. She suggested I come and live with her. Next thing we know, her old man's telling her to get shot of me. He's hired a PI to check into my background and found out I'd been in trouble over drugs. Her father was obviously horrified at the thought of his precious daughter being associated with someone like me."

Fin looked from Neal to Ava, as if expecting to be judged. "He got more than he bargained for, though. Ruth wasn't having any of it. She was shocked that he'd go to such lengths to control her, and she refused to stay in the flat any longer, or take another penny from him. Ruth's aunt, Lizzie, helped us out with a deposit and a month's rent, and so we got this place."

"Lizzie Hamilton lent you money?"

"Yeah. She's alright, is Lizzie. Very possessive of Ruth, though. I think it bothers Val a bit." His voice dropped. "You know what happened to Lizzie's son and her first husband, don't you?"

"The fire?" Ava said.

"Yeah. Ruth can't bear any mention of that. Or of her cousin, Will. I guess she and her cousin must have been pretty close."

Had they? No one had mentioned it. Ruth had attended the same private school as Hector, and Will had gone to one of the local comprehensives. They couldn't have had much in common.

Fin's remark about Lizzie being possessive of Ruth was interesting. As an outsider to the family, Fin was more likely to be objective. Ava thought of Val's display of jealousy when Neal suggested that Ruth and her son stay at Lizzie's. There was a tension between the sisters. That in itself was nothing unusual. Not all sisters got along like a house on fire — grim simile.

Neal was evidently of like mind. He said, "What was your impression of the relationship between the sisters?"

Fin seemed more relaxed now that he was no longer the focus of their attention. "Complicated one, that. According to Ruth, it's historical. Lizzie was always their parent's favourite. Val left home as soon as she hit sixteen and moved to London. Lizzie was regarded as the clever one, but she ended up being less successful than Val, financially speaking. Depends how you measure success, doesn't it? I guess Val was jealous of Lizzie being the golden child when they were growing up. Then, later on, she must have looked at Lizzie's dreary existence compared to hers and felt a certain satisfaction. Now she's jealous all over again because of the bond between Ruth and Lizzie." He paused. "Val once claimed that Lizzie saw Ruth as a substitute for her dead son."

Ouch. Val could have kept that to herself, Ava thought.

"Like I said, though, I get on okay with Val. She's been pretty good to us, especially since Cam came along." By good, Ava read *generous.*

"And she looked after us all when Ruth and I were sick recently. Val got up in the night with Cam, and Ruth and I slept the best we'd done for months."

Ava glanced at Neal, who nodded. Time to bring the interview to a close.

"You must be missing your family, Mr O'Shea."

"Yes. I'll be glad when this is all over and things get back to normal. If that's even possible, after all that's happened."

"Thanks for your time, Mr O'Shea. We'll let you get back to your work." Ava's eyes travelled to the laptop. "What are you studying, by the way?"

"History."

"Well, good luck with that," Ava said. Neal nodded approvingly. Fin escorted them to the door.

* * *

They were in striking distance of the car when Neal said, "Let's grab a bite to eat."

It was still a little early for lunch, but Ava offered no resistance. Like her, Neal had probably had an early, rushed breakfast.

"How about over there?" She pointed at a café on the other side of the street with a board outside advertising an all-day breakfast.

"Perfect. I only managed half a bowl of cornflakes this morning."

A few minutes later they were sitting at a table by the window, waiting for their 'Seven-ups' — seven breakfast items for five ninety-nine — and watching passers-by battling against the autumn wind.

"He seemed an intelligent, likeable young man," Neal said, referring to Fin.

"Obviously very much in love with Ruth. His face lit up every time he mentioned her name. And Cam, of course."

Neal tucked in with relish, devouring sausages and bacon like someone who'd been starving for days. Ava took a sip of coffee, not expecting much, and was pleasantly surprised. With added approval, she noted that the price included 'bottomless hot drinks.'

Only when his plate was half empty did Neal, meditatively pouring his tea, remark on the interview. "Fin's angle on the Val, Ruth and Lizzie triangle was interesting."

"I thought it was a bit unkind of Val to taint Lizzie's love for Ruth by suggesting that she was compensating for losing Will." Ava chewed her sausage ruminatively. "I wonder why we've never thought to ask where Ruth was on the night of the fire."

Neal looked up from buttering his toast.

"I mean, we've heard that Lizzie blamed Russ for Will's death because he stayed at work late instead of picking the boy up on time. Will and Ruth were the same age, weren't they? So who was looking after Ruth that night?" She gave a shrug. "There's probably some utterly obvious answer."

Ava held her cup aloft for a refill. Her third. Now she'd need to pee. How embarrassing. Then again, Neal had just started his second pot of tea . . .

"PJ's going to look at the Ruth angle. Maybe she'll dig something up," Neal said.

Ava asked if he thought Fin's story about Dana and the drugs let Hector off the hook too conveniently.

"Their stories matched. Then again, Ruth would have been in touch with Fin. They had time to make sure they told the same tale. Fin was clearly uncomfortable talking about the drugs thing with Dana, but that could be because of his past."

"So, is Hector in the clear? About the drugs? We only have Fin's word for it that he witnessed Dana taking coke in their bathroom. Fin could easily be back in the drugs game himself. They aren't exactly living in the sort of luxury Ruth was brought up in. He might even have come to some arrangement with Dana."

"If he is dealing, he's not living large on the profits. How is he funding his studies? Do we know?"

"I checked. He won a scholarship, but it's barely enough to live on. Certainly not enough to provide any extras for Cam. He might have been tempted back into his old way of life to make things easier."

"Val's helped them out," Neal said.

"Fin's another one who doesn't have an alibi for the time of Dana's death. He claims he was in Cambridge, at home, alone, working into the early hours. It's not inconceivable that he could have driven to Stromford, killed Dana and driven back." She paused. "Except Ruth had the car. But there are ways around that."

"Hmm . . ." Neal didn't look convinced.

Ava was contemplating another refill when Neal asked if she was finished. She excused herself and went to the loo, and when she returned she found that Neal had paid for both of them. He refused to let her pay her share. "Your turn next time."

Pleased to think he anticipated a next time, Ava took over the driving. To her surprise, Neal dozed off along the endless stretches of boring motorway. Ava didn't mind. She was content to listen to the sound of his gentle snores and go over the case in her head. Before long, though, she began to feel the pressure on her bladder and she was obliged to pull into a garage. When the car stopped, Neal started awake and began apologising for falling asleep.

After using their facilities, Ava felt obliged to buy something. Her gaze fell on a coffee machine, but she chose some chewing gum instead. As she was waiting for her change, the pictures on the front cover of one of the gossipy magazines caught her eye. She took a closer look.

"Shit!"

The assistant glared at her. "Pardon?"

She grabbed the magazine and said she'd have it too.

Not wishing Neal to see it, Ava squashed the magazine into her handbag. There had been a number of pictures on the cover, but the one that caught her eye was tucked away in the bottom corner. It showed Myrna's smiling face, accompanied by the caption, *Myrna McCloud to tie knot with American musical director Joey Brighton.*

Ava walked back to the car, her mind in turmoil. By the time she climbed into the seat beside him, she had convinced herself that Neal had been the one to contact Myrna. He wanted to stop the wedding.

Chapter Twelve

Ruth woke to the sound of Cam wailing. She waited a few minutes, hoping her mother might come and take him downstairs, but for once, Val must have been sleeping soundly. When Cam's cries became more insistent, Ruth tossed her bedclothes aside and padded across the room to his cot.

Ruth didn't even try to soothe him back to sleep. He was already standing up with his arms raised to be lifted. Ruth took him into her arms and caught a sharp whiff of ammonia. With a sigh, she gathered what she needed to change him and set him down on the mat to remove his wet nappy. He was gurgling now, content and wide awake, his eyes bright and full of mischief.

"Oh, Cam," Ruth said. "Won't you go back to sleep for Mummy? She's so tired."

"Dadadadada," Cam babbled, his eyes searching the room for Fin.

"Daddy's not here," Ruth whispered, despairing. Cam continued to babble, louder now, and Ruth kept expecting her mother to appear in the doorway. Would she ask Ruth to quieten him, or take him downstairs herself to let her daughter sleep? But Val did not appear.

Ruth picked Cam up and carried him downstairs, shuddering as they passed the study. In the kitchen, she warmed some milk in the microwave, hoping it might make Cam sleepy.

Hand in hand, they walked across the wide hallway and into the big airy lounge. Through the windows overlooking the garden, she could see that the moon was out, casting its silver light across the lawn. At least it wasn't cold like it was in her house in Cambridge when she had to get up in the night.

Val had tidied Cam's toys into a big plastic tub, and he made a beeline for this, while Ruth sank, exhausted, into the sofa. Her depression wasn't as bad as it had been, during those endless dark days after Cam's birth when she'd felt drained and empty, going through the motions of new motherhood without enthusiasm or even love. Fin had been the one who coped with it all.

Cam wasn't the only one who missed Fin. Ruth pushed herself up from the sofa and went into the kitchen to make a cup of camomile tea. She could hear the clock tick on the wall, and the tinkle of a toy Cam was playing with in the lounge. Otherwise, the house, enwrapped by the walls of the old hall, was hushed and still in a way that their little Cambridge house never was. The silence felt like a pause. As if she had no past or future, only that moment in the middle of the night. Some lines from Eliot came to her mind. "A still point in a turning world."

The tinkling was in the room with her now. Cam tottered over to her and clung to her leg. She stroked his head. He rubbed his eyes, fighting sleep.

"Come on," Ruth said, and they returned to the sitting room. Ruth carried her mug of tea, though she knew she shouldn't. She, of all people, should know never to assume that the worst wouldn't happen. But she returned to the sofa, and Cam to his box of toys, unscathed. No scalded child, no tea stains on the creamy carpet.

Cam pulled some trains and pieces of wooden track out of the box and began building a railway. Ruth sipped her tea and waited for him to grow tired. At least he was playing by himself, not tugging at her to join in. Her eyes closed and she drifted into a light, fevered sleep.

Will's pale, accusing spectre swam into view, and Ruth woke with a jolt, spilling hot tea over her thighs. She looked around dazedly for Cam and saw the abandoned, half-built train track, and Thomas the Tank Engine lying on his side, one reproachful eye staring fixedly at the ceiling. "Cam?"

Ruth roused herself, and went in search of her son. In the hallway, she found a trail of discarded toys leading into the study.

She found Cam, sitting on the floor by her father's desk. Somehow he'd managed to reach the bronze horse that Ruth had so coveted as a child. He was turning it over, wonderingly, in his hand.

Ruth suppressed an urge to snatch it from him. *That's mine*, whined a small, mean voice inside her head. Almost immediately, she felt a rush of shame.

She crouched on the floor beside Cam, and told him that the horse had belonged to his grandad, and how she'd loved playing with it as a child. But Cam wasn't interested. Ruth tried to coax the statue from him, but he grasped it tighter in his little fist and refused to let go. In a sudden fit of temper, he raised his arm and hurled it across the room. Ruth watched in horror as it struck the corner of the marble fireplace with a sickening crack.

"You horrible child!" She picked up the horse and inspected it. It appeared to be undamaged, but tears pricked her eyes anyway. She felt like shaking Cam. Instead, she shouted, "You horrible, spiteful little boy!"

"Ruth!" Ruth spun around to see her mother standing in the doorway, wearing the Chinese silk dressing gown that Ruth's grandfather had brought back from Malaya where he did his national service in the fifties. It had red-and-gold dragons down either side, and had once belonged to Ruth's grandmother. It, too, Ruth had coveted in her childhood. She sniffed. Might as well give Cam a pair of scissors and let him rip it to shreds. He spoiled everything.

"Go back to bed!" Val ordered in that stentorian voice Ruth remembered so well from her childhood. "I'll see to Cam."

Ruth opened her mouth to protest, but at that moment she couldn't even look at the wailing Cam, so she slouched from the room, only just remembering to thank her mother.

In the quiet of her bedroom, she cried into her pillow.

After her father's body was released by the coroner, after his funeral, she would go back to Cambridge. But was it really going to be that straightforward? Two people were dead.

"Oh, Dad," she whispered into the darkness. "I don't know if I can keep our secret for much longer."

* * *

PJ and Tom met Nathan Brewer at his house share. It was his day off work and he was spending it catching up on chores. He was in the middle of ironing when they arrived. "Sorry about the mess," he said, showing them into the kitchen. "My housemates aren't all as tidy as me."

Tom had lived in house shares in London, and in Hertfordshire. He knew what it was like. Now he could afford to rent a place of his own in Stromford, where his salary went a bit further. He smiled. "No worries, mate."

Nathan cleared stuff off the chairs so they could sit. "I was gutted to hear about Dana. Do you know who did it yet?"

Tom shook his head. He brushed the seat before sitting down. "I know you split up a while ago, but it would be interesting for us to hear your impressions of Dana. You met at Glastonbury, didn't you?"

"Yeah. She'd travelled from Essex with a friend, but the friend got a text from her mum saying her boyfriend had come off his motorbike and was in a pretty bad way. So Dana was on her own. She sort of latched onto me and my mates."

"Lot of drugs at these festivals," Tom said. "Was Dana into all that?"

"That's kind of why I split up with her," Nathan said. "I don't want to sound disrespectful or anything now that she's dead, but she had a bit of a problem with drugs."

"When did you first realise that?"

"Well, at the festival. She was trying to get me and my mates to smoke dope, but we weren't interested."

Nathan struck Tom as being a nice, conservative boy, unimaginative and rather old-fashioned. The type to fancy the girl next door. His use of the expression 'latched on' was interesting. It suggested Dana's company had not been entirely welcome. He suspected she'd sensed an opportunity to exploit in the mild-mannered Nathan.

"Dana travelled back to Stromford and sort of stuck around, didn't she?" PJ said. All of this they knew already, from the PC who had taken a statement from Nathan previously.

"Yes. She kind of attached herself to me. I agreed she could stay here for a couple of days, but she took that to mean she could stay as long as she liked. She wasn't really my girlfriend as such . . ." Nathan coloured.

"Sorry to have to ask you this, Nathan, but did you have a sexual relationship with Ms Schell?" PJ asked. Nathan's colour intensified.

"Yes."

"Was Dana using when she stayed here?" Tom asked.

"Yes."

"Do you know what she was taking?"

"Cannabis. Pills. Legal highs."

"Cocaine?" Tom asked.

Nathan shook his head. "I don't think so."

"So, would it be fair to say that Dana was quite open about her drug use?" PJ said.

"She didn't make a secret of it. My housemates gave me an ultimatum, get rid of Dana, or they'd tell the landlord." Nathan wasn't the brightest. It took a moment or two for him to realise what he'd said. His eyes widened.

"Relax," Tom said. "We know you didn't mean that literally. So you asked Dana to leave. Was that the end of your relationship as well?"

"It was never really a relationship," Nathan reiterated.

"Did Dana make any other friends in Stromford that you were aware of? Either when you were with her, or afterwards?" Tom asked.

"I saw her in town once with an old bloke. He looked well-off. His suit, like, it wasn't from Next or Primark. Know what I mean?"

"Can you describe him?" Tom said.

"Old. Like fifty or something? Good-looking, though. Distinguished. Grey hair . . . Not young." Nathan seemed to struggle to move beyond the man's age. He shook his head. "Sorry, just old and well-dressed."

"Average height? Tall?" Tom prompted.

"Average?"

Could be Paul Cornish, but he wasn't the only well-dressed, middle-aged man in town. Tom had been hoping for a description fitting Hector Cornish.

But Nathan wasn't quite finished. "She worked for Ruth Marsh's dad's business partner, didn't she? I read it in the *Courier*."

"You know Ruth?"

"Not really. I knew her cousin, Will. He was a mate of mine at school. He died. In a fire." From his expression, Nathan was still cut up over the loss of his friend. "Ruth Marsh went to the private school, the posh one up at the cathedral. I went to Stromford Hill High, just along the road."

Just along the road. A million miles apart. Tom sighed inwardly.

"I used to see her waiting for her mum to pick her up from school. She smiled at me once. When I was with Will." He'd fancied Ruth, Tom realised. "Poor old Will. Wonder what he'd be doing if he was here now?"

"Sorry, mate," Tom said.

"I never bought it, what they said about that fire." Nathan looked at Tom, and then PJ. "They reckoned it was started by a cigarette end, but Will was like me, he was never into smoking, it made him sick. And he was an athlete. He was training for a triathlon at the time. He'd never have taken up smoking."

"Did you raise your concerns at the time?" Tom said.

Nathan shook his head. "Should have done. Wouldn't have brought him back, though, would it?"

"Thank you for your time, Nathan." Tom extended a hand.

Nathan shook it. "I'll get back to my ironing, then. My mum's always offering to do it for me, but I don't like to burden her. She's got enough to do with my brothers and sisters still at home."

"So who did the cigarette end belong to?" PJ asked, the minute they were outside and walking away from Nathan's place.

"Probably was Will's. Nathan isn't the brightest, is he? Will could have been concealing it from him because he knew Nathan would disapprove. He's an old-fashioned sort of lad, isn't he?"

PJ nodded. "Reminds me of my little cousin, Bruce. Nineteen going on forty. Might be worthwhile checking out the reports on that fire, though, don't you think?"

"Absolutely."

"How are you getting on with Lesley Curran?" PJ asked, sneaking a glance at him.

"Er . . . She asked me to accompany her to a restaurant the other night. Said it was work related, but made it clear she had plans for afterwards. Wasn't best pleased when I made my excuses."

PJ smiled. "She's an attractive woman."

Tom stared at her with a look of disbelief. "She's like fifty-five!"

"Fiftyish, more like," PJ said.

"Well, I'm twenty-six. I prefer women closer to my own age, thank you."

"You know, if she makes you feel uncomfortable, you don't have to put up with it," PJ said. "Tell Neal. He could appoint Ava or me as her main contact instead."

"Thanks, PJ."

"Yeah, well, we women have had to put up with that sort of thing for ever. We're used to finding ways to support each other. No reason for anyone, male or female, to suffer in silence."

* * *

Fin held the curtain aside and watched the two police officers retreating down the street. Had he managed to convince them? Ever since Ruth had called to tell him about Hector's request, he'd been seething with rage. Hector had made a promise. You don't renege on a promise. Even in the murky world of drug dealing that he'd inhabited in his youth, your word counted for something.

Fin's life seemed to be unravelling at a frightening pace. Ever since that chance meeting with Hector Cornish and Dana Schell in the Grafton Centre, he'd worried that everything he'd worked so hard to achieve was being undermined by factors outside his control.

A couple of days after Hector and Dana came round for dinner, Fin encountered Hector again. Not by coincidence, Fin suspected. Hector had crept up on him as he was walking across New Square Park. He'd tapped Fin on the shoulder, making him jump.

"Hey, Fin. Great night the other night."

Was it? Fin didn't think so. Hector had made him feel threatened in some vague way, even before he'd claimed to know a secret about Ruth's past. Then there'd been Ruth's odd behaviour (prompted by Hector's remark about a secret?) She hadn't returned to excuse herself after leaving the table. This lapse in good manners had surprised Fin. He'd found her curled up in bed. "Did Hector say something to upset you?" he asked, only to be met with a stony silence.

Hector and Dana overstayed their welcome by a big margin, finally leaving at around two in the morning, having exhausted all the alcohol in the house.

The following morning, Ruth apologised to Fin for leaving him to entertain their guests alone. Sensing that she didn't want to talk about it, Fin simply nodded. He hoped they'd seen the last of Hector Cornish.

Turned out Hector had other plans. Hence the 'chance' encounter in the park. He invited Fin to have a chat, selecting a seat away from the lunchtime workers, out in force to enjoy the unexpected sunshine.

"I've got a proposition for you," Hector began. "A business proposition."

"No" was Fin's immediate, instinctive reply. He didn't trust Hector and he had an inkling of what Hector was about to say. He wondered how much Hector knew about his past. Ruth's father was in business with Hector's father, so he could easily have told him about the private investigator and his findings. "I'm a full-time student and I'm about to be a father. I don't have time for anything else."

Hector sat, legs splayed, arms stretched out along the back of the bench. He let out a long sigh. "That's a real shame, Fin, my man. On more than one level."

Fin followed Hector's gaze to a trio of young women sitting a few benches along, on the opposite side of the path. They all had sandwich boxes perched on their mini-skirted thighs, knees tightly clenched. "What's that supposed to mean?" he asked, squinting in the midday sun.

"That 'little secret' of Ruth's that I referred to the other night." Hector gave a slow smile, his eyes never leaving the group of young women. "You know. The one you know nothing about." Hector turned his head slowly towards Fin and their eyes met. Hector's gaze was like a cold dart.

"Ruth and I don't have secrets from each other."

A mocking laugh. The dart pierced Fin's armour, its chilly poison sapping his confidence.

Hector spread his legs still wider. "Once upon a time, not so long ago, there was a fire . . ."

Anger surged through Fin. "Stop!" he said, loud enough to attract the attention of the young women opposite, who all looked in their direction. Hector gave them a half-wave and one of them waved back. The others giggled, and they resumed their conversation.

"So? What? You don't want to know Ruth's secret?" Hector said.

"No." Fin choked on the word. If Ruth had a secret, he would hear it first from her lips, not from this arrogant bully.

"Tell you what," Hector said. "You go home, talk to Ruth. I'll call you tomorrow. Then we'll do business." A pause. His gaze was full of malice. "Or not. It's up to you." Hector sighed. "Ruth's such a fragile flower, isn't she? Mentally, I mean. Has been ever since . . . Oops, sorry, you don't want to know, do you? All I'm saying is it would be a shame if something pushed her right over the edge, wouldn't it?"

With that, Hector stood up and walked off, swaggering as he passed the trio of women. He bowed slightly and Fin heard him say, "Ladies." No doubt they thought him very *galante*.

So Fin and Ruth talked, late into the night. No more secrets. And when Hector called him the following morning, Fin was ready to do business.

He'd already guessed what Hector's business proposition would entail.

"We're going to London. I want you to introduce me to your mate, Liam Sharp." Fin recoiled silently. Hector must have spoken with the PI that Russ Marsh hired. "I'll pick you up in half an hour." He cut Fin off before he could protest.

Hector arrived exactly thirty minutes later. "He's here," Ruth said dully, turning from the window. There were dark shadows under her eyes. She had lost that aura of mystery that had first attracted Fin. To his surprise, his feelings for her, though more complex now, were unchanged. If anything, he loved her more.

"This is crazy," she said. Fin nodded. "How does he even know about your past and . . . and Liam Sharp?"

"I think you can work that one out," Fin said dryly.

"My father must have talked to Hector's parents about the PI. But he must know you've had nothing to do with Liam or the drugs scene for years! And why Liam? It's easy enough to get hold of drugs in Cambridge if you want them."

"I don't think Hector wants drugs for himself. He talked about a 'business proposition.' I think he wants to meet a supplier and set himself up dealing in Cambridge."

Hector's car was parked on the double yellow lines outside their front door.

"Back soon," Fin said to Ruth. She'd returned his kiss but he could tell she was distracted.

"You know this is crazy, right?" Fin said to Hector, pulling on his seatbelt. "Liam might not even be living on the same estate."

"Don't think I haven't done my homework. Russ Marsh's PI was more than willing to talk," said Hector, confirming Fin's worst suspicions, "and he was happy to let me have Liam's details for a small fee. Your mate's still living in the same area. I've got his address."

"He won't remember me, and even if he does he won't want anything to do with me," Fin said. "I told him years ago that I was through with everything."

"He remembers you."

Now Fin gazed at Hector in astonishment. "You've spoken with him?"

"He can't wait to see his old buddy. And he's happy to do business, as long as you'll vouch for me. All I need from you is an introduction. Did you really take the flak for his kid brother? How stupid are you?"

Fin said nothing. How could he explain that taking the fall for Darren Sharp had rerouted his life? He glanced nervously over his shoulder, at a black leather sports bag resting on the back seat, fat with Hector's money. He wanted nothing to do with any of this. He thought of Michael Corleone in *The Godfather*, and that line about being pulled back in just when he thought he was out.

True to his character, Hector drove as though he owned the road. He was an aggressive, reckless driver, taking the bends too fast, harassing other drivers, speeding. Fin shut his eyes, and his thoughts returned to the past.

Liam Sharp had pulled Fin in when he was twelve years old. Liam was eight years older. His younger brother, Darren, had attached himself to Fin when they were at secondary school. Darren wasn't the brightest kid on the block, and Fin had looked out for him. It had brought him to Liam's attention. Unlike his brother, Liam was no fool. Young as he was, he was already a successful 'businessman,' albeit on a small scale. Recognising Fin's intelligence, he'd put him to use as a runner. Fin could still remember the buzz of earning his first serious money, cash-in-hand.

Soon he was working fifteen-hour days for Liam. Running around with a mobile phone and a shank, he'd felt like a king. School was a distant memory. Darren was a runner too, but he lacked Fin's alacrity and presence of mind. He'd got himself into trouble a couple of times, and Fin had got him out of it, earning him Liam's respect.

Fin's career had ended because of one of Darren's mistakes. Fin had been the one hauled up against the panel, and he'd done the community service. The experience had been life-changing. That's when he'd realised he was living the wrong life. The community service showed him the joy of learning and education. They'd told him at school that he was clever. One teacher had said his IQ was 'in the stratosphere.'

A sympathetic youth worker had become his mentor, encouraging him to challenge and stretch himself beyond his limits. He developed into an A-star student, and acceptance at Cambridge had been the icing on the cake.

Now Fin was living a life so far removed from those days that he couldn't imagine him and Liam even speaking the same language. Nowadays he had more in common with the despicable Hector. They'd both spent the past few years in an institution that cultivated a sense of superiority and entitlement. Fin thought guiltily of the two hundred pounds he'd paid to attend his first college ball, when he'd swigged champagne from a bottle and behaved like a decadent toff, served by waiting staff that he treated with disdain. He shuddered. That had been the wrong life too. Thankfully, he'd managed to find his true self in academia.

Fin became aware of Hector speaking to him. "Recognise your old stomping ground, do you?"

They had been driving through London for what seemed like hours. Most of it was unfamiliar to Fin, who'd rarely strayed beyond his territory in the East End. Now, some familiar landmarks loomed into view: the Tube station and gardens at Bethnal Green, the Museum of Childhood, where he vaguely remembered being taken as a young child, before his parents lost interest in him altogether. The college where he'd studied for his A levels.

According to the satnav, they were arriving at their destination. The streets brought Fin's childhood and adolescence back like a smack in the face.

Despite the money he must have accumulated, Liam still lived modestly, in a terraced house within a quarter of a mile of the estate he'd grown up on. Of course he did. He was territorial. Fin wondered what he did with his profits these days, how he cleaned his money. How he'd evaded a prison sentence all these years.

Despite the area's recent gentrification, Hector's flash car made the neighbourhood seem shabby and grey. There was no correspondingly expensive car outside Liam's house. He wasn't stupid. Nothing shouted *drug dealer* louder than an ostentatious lifestyle.

This was all real. He wasn't dreaming. Fin went into defensive mode. "Just don't say or do anything to piss Liam off. Leave all the talking to me. Liam can be . . . volatile." That was putting it mildly. Fin had seen Liam cut someone's ear off for lying to him. When Fin thought of it now, it amazed him that there had once been a time when he hardly flinched at such brutal behaviour. How readily things become normalised. Back then, Fin wouldn't have believed he would one day blow two hundred quid on a ticket to a college ball.

Fin rang the bell and was surprised to see Darren open the door. He'd been expecting one of Liam's muscle men. Not that Darren was lacking in muscle. He looked like he'd been lifting since Fin saw him last.

Fin bumped fists with Darren and they embraced, Fin conscious of his own puny frame. He was almost touched at the outpouring that followed. Darren had evidently missed him more than he'd missed Darren. Unlike him, Darren hadn't moved on.

Fin introduced Hector. Darren's expression made it clear that his presence was tolerated only because Fin had vouched for him. They were led into a room at the back of the house, where Liam sat on a garish red leather sofa, his arm around a girl who looked like she ought to be in school. She eyed Fin and Hector with suspicion and left the room.

Fin went over to the sofa and Liam, still seated, grasped his arm with both hands. "Fin. Good to see you, man. It's been too long."

"Likewise," Fin said.

"So, Fin, my man. I hear you got yourself a fancy education."

Fin smiled. Suddenly Liam stood up and embraced him, slapping his back so hard it sent him off balance. Liam grinned. "All that learning's made you soft."

Fin's eyes turned to Hector, hovering awkwardly in the doorway, holding on to his leather bag protectively. It gave Fin a certain amount of satisfaction to see him so ill at ease. The rich brat was way out of his comfort zone.

Finally, Liam squinted over at him. "Introduce me to your friend."

Hector moved forward a pace. Their gazes met in mutual suspicion, two predators circling round each other.

"So, this Hector is your friend."

Between gritted teeth, Fin managed, "Yeah, he's okay. You can do business with him." Liam nodded, still appraising Hector.

"I'm doing this as a favour for my old friend Fin here, who did time for my baby brother. I trust him."

Fin prayed that Hector would keep his mouth shut. To his relief, Hector only inclined his head in acknowledgement. They got down to business.

An hour later, Fin and Hector were back on the road, bags of white powder having replaced the notes in the black leather bag.

* * *

Fin let the curtain drop. He was furious at Hector for involving him and Ruth in his murky affairs again. For the first time, he was angry with Ruth too. And, inevitably, with himself, for entertaining Hector's demands in the first place. Surely there were other things he could have done to help Ruth? In fact, he'd suggested as much at the time, but Ruth had screamed like a crazy person when he suggested that she confront her past. It frightened him.

A terrible thought now formed in Fin's mind. What if Hector had killed Dana, and he and Ruth had just helped him get away with it?

Fin had a sudden urge to run after the police officers, but instead he turned away from the window, crossed the floor to his laptop and went back to work.

Chapter Thirteen

PJ stared at the words on her computer screen until her vision blurred. She was reading the reports on the fire that had killed Lizzie's son, Will, and led, indirectly, to her husband committing suicide. She'd read everything twice over and could find nothing to suggest that the incident had been anything but a tragic accident.

"Nothing," she said to Tom, who was sitting at the PC opposite her, absorbed in his own research. He looked up. "Nathan was right," she went on. "Cause of the fire was a cigarette. A butt was retrieved from under the sofa in the living room. The sofa caught alight. It was an old one, not fire retardant. Ash from the burning sofa extinguished the cigarette and covered it over. That's what made the investigators pretty confident about the cause. Will's body was found in the room where the fire started. He was overcome by toxic fumes."

"Shit. Poor kid. Did anyone else in the household smoke?" Tom asked.

"No. The report says his parents were astonished to hear that he'd been smoking. Like Nathan said, Will was a keen athlete. Still, I did plenty of stuff my parents would've been shocked about if they'd known."

Tom looked sceptical. It irritated her that he thought her so conventional and boring. "What if Will had company that evening?"

"Nathan?"

"I was thinking of his cousin, Ruth Marsh." PJ frowned. "Ava raised the question the other day. If Will's parents and Val Marsh weren't around that evening, what do you suppose Ruth was up to? She would have been, what, fourteen at the time?"

Tom shrugged. "At a friend's house, most likely."

"The police spoke with Will's parents, obviously, and with Val and Russ Marsh. Ruth isn't mentioned. No reason why she would be, really, I suppose. Still, Ava's asked me to look into it."

"You're not seriously thinking Ruth could have been responsible for the fire?" Tom said.

"Not really, but let's see what Val Marsh has to say about the incident."

PJ called Val. As luck would have it, she was home, but when they were admitted into her house half an hour later, PJ and Tom discovered that she wasn't alone. She showed them into the big airy room with a view, where her sister was sitting next to her daughter on the sofa, both engaged in trying to soothe a grizzling Cam.

"He's got a temperature. Been off all day. I'll take him upstairs, see if I can settle him down for a nap," Ruth said, picking up the protesting toddler. Val indicated a couple of chairs, and they sat down.

"What is it this time?" she asked rather rudely.

With an apologetic glance at Lizzie, Tom said, "We'd like to ask you some questions about the night of the fire that Will died in, if that's okay?"

"Why on earth do you want to bring that up?" Val exclaimed. "No, it's not okay, actually. My sister doesn't need you people dredging up her heartache on a bloody whim."

"It's alright, Val," Lizzie reassured her sister. "I don't imagine the officers are acting on a whim. If they need to ask about the fire, they must have a good reason." She looked at PJ.

"Oh, yes, of course," PJ stammered.

Tom got straight to the point. "Mrs Marsh, was your daughter a smoker?"

Val stared at him. "What?"

"The fire that killed Will was started by a cigarette. Will didn't smoke. Did Ruth?"

Val grasped the arm of her chair as if to stand up, but she remained seated, still holding on. "Are you serious? I don't believe this. My husband is dead, shot through the head, and the best you can come up with after a week of investigation is an irrelevant question about a tragedy that took place eight years ago! What the hell is wrong with you people? Are you trying to say Ruth started the fire that killed Will? Maybe she blew her father's brains out too, despite being nearly two hundred miles away at the time."

Lizzie eyed Tom and PJ, her gaze icy. "Where are you going with this? Do you think Ruth was with Will the night of the fire?" She turned to Val. "Ruth was at a sleepover that night, wasn't she, Val?"

"Yes." Val seemed calmer now. "They were revising for an exam at school. The police didn't seem to be interested in what Ruth was doing at the time. Like Lizzie, I'd like to know where you're going with this."

PJ was starting to wonder herself. She was about to suggest they call Ruth down so that they could ask her to confirm her whereabouts the night Will died when, as if on cue, Ruth's voice called out from upstairs. There was an edge of panic to her voice. They all rose and made for the hall.

Ruth was halfway down the stairs, holding Cam. He hung, limp, in her arms. "Someone call an ambulance," she wailed. "Cam's a lot worse, and he's got strange blotches. I think it might be meningitis."

* * *

Ruth had gone in the ambulance with Cam. PJ offered to drive Lizzie and Val to the hospital, but Lizzie had insisted that she would drive her sister.

"How annoying is that?" Tom said, his eyes on the departing vehicles. "Just as we were getting somewhere."

PJ turned on him, bristling with annoyance. "Firstly, we weren't getting very far. Secondly, show a bit of flipping compassion, Tom Knight. That baby is very sick."

"Bit of a coincidence, you've got to admit, her bringing the kid down like that, just as we're about to question her."

"Oh, come on," PJ said. "Ruth couldn't possibly have heard what we were talking about from upstairs."

Tom shrugged. "Just sayin'. He didn't look that bad to me. There was no need for all that drama."

"Meningitis is a serious illness, potentially fatal. I think Ruth was entitled to panic."

"Hmm. More likely to be a viral infection of some sort."

"So, you're an expert on baby illnesses now, are you?"

"Babies get a lot of bugs," Tom said. "I have two nephews. They seem to have a temperature more often than not. My sister goes through gallons of Calpol. That's paracetamol for kids."

"I know what Calpol is. I have nieces and nephews too, you know," PJ snapped. "Look, I'm going to go down to the County to see how he is. No need for you to come. Just drop me off, and I'll walk back to the station."

"Okay," Tom said.

Actually, PJ secretly shared Tom's scepticism, if not his lack of empathy. There had been other issues to bring up with Val and Lizzie, but even if she managed to corral them at the hospital, it would be inappropriate to follow them up there and then.

Tom dropped her at Accident and Emergency. PJ walked through the double doors into a bustling reception and waiting area. PJ hated hospitals. They were all too familiar to her from her days as a PC. On her last visit, she'd arrested a drunken lout for assaulting a member of the nursing staff, and was landed a black eye for her trouble. She wasn't particularly nostalgic about her days in uniform.

She couldn't spot Val and Lizzie in the sea of people either waiting to be triaged, or to hear news of relatives. PJ approached the counter and waited to speak with the receptionist behind the Perspex safety panel. After a minute spent listening to the man in front of her complaining bitterly about the waiting time, PJ moved in front of him, flashing her badge. With a hostile look, he gave way and slouched back to his seat, still complaining.

The receptionist mouthed, *Thank you.*

"I'm enquiring about Cam Marsh,' PJ said. 'He would have arrived about twenty minutes ago in an ambulance, with his mother, Ruth Marsh."

The receptionist scrolled through the spreadsheet on her computer. "They're in the A&E Assessment and Treatment area," she said, nodding at the swing doors. "I'm sorry, but I can't let you go through."

"I know. I wonder if you could tell me if Cam's gran and aunt arrived around the same time. I thought they'd be in the waiting area."

"Yes, they did. I advised them that only the child's mum could go into the treatment area with him. I think I heard one of them suggest going upstairs to the canteen."

"Thanks," PJ said. She hesitated. "You know, you shouldn't put up with abuse from people like that guy."

The receptionist shrugged. "All part of the job."

"Well, it shouldn't be." PJ received another shrug.

PJ followed the maze of coloured directional lines up two flights of stairs, and arrived at a crossroads. Here, the signs ran out. A helpful porter directed her up another flight of stairs, where the sound of dishes clattering and an aroma of food told her she was on the right track.

One wall of the canteen was made up entirely of windows, taking advantage of the sight of the cathedral, within touching distance so it seemed.

Val and Lizzie were seated with their backs to PJ, facing the window, but it didn't look as though they were taking in the view. PJ walked towards them, automatically softening her footsteps. As she drew nearer, she could hear the two women and make out their heated discussion.

". . . That's rich coming from you. Buggered off to London the first chance you got. I was the one who had to look out for Mum and Dad."

"Here we go again. You're so predictable, Lizzie. Just for once, I wish you'd stop to wonder why I had to get away."

"Why? Because you thought I was Mum and Dad's favourite? That was all in your mind, Val. Mum and Dad went out of their way to treat us the same. In fact . . ."

Even from a distance, PJ could see how Val held her anger tightly coiled inside her. Her shoulders were stiff, quivering rather than shaking outright. PJ knew that Val's protective outer shell could be regarded as cold, lacking in empathy. But PJ, deeply empathic herself, thought she saw something else in Val. She was hurting, the way a person does when they have an old, and still raw wound. It seemed to her that the sisters were playing a familiar game. It had been going on since time immemorial, and there were no winners.

"Shut up, Lizzie. Please."

Lizzie did shut up. She'd glanced over Val's shoulder and spotted PJ eavesdropping. Val swivelled around.

Well, this is awkward. PJ felt herself redden. "Hi. I followed on to see how Cam is. Have you heard anything yet? Is he okay?"

"They're assessing him now," Val said. "One of the paramedics caught up with us after he'd dropped Ruth and Cam off. He doesn't think it's meningitis. Wrong sort of spots, apparently."

"Well, he's in good hands," PJ said.

Val's phone rang. "Ruth," she said. "Hello, Ruth?"

PJ waited, hoping to hear that baby Cam was out of danger. She smiled at Lizzie, who was straining to hear her sister's every word.

"Try not to worry. He's in good hands," Val said, repeating PJ's words into the phone.

"Well? How is he?" Lizzie asked as soon as Val ended the call.

Val was looking relieved. "They're not sure. Probably some sort of virus. But not meningitis. He's a bit dehydrated, and they're giving him fluids."

"Thank goodness." Lizzie embraced her sister, all hostilities forgotten — or suspended, at least. PJ felt like an intruder. She gazed around the canteen. Soon she'd be back here with Steve. "I'll be off then," she said. "I hope Cam will be okay." She turned to go.

"Detective Jenkins." It still gave PJ a little shiver of pleasure to hear herself addressed in this way. She looked at Val.

"Thank you for coming. I appreciate your concern."

PJ inclined her head and walked away. She could sense Val's eyes upon her. *Don't think I've forgotten about Ruth. I'll be back to ask more questions.* PJ sighed. Ruth had won herself a reprieve.

* * *

Lying in bed that night, Jim Neal reflected on his meeting with Myrna. He knew that Ava had been fishing for information on their drive to Cambridge, but he hadn't felt ready to talk with her yet. He needed some kind of hiatus, a breathing space before he could move on with his life. And there was the case, of course. But then there was always going to be a case.

It had been unsettling seeing Myrna again. They hadn't met face to face in years, and the sight of her walking towards him across the police station car park had reeled back the years at a dizzying pace.

At the time they'd parted, back in Edinburgh, Myrna had been determined to make a name for herself in the music world. Opera was her first love, but her voice was still immature and she had gone off to London to train. In the meantime, she'd accepted minor roles in musicals, and was now becoming known in musical theatre.

Neal had looked her up online from time to time, so he already knew that she'd changed her hair colour and looked a lot more polished than when they were together. But no picture could evoke the strange mixture of feelings he'd experienced on seeing her for real.

She'd walked up and kissed him right away. He'd kissed her back before he knew what he was doing. The sensation of feeling her lips on his was so familiar.

His friend Jock always said that Myrna was an enchantress, and she'd bewitched him. Looking at her after so many years, Neal could almost believe that the spell had never been broken, only pulled taut and Myrna was now rewinding the thread.

Myrna had been the first to pull away

"Jimmy. What a welcome!" Myrna stepped back and looked him up and down. "Still the handsome devil, I see." She linked arms with him, as if it were the most natural thing in the world. Catching sight of Tom and Ava's car just turning out onto the main road, Neal experienced a twist of anxiety.

"So where are you taking me, Jim?" Myrna asked. Her accent took him right back to the West Lothian village they had both grown up in.

"There's a nice little Italian in the cathedral quarter that you might like. Italian used to be your favourite food, if I remember rightly. Though things change, of course."

"Oh, I still adore Italian food."

Neal led Myrna through a cobbled alleyway, a shortcut through to the top end of the High Street and the start of the Long Hill. "Just like an Edinburgh close," Myrna remarked. "Don't you miss it, Jim? I never thought you'd leave Edinburgh. Remember all those times we'd bunk off school and catch the bus into town, and just walk and walk?"

"I remember," Neal said, somewhat wistfully. It was true. He did miss Edinburgh, but he'd made a life for himself and Archie here in Stromford. And unless he was mistaken, Myrna's home was in London now.

"No harm in a wee bit of nostalgia, is there, Jimmy?"

"I suppose not." He wondered whether he should tell Myrna the reason why he'd left Edinburgh. How he'd needed the promotion to make a better life for Archie. House prices were cheaper here. No need to mention any of that. He was happy enough with his choices. He'd been the one who wanted to be a parent. He'd pleaded with Myrna to carry their child to term, with the promise that she would never have to bear any of the responsibility.

"This is it," he said, stopping in front of the little restaurant where he, Maggie, Jock and Archie came to eat regularly. They went inside and the waiter greeted Neal with a friendly, "Ciao," and a questioning glance at Myrna. A couple of women were enjoying a meal and a bottle of Prosecco. They looked up as Myrna and Neal settled themselves at their table. Probably assumed they were a couple.

Myrna looked around, and Neal noticed her grimace of distaste. She never used to be so particular. "Not what you're used to?" he asked, amused. Myrna assured him she was perfectly happy with the restaurant, such as it was, but this was only the first in a string of criticisms.

She couldn't find her favourite dish on the menu. The wine tasted peculiar and she sent it back. Her pasta wasn't al dente, could they do it again. In fact, it had put her off, could she order pizza instead. Her voice was too loud and her tone with the staff brusque, almost arrogant. Despite the evidence of his eyes, Neal began to wonder if this really was Myrna sitting opposite him. Surely she hadn't always behaved this way. Soon, he found himself cringing with embarrassment for her and as soon as she went off to the toilet, he apologised to the staff. How many other things had he failed to notice about Myrna back then?

Myrna dominated the conversation throughout the meal. That was nothing new, Neal recalled. He'd always been the listener in their relationship. He'd been so besotted with her that he'd been content to look at her, not really caring what she said, just unable to believe his luck that she'd chosen him to talk to. Now it took him no time at all to realise that Myrna really only had only one topic of conversation — Myrna.

Myrna had talked non-stop, but she hadn't once mentioned Archie. Only once they had ordered dessert, and then coffee, did she.

"So, how is our boy?"

Our boy. Neal's heart filled with dread. Since Myrna's phone call, he had been preparing himself for this. For what Maggie kept referring to as 'Myrna's hidden agenda.' Maggie had run through all the possibilities the previous evening, after Archie was asleep.

She's got some incurable disease and wants to see Archie before she dies. This theory topped Maggie's list, followed by the one that Neal hated most: *Archie isn't yours.* The look on Neal's face when Maggie came up with this one had made Jock bellow with laughter. "For pity's sake, Jim, have you not looked at the laddie lately? Archie's your bloody double. And, Maggie, you need to stop watching so many soaps."

Neal's imagination was less fertile. He'd assumed that Myrna could have only one reason for turning up in Stromford — she had suddenly changed her mind about being involved in Archie's life. He'd lain awake for hours the night before, worrying that Myrna planned to whisk Archie off to London to live with her.

Before he could comment, Myrna gave a hearty laugh. "You don't have to worry about me getting all maternal and trying to take Archie away from you. Nothing's changed on that front, Jim."

Neal was overwhelmed with relief.

"Look at you. Is that what you thought?"

"It did cross my mind." *Understatement of the decade.*

"I expect Maggie's been twisting the knife. She never did like me."

"That's not true." *Liar.*

"What's she doing these days, your sister?"

"Maggie's been living here in Stromford. She's getting married in the new year. To my friend, Jock."

"Jock Dodds?" Myrna's incredulous expression puzzled Neal.

"I slept with him once, you know." It was Neal's turn to look incredulous. "It was a couple of years after we split up, Jim. I never two-timed you if that's what the long face is about."

Neal stared out the window. Why had Jock never told him this? Did it matter? It wasn't as if his friend or his ex-lover had betrayed him. Did Maggie know?

"It was only the once. I was in Edinburgh doing a show in the Fringe. I bumped into a very drunk Jock and I seduced him, shameless hussy that I am. Even then he was carrying a torch for your sister. I never thought he'd get up the courage to ask her out, never mind marry her." She leaned across the table. "He wasn't nearly as good in bed as you, Jim."

Neal stole a glance at the Prosecco women, but they seemed not to have overheard. Or perhaps they were being polite. Maybe Myrna's voice wasn't as loud as he thought it was. And then he caught the eye of one of the waiters and he knew it was.

"You're as red as a beetroot," Myrna teased. "What happened to you, Jim? You never used to be such an old stuffed shirt. You used to be fun." She paused. "I can't believe you ended up being a copper."

I grew up, Neal was tempted to say, irritated at her mocking tone and the word 'copper.' But he had no desire to provoke her. If she cared to, she could complicate things for him and Archie.

He was still curious as to why Myrna'd come to Stromford. Was Maggie right in suspecting that she had some hidden agenda? The waiter hovered near their table and Myrna barked, in that unfamiliar, brash voice. "Can we get the bill?"

It was not until they'd left the restaurant and were sitting in a bar nearby that Myrna revealed the reason for her visit.

"You're probably wondering why I've come to see you after so long, Jim." Myrna laid a hand on his knee.

Here it comes. Neal braced himself.

"The thing is, I've met someone and we're getting married. He's a musical theatre director, an American. From Boston, actually."

It was worse than he thought. She was going to take Archie out of the country with her. A feeling of doom descended on Neal.

"It probably sounds a bit weird, but before I went ahead with the wedding plans, I wanted to be sure that Joey really is the one."

Whatever Neal had been expecting, this certainly wasn't it.

"You were my first love, Jimmy. We lost our virginity together. Remember how awkward it was that first time, at my parent's house, fumbling around with the condom in the half-dark?"

Neal nodded, wondering if it was too soon to feel relief. "Aye," he said, hoping Myrna wouldn't delve any deeper into that particular memory. He had a sudden vision of Sandy McCloud, Myrna's dad, eyeing them with suspicion whenever they came downstairs after an extended session in Myrna's bedroom. And his warning. "If you get my daughter in the family way, I'll tan the behind aff ye."

Myrna chattered on. "I suppose what I'm trying to say is that I've thought about you a lot over the years, Jim Neal, and I just wanted to be sure that I wasn't still carrying a torch for you. Before I go off and tie the knot with Joey."

Her grip on his knee tightened. So did Neal's chest. Was Myrna about to declare that it had been a terrible mistake splitting up with him after Archie was born? But she'd already said she wanted no part in Archie's life, hadn't she? Perhaps he'd misunderstood. Myrna's words filtered through his panic, slowly turning his emotion to elation.

". . . And after this afternoon, I can say, beyond any shadow of a doubt, that the torch is completely extinguished."

"Er . . ."

"So do I have your blessing, Jimmy?"

"Absolutely, one hundred per cent," Neal said, a little too effusively. Myrna grunted. "Oh. Right, well. I take it the feeling's mutual, then."

He felt easier in her company after that. Maggie had been wrong. There had been no hidden agenda. Or, there had, but the outcome was positive. It seemed to clear the air between them. More drinks followed, and before Neal knew it, the afternoon had given way to evening.

And then they were standing outside Myrna's hotel. There was an awkward moment when Neal wondered if he should kiss her goodbye and if so, would a peck on the cheek suffice. Then Myrna asked, "Want to come up?" Neal was appalled.

The air around them vibrated with Myrna's peal of mischievous laughter. Suddenly, Neal was reminded of the girl he'd fallen in love with. The girl who'd given him that wonderful, amazing gift of a child. His son, Archie.

"I thought it might be nice, you know, for old time's sake. But I can see that someone else has your heart now, Jimmy." Myrna kissed him on the cheek. "Whoever she is, I hope she appreciates you." Another chaste kiss, before she shooed him off, saying, somewhat enigmatically, "No regrets, Jim."

Neal walked home slowly, the past vivid in his mind and in his emotions. When he reached the cathedral, he paused and stood for a moment, admiring the ornate Romanesque stone carvings on the columns on either side of the west front doors. They rose up to form a series of arches, and every one of them was different. Some were decorated with geometric shapes, others with birds and beasts, real and fantastic. Neal had spent a pleasant afternoon in the summer, watching Archie sketch some of the designs for a school project. He'd taken pictures on his phone and downloaded them into a folder on his laptop. *Archie sketching the arches*. No, he had no regrets.

Back at his house, Neal closed the gate to his small front garden and strolled up the path. Maggie waved to him from the window, and met him in the hallway, bursting to hear the news.

They went into the sitting room at the front of the house, where Jock was reading a newspaper.

"Archie's asleep. I read him the last couple of chapters of *Stormbreaker*. It's bad news, isn't it?" Maggie said. "Myrna's been diagnosed with an inherited disease that affects the male line and you'll have to decide whether to have Archie tested."

"Where do you get that crap from?" Neal said. Over the top of the *Guardian*, Jock studied him closely.

Neal decided he'd better put Maggie out of her misery.

"Myrna's getting married and moving to the States. She hardly even mentioned Archie." His sister threw herself upon him and hugged him in jubilant relief.

"That's brilliant news! I can't wait to tell . . ." Maggie's voice tailed off. Jock had a sudden coughing fit and asked for a glass of water. Neal surprised them both by declaring he was having an early night.

Chapter Fourteen

Fin O'Shea stood at the nurses' station and looked down the row of beds. It was six thirty in the morning, the ward hushed and softly lit. His heart ached at the sight of Ruth, curled in a chair, loosely covered with a hospital blanket, asleep at their son's bedside. Her cheeks were flushed. Damp tendrils of brown hair curled around her forehead, and tiny bubbles escaped her pursed lips as she exhaled. Fin was overcome. He tore his eyes from Ruth and looked at Cam, fast asleep also, lying atop the covers, wearing only a nappy. A wave of tenderness engulfed him and he felt tears prick his eyes.

He settled into a chair beside Ruth, and waited. It was alright. Cam was going to be alright, he told himself. Ruth had assured him that Cam's condition wasn't life-threatening. When she'd first called, from an ambulance on her way to the hospital, it had seemed that his whole life was falling apart. Now he could allow himself a moment's respite from worry.

Ruth's had not been the only bad news he'd received that day. Fin sighed. He'd already had plenty to worry about, even before her call.

The previous afternoon, an unlikely caller had turned up at their house in Cambridge. The unexpected sight of Darren Sharp on his doorstep had set alarm bells ringing. Ordinarily, Darren wouldn't set foot outside his own territory, and his mere presence in Cambridge could signify only one thing. Trouble. He was right.

Fin had been expecting some kind of fallout from that day in London when he'd taken Hector to meet Liam. It had taken its time in coming, nearly two years. But now it had arrived in the form of Liam's brother, with a story Fin could hardly believe.

"It's bad, man," Darren had said, stepping into the house without invitation. "Your mate Hector's ripped Liam off, and you know what my bro's like when someone pisses him off."

Fin knew. He thought of the severed ear. The way Liam had flicked it casually across the room, as though it were the skin from an apple he'd just peeled and didn't want left sticking to his knife. His victim's screams hadn't provoked so much as a blink.

"Tell me what Hector did," Fin said.

It was worse than he imagined. A few weeks ago, one of Liam's dealers had been attacked in his home. His attacker had made off with twenty grand's worth of coke. The mystery man had been wearing a scarf to cover the lower half of his face — one of those with grinning skeleton teeth — and ski goggles. It had taken a little time, but Liam had managed to bribe a corrupt police buddy to get hold of the CCTV footage for the area, and it had revealed a man fitting Hector's description getting into a flash red sports car parked several streets away.

"This has nothing to do with me," Fin said.

"That ain't how Liam sees it."

"I introduced Hector to Liam, that's all. I can't be held responsible for his actions."

"C'mon, man. You vouched for him. Way Liam sees it, that means you are responsible."

Fin's head reeled. Of course. Everything was black and white in Liam's world.

"Wh-what am I supposed to do?"

Darren had a plan. "You take me to your mate and we beat the shit out of him to teach him a lesson. If he has the merchandise, I take it back to Liam. Problem solved."

"And if he doesn't have it?" Fin asked. He had a sudden vision of Dana Schell. Of the drugs the police recovered from her bedroom. Darren didn't answer. There was no need.

It was difficult for Fin to comprehend Hector's lack of judgement, his sheer idiocy. Hector was an arrogant bastard. He probably believed that his ill-conceived robbery had gone without a hitch. In addition, he most likely thought he had nothing to fear from a low life like Liam. He was wrong on both counts. That was the problem with entitled pricks like Hector. They lacked all understanding when it came to those they presumed to be socially inferior.

Fin wondered if Hector's perspective would shift when he caught sight of Darren standing outside his front door. Would he wonder how the sleazy underworld of East End drug dealing could possibly find its way to his own doorstep?

But when Hector had answered the door to Fin and Darren at his luxury home in Marton Tower, he had a poker face that made Fin marvel that he ever lost at cards. Hector's gaze brushed over Darren, to Fin, who read the silent question in his eyes: *Why have you brought this piece of human garbage to my door?*

Before Fin could speak, Darren asked, "You going to ask us in, or what?"

Hector stood aside.

"Anyone else at home?" Fin asked.

Hector shook his head. "What's up?"

Darren stood looking around the wide hallway, hood up, shoulders hunched, hands stuffed in his jeans pockets. Fin realised it was up to him to do the talking.

"You were seen," he said simply. "Leaving the house in Stepney. Liam wants his property back."

Wisely, Hector didn't prevaricate. There was a moment's silence. Then he said, "I don't have it."

Fin felt a movement at his side. He twisted round in time to see Darren conjure up a knife out of nowhere."

"Whoa, steady on." Hector took a couple of steps backwards and collided with the sofa. He went down, sprawling across it, and in a beat, Darren was on top of him, pinning him to the sofa, knife at his throat.

"Where is it?" he said. Blood dribbled over his blade from a nick in Hector's throat.

The poker face had disappeared. Hector's panicked eyes darted to Fin. "Remember Dana?" A nod. "That crazy bitch stole it from me."

"Who the fuck is Dana?" Darren snarled.

"Hector's ex," Fin said.

"Where is she?"

"She . . . she's dead," Hector said.

Hector's eyes were wide. He was probably seeing his life flash before him. Fin intervened. "Darren. Mate," he said, thinking fast. "Killing him's not going to achieve anything." To Hector, he said. "Tell me this wasn't the coke the police found in Dana's room?" Hector signalled his agreement with his eyes, a nod being too risky with a knife against his throat. Fin linked his fingers behind his neck and paced the room. It was even worse than he'd thought.

"What's going on, Fin?" Darren demanded.

Fin explained.

"Liam's not going to like this," Darren said. His tone suggested he wasn't looking forward to breaking the news to his brother. His grip on the knife never slackened while his slow mind processed the information. Fin's thoughts, on the other hand, were racing.

"Give him some time?" he said, at last. "If he can get Liam's property back, then all's good, isn't it? Dal? A couple of weeks, mate. That's not a lot to ask, given what I did for you. Right?"

Moments passed while Darren considered the deal. He was a slow thinker, but in this situation that was a good thing. If Liam had sent anyone else, odds were Hector would be disfigured, or dead, already.

"Two weeks," he said at last, apparently regarding that as fair recompense for seven months of Fin's life. Darren slid the knife from his right hand to his left and landed Hector a punch in the face. Then the knife disappeared, and he laid into Hector with both fists, while Fin stood by, flinching at every blow, but knowing better than to intervene. Darren needed to walk away from this encounter with his pride intact. To his credit, Hector seemed to grasp that some kind of immediate reparation was due, and he took the blows without any attempt at retaliation.

By the time Darren had finished, Hector looked like his mother's worst nightmare, but at least he was alive. And nothing had been cut off.

"Two weeks," Darren repeated, finger in Fin's face. "Liam ain't gonna like it, but it is what it is." He turned to Fin. "And no more favours. You and me, we're quits now."

And then he was gone. Out the door, having checked up and down the corridor — out of habit. In Darren's world, you expected trouble to arrive from any direction.

Fin closed the door and pulled Hector to his feet. Only the whites of his eyes were visible under the bloodied pulp of his face. "Fucking low-life little shit . . ." Hector sputtered. Fin's patience snapped.

"You just don't get it, do you? You fucking moron. He could just as easily have killed you. What the fuck possessed you to steal from someone like Liam? I told you not to piss him off. How many kinds of stupid are you?" Hector staggered across the floor. "Tell me you can pay Liam back, Hector." No answer. "Hector?"

"I need to get cleaned up. Wait here." Hector said, but Fin followed him into the bathroom, unwilling to let Hector out of his sight until he had an answer to his question.

"Was that even true, what you said about Dana stealing the stuff?"

Hector dabbed at his nose delicately with a damp facecloth. "Not exactly. She was looking after it for me."

"Did you . . . ?"

"Did I kill her? No, but I bloody well might have if I'd got my hands on her first."

"You're despicable. I need to know how you're going to sort this, Hector. I know Liam. He won't stop at making you pay for shitting on him. And, far as he sees it, I vouched for you, which means I'm in the shit too." He didn't dare articulate his fear that Liam might go after his family. Fin pulled Hector around to face him. "So I'm asking you again. How are you going to fix this?"

Hector spat into the sink. Both of them stared at the bloody streaks on the sparkling porcelain.

"I'll have to speak with my father," Hector answered between gritted teeth.

"See that you do that. ASAP," Fin said.

He had seen himself out and walked out into the night. But he was too wired up. He couldn't go to the hospital to see his family like that. Ruth would know immediately that something was very wrong. He'd walked all night and finally come to rest next to Ruth, at their son's bedside, calm enough to pass her scrutiny.

A low moan from Ruth as she repositioned herself on the chair interrupted Fin's thoughts. He held his breath. Those thoughts mustn't contaminate their reunion. Ruth's eyes flickered open and darted straight to Cam, giving Fin a moment to compose himself.

"He's okay, I think," Fin whispered.

"Fin?" Ruth's eyes widened. She rose stiffly, rubbing her legs. She must have had an uncomfortable night. Ruth embraced him, and he held her, burying his face in her hair and breathing in her familiar, much-missed scent.

"I'm sorry about that whole thing with the police. I didn't know what else to do."

"Shh. It's alright. I think they believed me."

"Do you think Hector killed Dana?" Ruth asked.

"I don't know."

Fin considered how much to tell Ruth about the developments of the past few hours. He calculated they were all safe until the two weeks were up. There was no sense in giving her anything more to worry about. For now, they had to focus on Cam.

Fin pulled up a chair next to Ruth. Side by side, they sat in watchful vigil over their little son.

* * *

Jim Neal kissed his son goodnight. He hadn't mentioned Myrna's visit to Archie. A couple of years ago, he'd agreed to let Archie write to her, but the letters had gone unanswered. He suspected that Archie had looked his mother up on the Internet, but not so often now.

Downstairs, Neal poured himself a Scotch and retreated to his study.

There, he brooded on the case. Almost two weeks had gone by since Russell Marsh's murder. Neal was always hypersensitive to the passage of time in a murder investigation. Every day had consequences in terms of resources, evidence gathering and motivation. Not that he needed to worry about his team losing momentum, particularly as they had not one but two concurrent investigations to keep them on their toes. Neal was increasingly interested in the family angle, particularly in the 'intertanglement,' as PJ so aptly put it, of their affairs.

Finally, Neal brooded about Ava Merry, recalling how quiet she'd been on the drive back from Cambridge. He'd sensed that she'd been glad to get out of the car on their return to Stromford. They'd hardly spoken since. Neal sipped his whisky, ruminating for some time before calling it a night and going to bed.

The following morning, he was at his desk before anyone else arrived. He put his head down for a couple of hours, working steadily. When at last he looked up, he could see the office outside was no longer empty.

PJ, he noted, was not at her desk. Was it today her partner, Steve, was having his ultrasound? Tired of staring at his screen, Neal left his office and joined Ava and Tom.

"Tom, I hear you and PJ were involved in a bit of drama last night," Neal said.

Tom looked blank. "What? Oh, yeah, the baby thing."

"PJ told me you were slightly sceptical about Ruth appearing with a sick Cam just as you were about to question her about the night of the fire," Ava said.

"She called you from the hospital?"

"Yes. Cam's okay. But he really was very ill."

"Shit."

"Okay, Tom," Neal said, "your detective instinct must have been in overdrive."

"I'd probably have thought the same," Ava said. "Anyway, PJ's going to speak with Ruth. I think she's the best person to deal with her at such a sensitive time." The others nodded.

"What did you and PJ glean from speaking with Dana Schell's ex- boyfriend?" Neal asked Tom.

"That Nathan Brewer wasn't really her boyfriend. Basically, she was abandoned by a friend at Glastonbury and hooked up with Nathan and his mates. Came back to Stromford with them and sponged off Nathan for a bit."

"Until she got the live-in job at the Cornish household?"

"Yeah. Oh, and she was into drugs. But not coke, as far as Nathan knew. So what Ruth and Hector claim about her coke habit may or may not be true."

"Anything else?" Neal asked.

"Nathan mentioned the fire that killed Will. They were mates at school, apparently," Tom said.

"The Cathedral School?" Neal asked.

"No. Stromford High. Nathan sort of knew Ruth Marsh because she was Will's cousin. You could tell he was cut up about losing his friend. Still resentful about it. The fire was started by a discarded cigarette, but Nathan said Will was sporty. He didn't smoke. Nathan found it hard to accept."

"And you and PJ were following up on that last night, just before Cam was taken ill?" Neal asked, still catching up.

"Yeah," Tom said. "Ava asked PJ to find out where Ruth was on the night of the fire, and we wondered, could she have gone round to Will's?"

"Interesting," Neal commented.

"I'm worried that we're getting sidetracked with all this. I'm still thinking this case is about the drugs." Tom reiterated his earlier theory. "Maybe Hector Cornish goes round to Russ's. Demands even more money. Russ refuses . . ." Tom made a gun of his fingers and put them to his temple. "Bang!" He stumbled backwards. Neal gave a disapproving grunt.

"And Dana? What was Hector's motive for killing her?" Ava asked.

Tom shrugged. "Again, something to do with drugs."

"Or money," Ava commented.

"That reminds me. Lesley Curran left a message for me this morning saying she might have something for us on the money angle. She's coming in . . ." Neal glanced at his watch. "Any time now, actually."

As if conjured up by his words, Lesley walked into the office. "You're going to love me," she said. She was addressing all three of them, but her eyes seemed to linger on Tom.

"What have you got, Lesley?" Neal asked.

"Did someone say coffee?" Lesley said, and began unpacking her laptop.

Ava went off to the kitchen, muttering something about bribery.

"I've been looking at all the usual stuff. Bank activity, of course, so withdrawals, deposits, credit and charge card accounts, yada yada yada, but also Russell Marsh's own accounts held on his laptop." Lesley was a fast talker and her fingers darted over the keyboard as she spoke. "Don't worry, I've followed all the legal pathways for obtaining information."

She didn't have to say it. Neal knew that Lesley was well-versed in the intricate web of legislation involved in the investigation of financial crimes. Failure to comply could result in evidence being inadmissible in court.

"Russ Marsh's business affairs are squeaky clean," Lesley said, smiling at the sight of the giant coffee mug heading her way, courtesy of Ava. "But before you all become despondent, I have two words for you." She paused and sipped her coffee, presumably to keep them in suspense. "Paul Cornish."

"You've got something on Russ's partner?" Neal frowned.

Lesley looked annoyingly smug. "As you know, Cornish and Marsh was founded after the two men had had successful individual careers in the City. They became financial advisers and investors. And they had good instincts. Most of the businesses they've invested in have gone on to give them decent returns on their money."

"So they hold shares in these companies?" Tom asked.

"That's usually how it works." Lesley winked at him. "It would appear that Paul Cornish also had projects of his own on the side."

Lesley certainly had their interest. Neal could practically hear the buzz of Tom and Ava's brains spinning around the possibilities.

"Anyone got a biscuit? I skipped breakfast and I'm famished."

"I've got one of those energy bars." Tom fished around in his drawer and produced a rather squashed-looking specimen.

"Er . . . thanks. I'll pass." Lesley eyed the bar with distaste. It was all a performance, of course. She had something for them and she was enjoying drawing it out as long as possible.

But Neal didn't have all day. "Get to the point, Lesley," he urged.

"Okay. The short version. Last year, Paul Cornish invested money in a local construction company, Ballgreen Construction."

Ava and Neal exchanged glances. Ava said, "That's the name of the company that built Marton Tower, where Paul Cornish has a penthouse. His son, Hector, is living there at the moment. I saw pictures of Paul in the foyer of the building. You know, on the building site, wearing a hard hat and a business suit, and holding a cement hoe."

Lesley nodded. "Paul likes construction. He's been involved in a series of projects across the East Midlands, everything from office blocks to housing developments. Apparently his father was a builder. Anyway, an electrician — a sub-sub-contractor working on the Marton Tower development — blew the whistle on Ballgreen. According to him, he was asked in the absence of the site manager to sign off on a consignment of cables that arrived a day early."

"Let me guess," Tom said, "there was a mismatch between the invoice and the size of the delivery?"

"Bang on. Our electrician kept his mouth shut, but he did keep his ears and eyes open and, well, I'm sure you can guess what sort of other activities he observed."

"Ghost workers," Ava said.

"Fake overtime claims," Tom chorused.

"And the rest." Lesley nodded. "There was an investigation and Ballgreen admitted to corrupt practices. Paul Cornish came out of the investigation untainted. He was only involved in investing in the company." Lesley's expression told another story.

"Have you got anything concrete on him?" Neal asked.

"I've done some digging and delving into the accounts of the various businesses Paul Cornish has been involved with. Many of them have been remarkably profitable." Lesley reeled off a few examples. "Restaurants dotted across the East Midlands. Dry-cleaning shops."

She listed a few other examples.

"Compared to peer businesses, Paul's have been banking a lot more money. I ate dinner in a few of the restaurants Paul's involved with." She paused and looked at Tom. "Tom joined me on one occasion. I was practically the only customer on some of the busiest evenings of the week. But the profits tell a different story."

"Are we talking about money laundering?" Ava asked. The types of businesses Paul Cornish was investing in were the sort typically used for that purpose. Service industries, where cash could be put through the till with no questions asked.

"Drugs," Tom said, tapping the side of his nose. He looked smug. To both Neal and Ava's annoyance, he was probably right.

"Lesley?" Neal prompted.

"Paul Cornish has shares in several businesses that would lend themselves well to money laundering." She sighed. "I'll be honest. This is potentially a huge investigation. It could take months to gather enough evidence to go to court. If the evidence even exists. *And* if we can prove it leads back to Cornish. I suspect Paul will have covered his tracks. If you could slap a conviction on him for killing Russ Marsh or Dana Schell, it would probably take less time. Maybe one or both of them got wind of what Paul was up to, and got themselves killed as a result. And not necessarily by Paul in person. If he is money laundering, we need to be asking, who for? He's likely to be associating with some very nasty people."

Neal's thoughts were racing. There was something agitating his brain. Suddenly he knew what it was. "That electrician. The one who blew the whistle on Ballgreen Construction. Do you have his name?"

"It was kept confidential at the time, of course. I can divulge the name to you in strictest confidence." Lesley did the computer equivalent of fumbling around with paper files.

"Here it is," she said at last. "His name was Stephen Hamilton."

Chapter Fifteen

"No wonder Stephen Hamilton seemed so nervous when we interviewed him. He made out he was worried about having to confront Paul Cornish about his loan, but he must have been wondering whether Cornish had something to do with Russ's death," Ava said. She and Neal were in a small industrial estate, approaching the unit where Stephen's electrical contractor's business was located.

Ava drew up and parked outside. Before they set off, Neal had asked her to check that Stephen was available and not out on a job. According to the employee she spoke to, Stephen would be in his office all morning, going over the weekly accounts.

They entered the unit under a rolled-up shutter door, and stepped into a small, open office space. There were two desks, and a kitchen area, with a table and an assortment of odd chairs. Stephen Hamilton was hunched over a computer. Next to him sat a woman, presumably his accounts and admin assistant. They looked up as Neal and Ava walked in.

"Mr Hamilton, is there somewhere private we can talk?" Neal asked.

"Would you mind going out for an hour, Lorna? Take an extra half-hour's lunch," Stephen said.

Lorna looked as though she'd much prefer to stick around and hear what Neal and Ava had to say to her boss, but she gathered up her things and headed for the door.

Stephen pulled up a couple of chairs and placed them in front of his desk. He retreated to the other side, regarding Ava and Neal with suspicion.

"Mr Hamilton," Neal began, "as part of our investigation into Russ Marsh's death, we've been looking into the financial affairs of Cornish and Marsh. Our financial investigator has uncovered a report into a construction contract that Russ's partner, Paul Cornish, financed, independently of him."

Stephen's foot tapped against the floor. He placed a restraining hand on his knee.

"Mr Hamilton, we know that you blew the whistle on certain practices that you observed while working as a sub-contractor on the Marton Tower development."

"I were told my anonymity would be protected."

"It has been disclosed only to us, as an item of interest in a murder investigation." Stephen's eyes widened. "Paul wasn't found guilty of any wrongdoing, but . . ." Neal paused, watching Stephen closely, "do you have any reason to believe that Paul Cornish is corrupt, or that Russ Marsh might have found out?"

They waited for Stephen's response. Minutes seemed to tick by.

"I . . . I wanted to tell you last time we spoke. If it hadn't been for Lizzie . . . I didn't want her worrying about it."

"Go on," Neal said gently.

"I didn't think it were that relevant, anyhow. Even though Paul Cornish invested in the project, he weren't to know what were going on at the site." Stephen sighed deeply. "Site foremen got the blame, didn't they?"

"I believe so," Neal said. This was what Lesley Curran had told them. There had been no wider investigation into Cornish and Marsh's business affairs at the time, because those responsible for corruption on the site had seemed to fall out of the woodwork, and were speedily arrested and convicted. Now that Lesley was on the case, a more rigorous investigation would proceed, leading into who knows what labyrinthine tunnels of deceit and corruption. Even so, there was no guarantee that Paul would be linked to any of it.

Financial crimes required exhaustive investigation and could become mired in detail. As Lesley had hinted, it would be easier to put Paul away for murder. Had Paul murdered Russ? Neal thought him the most likely suspect. Then again, he must have known that killing Russ would bring an investigation down on his head. Still, it would have taken care of the immediate danger of disclosure, and bought him some thinking time.

"You haven't answered my question, Mr Hamilton. Do you believe Russ Marsh was aware of, or involved in any corruption? Did you suspect Paul Cornish of corrupt practices?" He paused. "Did you tell Russ you were the whistle-blower on the Marton Tower affair?"

Stephen shook his head. "I don't think Russ were involved. He were a good sort. And no, I never told him about Marton Tower. But I know he had some worries about his business. So Lizzie told me anyhow. Val mentioned it to her. I can sympathise with anyone who worries about business matters. I keep this place ticking over, but I'd just as soon be a jobbing sparky."

Neal felt like they were wading through treacle. Their interview with Stephen, though necessary, was proving to be a waste of time. And then, out of nowhere, he threw them a golden nugget.

"I tell you what though, that affair between Russ and Gail Cornish were far from over."

"What do you mean?" Ava asked.

"I stopped by the house to drop off a pie that Lizzie had made one night when Ruth were away in Cambridge, and Gail Cornish were there."

"Why didn't you mention this before?" Neal asked

"I never thought. And I didn't actually see her. I could smell perfume in the air. I noticed because it's the one Lizzie wears. Coco Chanel. Val can't stand it. And I saw a pair of shoes in the hall. Them ones with the red soles. I told Lizzie when I got home, and she said Val never wears shoes like that."

Neal stood up. "Thanks, Mr Hamilton. That's all for now. We'll be in touch if there's anything else."

Back in the car, Neal and Ava pondered this latest piece of information.

"He never thought to mention it." Neal shook his head.

"Why didn't Lizzie Hamilton tell us? Surely she must have realised it was relevant to our investigation?"

The answer was obvious. "To protect her sister," Neal said. "Val Marsh had just found her husband in his study with his brains blown out. Lizzie probably wanted to spare her the upset and embarrassment of finding out that her husband was still carrying on an affair with Gail Cornish. No doubt she's been biding her time, waiting for the right moment, or wondering whether to let on at all. And, perhaps she just didn't regard Gail Cornish as a potential killer."

"And, as Stephen Hamilton pointed out, he didn't see Gail in person. A lot of women wear Coco Chanel. Including me," Ava said. "Well, Val's going to have to learn about it now. Unless . . ." She considered the possibility. "Unless she already knows? A jealous spouse — one of the oldest motives in the world for murder."

"Except she was in Cambridge the night her husband died. Bit of a stretch to believe she could travel to Stromford, shoot Russ and travel all the way back without being missed."

"But not impossible."

"Highly improbable. Let's bear it in mind, if it comes down to eliminating the impossible," Neal said, but his feeble homage to Sherlock Holmes fell on deaf ears.

* * *

PJ left Steve and made her way through the labyrinth of corridors to the children's wards. She eventually found Cam in a private room, Ruth keeping watch at his bedside. PJ sat down on an empty chair next to Ruth, and laid her hand on her shoulder. To her surprise, Ruth collapsed against her, weeping.

At first, PJ thought she was crying with relief. Cam's drip had been removed, and she thought he looked a healthier colour. For a few moments, PJ comforted Ruth, gazing over her shoulder at the gentle rise and fall of the infant's chest. Her own sadness over Steve mingled with Ruth's, and she was glad of the contact. Finally, Ruth shifted, and raised her head. "Sorry."

"What for?" PJ said. "How is Cam doing?"

"He's much better. Sleeping it off, it seems. He just looks so fragile lying there."

"He's very lucky to have such an attentive mum."

"I know I should be glad, but I can't stop thinking about what might have happened. He might have—"

"He didn't. He's here, and the two of you are going to be together for a very long time." PJ choked back a sob.

"Are you okay?" Ruth looked at PJ with concern. "You're a kind person. There aren't many genuinely kind people around." PJ managed a weak smile and pushed her own problems aside.

"Fin's been here," Ruth said. "He's just gone off to get a few things from the shop."

They sat quietly for a while. The ward was strangely peaceful, despite the constant hum of the monitoring equipment and the voices at the nursing station in the corridor outside.

Ruth cleared her throat. "What you said just now about there being nothing to be sorry about. You were wrong." A prolonged silence followed.

PJ waited. Her grandmother had told her to always be a good listener. Granny never knew just how useful her advice would be.

"I was fourteen years old . . ." Ruth began.

PJ held her breath. She had long believed that Ruth was key to this whole mystery. Ruth would have been fourteen when Will died in the fire. Was this what she was on the point of telling her about?

"My mother and my aunt had gone away for the weekend to a health spa. Aunt Lizzie couldn't afford luxuries like that, and my mum was treating her. I was supposed to be spending the night at a friend's house. Dad . . ." Ruth's voice trembled, reminding PJ that Cam's sudden illness was not the only trauma Ruth had suffered recently. Ruth had also just lost her father.

"My dad was supposed to pick Will up and take him to a football match. They were going to grab a burger on the way. Then Dad phoned and said he was going to be held up at work. Will wasn't answering his calls and Dad wanted me to go round and give him the message. I was annoyed because I had plans of my own for the evening." There was self-disgust in Ruth's tone.

"I knew Dad would lose track of the time. He always did when he was working. I remember I was in a bad mood after he called. I hadn't told my parents, but I wasn't really staying at my friend Bea's that night—"

A frantic beeping started up from a room further down the corridor, followed by a burst of activity and voices speaking in urgent, subdued tones. PJ and Ruth exchanged looks. They both glanced at Cam, and a lump rose to PJ's throat. Minutes passed, the corridor now ominously silent. And then, nurses' voices again, sounding cheerful. Crisis over, PJ hoped.

"I wasn't going to Bea's. I'd arranged to meet Hector Cornish." PJ gave a start. "Hector knew some older kids who were having a party. He'd got some booze and, well, some dope. I'd never had it before. Hector said it would be cool."

"And you were at the party with Hector Cornish when your father called you?" PJ asked.

"Yes. We were out of our heads," Ruth said. "Hector didn't want me to go to Will's to give him the message, but I was worried Dad would be angry if I didn't, so I decided I must. I knew I'd have to go back to my house afterwards with Will, so Hector was pissed off about that. It spoiled all our plans for the evening."

"Did Hector go to Will's with you?"

"What? No, I mean, yes. He came as far as my aunt and uncle's house and then he left. I knocked on the door and Will answered straightaway. That irritated me. I remember thinking if he could hear a knock at the door, why couldn't he have answered his phone?"

"What happened next?" PJ asked.

"Will said he was sorry. He'd forgotten to charge his phone up, and he hadn't heard the landline because he'd been playing a computer game and had his headphones on. I behaved like a spoilt brat, started shouting and screaming at him. I was still high, and drunk as well by that time. Everything was starting to spin, you know, the way it does when you're that drunk." PJ nodded.

"I remember staggering into the sitting room and lighting a cigarette that I'd got from Hector. Will was a bit shocked — he wasn't into smoking. He was really keen on sports. I kept saying he was boring, and trying to get him to have a ciggie."

Poor, naïve, sheltered Will. PJ thought of how that evening had ended for him and her heart ached for the boy.

"It was about nine o'clock. My dad rang to say that he was going to be a couple more hours. I was going to go back to the party. I didn't want my dad to find me at Will's house in that state, but . . ."

Up to that point, Ruth's voice had been steady. Now it began to quiver. "Oh, Will, I'm so, so sorry," she whispered. PJ held her breath. "I . . . I remember I was lying on the sofa, smoking one cigarette after another. Will kept lecturing me about how bad it was for my health. He was probably worried his parents would smell it when they got home, and think it was him. After a while he went upstairs to get some bits together. He was supposed to be spending the night at our house. I was going to go, but suddenly I felt really tired and a bit sick . . . I . . . must have fallen asleep."

Both of them looked at the sleeping Cam.

"With the lighted cigarette in your hand?"

Tearfully. "Yes."

This was the secret that Fin had alluded to when the DI and Ava interviewed him. The root of all Ruth's sadness.

"It must have fallen from my hand. The sofa caught alight. It was by the window and the curtains went up too. It all happened so fast. Within seconds, the room was full of thick, black smoke. I remember coughing and calling for Will. And then I managed to find my way to the door and into the hall. I felt sick and I went outside."

Oh, Will, thought PJ. She remembered from the reports that he had been found in the sitting room, having died from smoke inhalation. What no one knew was that he had also died a hero. He had heard Ruth's cries for help and gone to her aid, thinking she was still in the sitting room.

PJ felt a sudden stab of anger, then she was ashamed of herself. Ruth had been stupid and thoughtless but she had also been fourteen years old, and out of her head on drink and drugs. To her credit, Ruth hadn't excused her behaviour. She didn't claim it had been an accident — which it had. PJ was a bit hazy on the law concerning arson, but she had a fair idea that no judge would rule that Ruth's behaviour had been deliberate, particularly given her age. Still, her sympathies were with Will.

She asked, "Why didn't you ever tell anyone what really happened?"

"I . . . I told my father."

"Tell me what happened after you left the house."

"I was scared. I just wanted to get away from there. I . . . I couldn't think straight." Ruth looked at PJ, her expression full of self-loathing. "The worst thing is that I didn't even give Will a thought until afterwards."

"When did you call your father?"

"After about twenty minutes. He picked me up from several streets away. He tried to get to the house, but the police had already cordoned off the street, and a fire engine was there. Dad said the fire officers would get Will out, if he hadn't got out already. He said there was nothing more we could do. He took me home, and then he went back. That's when he found out that . . . that Will . . ."

A neighbour had raised the alarm, PJ knew. None of the reports had mentioned a girl fleeing the scene.

"Dad said he would take the blame for putting his work before picking up Will. He told me to stick to my story that I had been staying at my friend's house. He said no one needed to know what really happened that night. He said there was no point in Aunt Lizzie and Uncle Craig finding out it was me that started the fire."

PJ was about to reach out and reassure Ruth, tell her it had been an accident, when they heard a gasp. They turned around to see Lizzie Hamilton standing in the doorway, a hand over her mouth. The other clutched a balloon and a teddy bear.

"Aunt Lizzie!"

Bear and balloon slipped from Lizzie's fingers. The balloon bobbed just above the floor. The teddy lay splayed at Lizzie's feet. Ruth got up and took a step towards her. Lizzie backed into the corridor, and then she was gone. As if on cue, Cam woke up and began to howl.

* * *

Fin left the hospital after seeing Ruth and Cam, love and anger roiling in his gut. He was afraid. He'd planned on just going as far as the shop but instead found himself walking in the direction of Hector's apartment. He needed to be certain that Hector appreciated the urgency of their situation.

Adrenalin coursed through him as he waited for the security guard to buzz Hector. "This isn't bloody Trump Tower," Fin said. The guard gave a shrug.

Hector's door was ajar. In any other tower block this would have put Fin on the alert, but in this guarded fortress he felt no sense of danger. He walked in. Hector was lying on the sofa, watching TV. His eyes flicked to Fin, then back to the screen.

Fin erupted in rage. He strode across the room and grabbed Hector by the scruff of his neck, dragging him to his feet.

"For fuck's sake!" Hector exclaimed.

"Have you spoken to your father?"

At this, Hector's fear seemed to vanish. "Is that what you're all fired up about? Relax. It's taken care of."

Fin didn't know what to do with his anger. He stood there, trying to ratchet it down a few notches, when what he really needed to do was punch Hector in his already messy face. He counted to ten. "What do you mean, taken care of? How, exactly?"

"My old man's sorting it out."

Of course. Hector had a safety net not available to ordinary people. Ruth had one too, though she'd sworn off using it. As Ruth's partner, Fin had experienced something of the security such a thing provided. He knew that his son would never go hungry, never be homeless. Because, despite Ruth's protestations that she would never touch her father's money, she would never put pride before her child's needs.

"He's going to pay Liam for the coke?"

"Yes. It's all in hand. I rang him last night after you left. When I explained the gravity of the situation, he told me he'd take care of it."

Fin had what he'd come for. Nevertheless, he found that he wasn't yet satisfied. He drew back his arm and drove his fist into Hector's face. That was more like it.

Hector staggered backwards, his nose spouting blood afresh, but he made no move to retaliate. "Feel better now, do you?"

Fin wondered if Hector had any idea of the real danger Liam presented. Disgusted, he turned to go.

"Say hello to Ruth from me," Hector called after him. "Tell her not to play with fire again. Next time she might get burnt instead of screwed up to fuck." A laugh.

Fin's hands balled into fists. He wasn't satisfied after all.

Chapter Sixteen

Neal stared at the email that had just arrived in his inbox. It was from a DI Gary Blunt of the Bethnal Green Met, sent in the early hours of the morning. Blunt had requested that Neal contact him urgently. Neal glanced at the time at the bottom of his computer screen. It was early, but he was at work. Chances were, Blunt would be too.

Sure enough, Blunt picked up on the second ring. Neal had no clue as to what this man could be calling about. He was even more puzzled when Blunt launched into a story about a drug dealer that his team had had under surveillance. The dealer's brother had put in a 999 call, reporting that he and his brother had been shot at in his brother's flat. Liam had taken a shot to the head, but was still alive when Blunt arrived at the scene, ahead of the paramedics. There had been no sign of the brother, Darren.

DI Blunt had some information that he thought Neal might find interesting. In addition, he was hoping that Neal could assist with his investigation into the double shooting.

"Bear with me a moment," Neal said. He got up, tapped on the glass door of his office and beckoned to Ava and Tom. They hurried in.

Neal filled them in on his conversation with Blunt. "I'm putting you on speaker," he said.

"Liam Sharp died at six thirty this morning," Blunt said. "He'd been shot in the head at point-blank range. No one knows how he managed to survive that long."

"What have you got for us?" Neal asked, still in the dark about what the death of an East End drug dealer had to do with them.

"Liam was very talkative before the medics showed up. He was rambling mostly, about his brother, his mates, but the names Hector Cornish and Fin O'Shea also came up."

"In what regard?" Neal asked.

"Like I said, he was rambling, but he kept coming back to these characters, Hector and Fin. How they'd betrayed him. Stolen from him."

"Bethnal Green was Fin O'Shea's old haunt, wasn't it, Chief?" Tom said. "Could he have known this Liam character and his brother, Darren?"

"Did you recognise the name Fin O'Shea? He grew up on your patch, and we know he was once involved with drugs," Neal said to Blunt.

There was a pause. "No, but my predecessor covered my patch for twenty-odd years. Chances are he'd have come across him. I'll get back to you on that. In the meantime, what can you tell me about this Hector Cornish?"

"He's Stromford born and bred. Cambridge graduate. Wealthy parents. His father's business partner, Russ Marsh, was shot in the head a couple of weeks ago." It was beginning to sound like a lot of people were being shot in the head. "And a girl he was involved with, Dana Schell, was found dead a day after Marsh's killing. A kilo of coke was found in her room. She lived at Hector's parents' home, where she worked as a help. Both murders are currently under investigation."

"Well, this Hector Cornish is our only lead," Blunt said. "I think I need to pay you all a visit. I can be with you at say . . ." He paused, "two thirty. Think you can have this Hector Cornish available for questioning by then?"

"We'll bring him in."

"What about O'Shea?"

"He's in Cambridge."

"I'll make another call," Blunt said, and hung up.

"It seems that Fin and Hector are better acquainted than we'd previously thought," Neal observed.

"Drugs," Tom said. He just failed to say 'told you so.'

"So, what's going on?" Ava said. "Hector, Fin, East End dealer? What have they got themselves mixed up in?"

"Paul Cornish reckoned Hector had got in with a bad crowd, but I don't think he was referring to this Liam Sharp and his gang," Neal said.

"He was talking about the gambling crowd, wasn't he?" Tom said. "Hector ran up a lot of debt and his father cut off his allowance as a deterrent. What if it didn't work, and Hector carried on gambling? He would have needed a way of funding his activity. I reckon he got into the drugs game. Like we said before, those drugs in Dana's room were his. He was dealing to finance his gambling."

Neal thought this was probably about right.

"Fin introduced him to Liam," Ava said, and Tom nodded. "Hector somehow found out about Fin's past history — probably heard his parents talking about the PI's findings — and asked Fin for help setting himself up as a dealer. Fin did more than provide information, he provided a contact. His old mate, Liam Sharp."

Neal nodded. They might not have it exactly right, but surely they were on the right track?

"But Fin was out of the game," Ava said. "Why would he get back in? We speculated, didn't we, that Hector might have had something on Ruth and Fin. He blackmailed them to take part in what seemed like an obvious deception about Dana being a dealer."

"I think I might be able to shed some light on that." They turned and saw PJ standing in the doorway, looking tired and drawn. "I've just come from the hospital. I saw Ruth Marsh. Cam's a lot better." PJ glanced somewhat accusingly at Tom as she said this.

"That's very good news," Neal said.

"There was a bit of a to-do," PJ said. She related what Ruth had said to her — the truth about the events of the night of the fire that had killed Will. Finally, she got to the bit about Lizzie Hamilton's ill-timed arrival.

"Holy shit!" Ava said.

"Quite. Ruth and Lizzie are — or were — very close. I hate to think how this will affect their relationship. Not to mention Val Marsh. Russ made sure the truth never came out. He did it to protect his daughter. He made Ruth promise not to tell anyone what really happened."

"Lizzie's been blaming Russ for Will and her first husband's deaths, when really it was all Ruth's doing," Ava said. "I suppose Russ's urge to protect Ruth exonerates him a little."

"No. It doesn't," Neal said. As the only father in the room, he felt the need for clarity on this matter. "He was wrong on several counts, but most of all he was wrong to let Ruth grow up with no outlet for her guilt. He denied her the opportunity to atone or make reparations. Who knows what psychological damage that's inflicted on her?"

"Serves her right, if you ask me," Tom said. "Lizzie Hamilton's the one who's suffered most."

"Oh, Tom! You're so . . . so unfeeling." PJ had evidently still not forgiven Tom for suggesting that Ruth had faked Cam's illness.

"Well, she doesn't seem particularly maladjusted, does she?" grumbled Tom.

"I think she is. Didn't Fin say he was attracted to what he called 'a sadness' in Ruth?" PJ asked Ava, who gave a nod. "I think she's got terrible psychological scars."

Tom looked sceptical, but PJ continued. "The fire was a tragic accident, but I think Ruth truly believes she committed murder that night. After Lizzie left, I tried to calm her down, but she just kept saying it over and over. She was hysterical. She's an intelligent person, and she must know that in the eyes of the law she didn't murder her cousin, but her conscience says otherwise. She can't forgive herself. And now Lizzie Hamilton probably won't either." PJ looked close to tears.

"Well, obviously, this news could be significant," Neal said. "If, as you say, Hector Cornish was with Ruth Marsh earlier that fateful evening, did he put two and two together, and work out what part Ruth played in the tragedy? He was the only other person who knew that Ruth went to her aunt and uncle's house that night. This could be the information he used to blackmail Ruth and Fin into lying for him about Dana selling drugs."

"But surely Fin must have known Ruth couldn't be charged with anything? Why would he let himself be drawn back into the drugs game when Hector had no actual evidence against Ruth?" Tom said.

"He loves her," PJ said. "He understands how she thinks. And Ruth's mental state is fragile. Fin would have been worried about pushing her over the edge. *And* she was pregnant."

"I agree," Neal said. "I think Ruth Marsh will need a lot of counselling if she's ever going to come to terms with her actions that night."

"Could have saved herself a lot of grief and been up front about it from the start," Tom said. "If she's carrying all this guilt, you'd have thought she'd feel the urge to confess, purge herself and face the music."

"I think she was scared to. Her father forbade her ever to speak about it. Then her aunt started seeing her as a substitute for Will, and she was just too terrified of the effect it would have on Lizzie if the truth came out," PJ said.

"Well, it's out now alright," Tom said. There was no disagreeing with that. "So, are we saying this makes it more likely that Hector's our man, at least for Dana's murder?"

Neal was sceptical. "It doesn't make sense for him to kill Dana over the drugs, and then leave them in her room for the police to find."

"I agree," Ava said. "If he'd killed Dana he would have recovered the drugs from her room."

"Tom, arrange for Hector Cornish to be brought in for questioning. I want to see his reaction when Blunt mentions that an East London drug dealer died with his name on his lips," Neal said.

"On it, sir." Tom gave him a half-salute and left the room.

"Good work on finding out about what happened to Will, PJ," Neal said. "Do you think you could get Ruth to admit that Hector blackmailed her and Fin over Dana? It would be useful if you can get her to confirm that she and Fin lied to us about that. Preferably before Blunt gets here and we interview Hector."

"Yes, sir. I'll go straight back to the hospital now." Looking pleased at the praise from Neal, PJ hurried off.

* * *

DI Blunt had arrived ten minutes early, and was sitting in the kitchen drinking coffee and biting down on a giant McDonald's burger. He wiped grease from his chin. "Sorry. Skipped breakfast this morning and didn't fancy anything on the trolley they brought around on the train."

Neal nodded, thinking it wouldn't do Blunt any harm to skip a few meals. He was a big bear of a man, with a balding head and a soft paunch overhanging the belt of his trousers. He was impatient to get started on interviewing Hector Cornish. Hector had been brought in a couple of hours ago, and had already made rumblings about legal representation. By all accounts, he was in a pretty bad way. Tom had been present when he was brought in, and he reckoned Hector had a broken nose, and a cut that could do with some stitches. He'd been seen by a medic who'd confirmed that he was fit for questioning.

A mental image persisted from Neal's last meeting with Hector of an arrogant, entitled young man dressed in a onesie, posing as a bit of a fop, and feeling sorry for himself because his peers were taking advantage of his wealth. He'd been eager to represent Dana Schell as being a drug user. He'd practically accused her of prostitution, and of stealing from his parents. Dana had been a user, that much was clear, but nothing they had so far uncovered suggested that she had been dealing.

Tom appeared at the kitchen door, bearer of unwelcome news. "Hector's got himself lawyered up. He asked to make a call, phoned his dad and we've been advised not to proceed until their bloke arrives."

"As if we'd dare," Neal said. Blunt rolled his eyes.

Half an hour later, Neal and Blunt introduced themselves to Paul Cornish's solicitor, Julian Brattleby-Brown, outside interview room two. Brattleby-Brown's upper-class accent and condescending tone immediately grated. "Exactly what is my client being questioned in connection with, Inspector?" he asked.

"DI Blunt is investigating a murder in which Hector Cornish's name came up. We'd like to know what Hector's relationship with the victim was, and why he thinks this victim mentioned him in his dying moments."

Brattleby-Brown stroked his chin ruminatively, while Neal gave him the details of the investigation into Russ Marsh and Dana Schell's deaths, as well as the police's previous interview with Hector at his father's flat, in which he'd denied any involvement with drugs. Brattleby-Brown made a series of harrumphing noises as he listened.

Despite having heard an account of Hector's beating from Tom, according to whom, 'his face looks like a plate of raw meat,' Neal was somewhat shocked at the sight of Hector's bruised and bloodied features. His nose looked out of alignment, his lips were cracked and swollen. One eye was so puffed up it was practically closed. No one had mentioned the beating to Brattleby-Brown, and he immediately jumped to the wrong conclusion.

"Who did this to you?" He glared at Neal and Blunt.

"It wasn't the police, Jules," Hector said.

Jules. So Brattleby-Brown was a family friend.

"Care to tell us, who, then, Hector?" Neal asked. Hector didn't answer. He stared sullenly at the desk, refusing to meet Neal's eye. Neal guessed he was probably in pain.

He cautioned Hector and advised him that the interview would be recorded. He introduced himself and DI Blunt. Did he imagine it, or did Hector's good eye really flicker in alarm when he mentioned that Blunt was from the Met and was based at Bethnal Green?

"Mr Cornish, DI Blunt attended the scene of a shooting incident in Bethnal Green in the early hours of this morning. There were allegedly two victims, one Liam Sharp, who'd been shot in the head, fatally, as it turned out, and his brother, Darren, who was not present at the scene when the police arrived. It was Darren Sharp who put in the 999 call, in which he alleged that he and his brother had been shot. Liam lived long enough to talk to the police. He wasn't exactly coherent but he was able to give the police some details . . ." Neal paused.

Hector rubbed his nose with the back of his hand and winced. He said nothing.

"The thing is, Hector, Liam Sharp named you and Fin O'Shea . . ." Again, Neal deliberately left his sentence unfinished.

"What? That's fucking crazy. I haven't even seen Liam since—"

Brattleby-Brown's attempt to repair the damage was almost comical. He jerked about like a puppet, gesticulating and clearing his throat loudly. No doubt he'd cautioned Hector to keep his mouth shut unless it was to say, 'No comment.' With his first utterance, Hector had managed to screw things up.

"So you admit to having known and interacted with Liam Sharp, Hector?" Neal pressed.

"No. I didn't say that, I . . . Shit, I'm in so much pain here I can't think straight. That bloody medic wouldn't give me anything stronger than paracetamol."

"I'd just like to point out that we will also be interviewing Fin O'Shea. Is he likely to corroborate what you say? I'm asking you again, did you know and interact with Liam Sharp?"

Hector turned stiffly to Brattleby-Brown, who gave him a nod.

"I . . . yeah . . . I remember now. I went to London with Fin once. We were going to a concert. Fin wanted some coke. I don't do that stuff, but he insisted on going to see this dealer he used to know years ago. I waited outside when he went in to see . . . to see . . . this . . . Liam . . . was it?"

Nice try, Neal thought, irritably. "So you didn't meet Liam Sharp personally?"

"That's right, no, I never set eyes on him or his brother." Hector shifted painfully in his seat, "Wha-what did you say happened to his brother?"

Interesting that Hector was keen to learn the fate of someone he'd never set eyes on.

Blunt spoke up. "We don't know. We think he was shot too. Injured. There was a trail of blood leading out of the house. A neighbour said Liam's car was gone. I tell you what, though. If that lad's still alive, he'll be going after whoever shot his brother. Or anyone he thinks knows something about it."

Hector gave a shrug. It was hard to tell if his face had paled under those livid bruises, and his one good eye gave little away. Even so, Neal sensed that he was unnerved. *Good.*

Neal said, "Mr Cornish has been questioned already concerning the death of Dana Schell. I believe you are aware of this?" The lawyer gave a brief nod. Neal proceeded with caution. "There are certain elements of that investigation that may be . . ." He thought suddenly of PJ's word 'intertangled,' and wished he could use it. "Connected in some way to DI Blunt's murder investigation."

"Well, my client isn't your connection, even if his name did crop up in what to my mind is clearly some kind of drugs-related gangland killing. I suggest you concentrate your resources on locating and questioning this Fin character and leave Mr Cornish, who has clearly suffered a traumatic experience, out of it."

"Tell us what you know about the night Ruth Marsh's cousin, Will, died in a fire at his home, Hector." Neal decided that a sudden change of direction might unsettle Hector further.

"What?" Hector's surprise seemed genuine. Brattleby-Brown intervened immediately.

"What's this about now, Inspector? I haven't been informed of any further line of questioning. Is this relevant?"

Pompous git. Neal ignored him. To Hector, he said, "We know that Ruth Marsh was with you the night Will died, and that you accompanied her to Will's house."

Hector looked confused. "Surely you're not suggesting I had anything to do with that fire?"

"No. Ruth has given us a full account of what happened that night. She was high — on drugs and alcohol that she says you gave to her."

"Where are you going with this, Inspector Neal?" Brattleby-Brown intervened again.

Neal ignored him again. Pity PJ hadn't been in touch yet. Had she managed to get Ruth to admit that Hector had blackmailed her over the drugs in Dana's room? Neal pressed on anyway, putting his faith in PJ.

"You blackmailed Ruth, and her partner, Fin O'Shea, to lie to us about Dana Schell, didn't you? Those drugs we found in Dana's room were yours. Stolen from Liam Sharp. Dana was storing them for you and you panicked when we found them, so you hatched that stupid story about Dana being a drug dealer, presumably to deflect our attention from you. A complete waste of police time. But you're the one who's been dealing, Hector. To finance your gambling addiction."

"Prove it," Hector said. He grimaced. A thin line of blood trickled from his split lip and he wiped it away.

"We will, son." Neal looked at his watch. "One of my officers is interviewing Ruth Marsh again this afternoon. Now that she has confessed to starting the fire accidentally, she has no reason to be afraid that you'll reveal her secret."

Brattleby-Brown coughed and then requested a recess.

Neal and Blunt waited outside while the man briefed his client. Blunt lit up a cigarette and inhaled deeply. "Needed that."

"This Liam Sharp. How big is his operation?" Neal asked.

"Small potatoes, really, compared to the organised gangs we see these days. Mainly him and his brother, plus a few others. They've been on our radar for a while, but Liam was in the game long enough to know how to avoid getting caught. This Fin O'Shea took the rap for Liam's kid brother once. Claimed a stash found in Darren's rucksack belonged to him. You ask me, that was the making of him, gave him a way out of the life. Never looked back after he did his community sentence, so I've been told. But even after this amount of time, Liam would have felt obliged to grant him a favour by doing business with Cornish. But if Hector pissed him off, well . . ."

Neal listened, intrigued. He'd liked Fin O'Shea. He hoped fervently that the lad hadn't slipped back into 'the life,' as Blunt put it. "What's happened to Darren Sharp? Do you think he's still alive?"

"He took off in his brother's car, but it was found abandoned a few streets away. Either he's holed up somewhere in case whoever took a shot at him and his brother is still after him, or," Blunt met Neal's gaze, "if Darren had reason to believe that Cornish or O'Shea was responsible for the shooting in some way, he'll be looking for revenge."

"You mean he could be on his way to Stromford? Great. That's all we need."

"Look, I'm following up a lead coming here. I need to speak with this Fin character ASAP, but between you and me, this killing has all the hallmarks of a hit. A professional job. In and out like the invisible man. And believe me, even if any of Liam's cohorts did see something, they ain't going to talk to the police."

"But Darren might. If we can find him," Neal said.

"Yeah, well. Don't hold your breath."

An officer came to tell them that Brattleby-Brown was ready to restart.

Back in the interview room, Neal sensed a change in the atmosphere. Brattleby-Brown's manner towards them was distinctly less hostile. He even acknowledged their return with a brief nod. Neal restarted the tape.

"As you can see," Brattleby-Brown began, "my client is in poor shape, physically. He has been subjected to two separate physical assaults in the past two days. It is my opinion that he needs to go straight to A&E at the conclusion of this interview. But first, he would like to . . . ahem, tell his story."

Neal glanced at Blunt, wondering if he too was amused by Brattleby-Brown's attempt at cooperation. He said, "Okay, Hector, let's hear your story."

Hector spoke in a monotone. "I just remembered. Fin took me to see Liam Sharp."

"At your request?"

"Yes."

"Fin O'Shea hadn't seen Liam Sharp since he was sixteen years old. He probably never wanted to see him again. Did you blackmail Fin into arranging a meeting between you and Liam?"

"Yes. I told him that unless he cooperated, I'd make sure Lizzie Hamilton got to know that Ruth killed her son." Slightly inaccurate, but Neal let it pass.

"And the meeting was arranged in order for you to purchase cocaine from Liam Sharp with a view to selling it in Cambridge?"

Hector corrected him. "To buy some coke for recreational use only, yes. I never intended to sell the stuff."

"And you made subsequent trips to London for the purpose of purchasing cocaine from Liam Sharp?"

"Yes."

"Over how long a period?"

"Twenty, twenty-two months."

"And this was purely for your own personal use?" Neal's tone was disbelieving. "Why did you steal from Liam Sharp? Was your gambling addiction so out of hand that you couldn't even finance it from selling drugs?"

"I told you I wasn't selling," Hector still insisted. "I went there intending to buy and it was just . . . there . . . It was an, er, opportunistic crime."

"And this was the stash we recovered from Dana's bedroom."

"Yes. Dana was no innocent, you know," Hector whined. "She agreed to hide the stuff in her room in return for a cut. I wasn't lying when I said she was a druggie."

That much was true, but Dana used drugs for recreational purposes. It was unlikely that she'd been selling.

"Come on, Hector," Neal said, impatient now. "Tell us the rest of it."

"Darren Sharp paid me a visit early yesterday evening. Beat the shit out of me. Fin got him to agree to give me some time to pay back what I stole, or come up with the cash."

"Got yourself in a nice mess, haven't you, sonny?" DI Blunt said.

Brattleby-Brown weighed in. "My client is guilty of purchasing for personal recreational use only. He never sold the cocaine that came into his possession. The theft of the drugs was opportunistic."

Yeah, right. They'd recovered a substantial amount of coke from Dana's room, far more than an individual would keep at home for recreational use. Neal was in no doubt that Hector had intended to sell. He was equally certain that Brattleby-Brown would argue otherwise. He would magic up some mitigating circumstances and get Hector off with minimum damage to his reputation and future career.

"So, Fin got you a stay of grace. Tell me, just how did you intend to pay Liam back?"

And now Hector did look uneasy. "I hadn't worked that out yet," he muttered, picking at his bloodied lip. "There wasn't time before . . . this happened." Supposedly he meant Liam's untimely death.

"Who else did you tell about your predicament?" Neal asked.

A pause. "Only Fin knew. Maybe Ruth, if Fin told her."

"You sure about that?" Neal had picked up on the pause.

"I'm sure."

"Convenient for you, Liam taking a bullet to the head like that. If it wasn't for his kid brother running around like a loose cannon, you'd be able to sit back and relax," Blunt commented.

Brattleby-Brown gave an exaggerated sigh. "Mr Cornish was at home last night. He popped out to an all-night pharmacy to get some painkillers. The pharmacist will remember seeing a young man with a badly beaten face."

Neal didn't suppose for a minute that Hector had shot Liam Sharp. And yet, fatally wounded and dying, Hector and Fin had been all Liam could talk about.

"DI Blunt, do you have any more questions?" he asked. The DI shook his head.

"I have one more," Neal said. "How did you get the cash together to buy from Darren Sharp twenty-two months ago? Your father had already cut your allowance, so how did you afford it?"

"Russ Marsh gave me a loan."

"Just like that?"

"Yes."

"Did Russ lend you more money recently?"

"No."

If Hector was telling the truth, Paul had lied about the cause of the row between him and Russ. It wasn't about Russ lending Hector money. Unless he'd only recently found out about that.

The interview ended with a few concluding words from Neal, for the benefit of the recording.

"Watch your back, son," Blunt cautioned Hector as they left the room. He was warning Hector to look out for Darren Sharp. Blunt's words recalled something Neal had heard before. The quarrel between Russ Marsh and Paul Cornish, and Russ warning Paul to watch his back. And Lesley Curran had asserted that Russ Marsh might have got himself killed because he discovered that his business partner was involved in corrupt business practices.

And if Paul Cornish was involved with serious organised criminals, the last thing he — or they — needed was his son attracting the wrong sort of notice.

A scene played out in Neal's head. Hector, out of his depth, desperate, appealing to his father for help. Asking for money to pay off his debt to Liam. Paul Cornish, arrogant, angry at his son for tainting his home by bringing drugs into it, afraid that it might draw attention to his own much bigger involvement in the drugs game. Angrier still at a low life like Darren Sharp beating the shit out of his son, and daring to make threats on his life. Paul Cornish wasn't the type of man who would stand for that, no matter that the fault had been Hector's in the first place. What would Paul do? He wouldn't get his own hands dirty, certainly. He had powerful associates, the kind who could take care of his problems for him.

A hit. *In and out like the invisible man*, that's what Blunt had said of Liam Sharp's killer. Neal was convinced they were getting to the heart of the matter, but it brought him little sense of progress.

Chapter Seventeen

PJ decided to walk back to the hospital. She needed time to think, not just about the case, but also about her conversation with Steve earlier that morning. She was glad that no one at the station had asked how things were going. She couldn't have trusted herself to speak without bursting into tears. She felt like she was grieving already. All the hopes and dreams she'd entertained about their future together now hung in tatters.

At the hospital, she stopped to buy a couple of coffees from the café. One for her, one for Ruth. PJ had had to leave shortly after Lizzie's hasty departure, she wondered how Ruth had coped. Poor Lizzie. Life just kept throwing her blows. It did that to some people, heaping misfortune upon misfortune. What if this sad business over Steve was the start of a run of bad luck for herself? *Snap out of it.* It wasn't in PJ's nature to be miserable, but right now she felt a little self-pity was allowed.

PJ was glad to see a young man with Ruth when she looked through the window in the hospital room door. Must be Fin. She tapped, softly, because Cam looked to be asleep.

Fin opened the door and she handed him a cup. He looked dishevelled, and was that a speck or two of dried blood on his sleeve? PJ introduced herself. He could have her coffee. He looked like he needed it more than she did.

Ruth looked up wearily from the chair by Cam's bedside. "Fin knows I told you about the fire, as well as Lizzie overhearing what I said."

"It was an accident," Fin said. "She was only fourteen."

"I know," PJ said.

"Her father should have spoken up at the time."

"Sit down, Fin," PJ said. "There's another matter I need to discuss with you. That story you told us about Dana Schell being into drugs. Did Hector Cornish put you up to that?"

Ruth and Fin exchanged glances. There was no reason for them to deny it now. "Yes," said Ruth. "He was afraid the police would think the drugs they found in Dana's room belonged to him, so he wanted us to back up his story that they were hers. Are Fin and I going to be in trouble over that?"

For lying to the police and hampering their progress on an investigation? PJ was evasive. "Never mind about that for now. Look, is there anything else either of you need to tell me about? Hector Cornish is in a lot of trouble." PJ could tell from Fin's face that he was holding something back. "We suspect you introduced Hector to Liam Sharp," she said.

Fin sighed. "It's worse than you know." He gave Ruth an apologetic glance. "I'm sorry, love. I kept this from you because I didn't want you to have even more to worry about after Cam took ill. Hector stole a kilo of coke from Liam Sharp. Liam sent his brother to get it back or get the cash equivalent, but Hector no longer had the stuff. You lot picked it up from Dana Schell's room." He nodded at PJ. "Darren would have killed Hector there and then if I hadn't intervened and bought him some time to come up with a solution."

"Here's what you don't know," PJ said. "Liam Sharp was shot dead in the early hours of this morning. Before he died, he mentioned Hector's name to the police, and yours too, Fin. He was rambling, but he said Hector'd stolen something from him. Liam's brother, Darren, was injured. He survived but fled. His present whereabouts are unknown. Do you have any idea where he could be, Fin?"

Fin's eyes were wide with fear and disbelief. "Hiding out? In case the killer comes after him to finish him off too?" He paused. "Here in Stromford, looking for revenge?" His voice was shaky.

"But why would Darren connect the shooter to Hector," Ruth said, "or . . . or . . . Fin? Someone like Liam must have plenty of enemies."

"We don't know for sure that he has," PJ said.

Fin sat, staring at the floor. Then he looked up. "Hector said his father was taking care of it. I thought he meant his debt to Liam." He caught PJ's eye. "What if Hector's father . . . ?"

PJ whipped out her phone and called Neal.

* * *

Neal was on his way back to his office with Blunt when his phone vibrated. PJ's message sent a shiver of excitement through him. Hector had told Fin that his father would 'take care' of his problem. This seemed to lend substance to his surmise that Paul Cornish was behind the shooting of Liam and Darren Sharp.

Tom and Ava were at their desks. Neal beckoned to them and they joined him and Blunt in his office, where he explained his theory.

"If you're right, it's going to be practically impossible to prove," Blunt said, gloomily. "Tell me about the cases you're involved with, the ones that seem to intersect with mine."

Neal, with contributions from Ava and Tom, told him the story.

"Totally different modus operandi in each case," Blunt observed. "Dana's was the more careless of the two, but that doesn't necessarily mean you're looking at two different killers."

"I take it you've got your theories. If Marsh was onto Cornish's corrupt practices, Cornish would have needed to take care of him, fast, even though he must have known that his partner's death would inevitably turn the spotlight on him, and on their business affairs. I guess he had to take the risk and try to limit the damage," Neal said.

Ava reminded them about the text messages between Dana Schell and Russ Marsh. "Gail Cornish had an affair with Russ Marsh, and claimed it was a one-night stand. Paul gave Russ a black eye and it was allegedly all over and done with. But we've recently been given reason to believe that Gail and Russ carried on seeing each other. If so, Dana was certainly well-placed to discover it. It's still the most credible explanation for her trying to blackmail Russ."

"Poor Russ," Neal said. "He suspects his partner — whose wife he's still carrying on with — of corruption, and then Dana tells him she knows his secret and wants paying for her silence. Add to that his estrangement from his daughter, and it's a wonder he didn't commit bloody suicide."

"Have you managed to speak with either of the wives about the affair?" Blunt asked.

"Not yet. It's been on the list of questions that need answers, but Val Marsh's grandson was suddenly rushed to hospital. He's out of danger now, so it's probably time to have that conversation, both with her and Gail Cornish."

Tom, who had been quiet for a bit, said, "Do you think Gail Cornish knew what Paul was up to? The money laundering, I mean? Surely she must have had her suspicions?"

"She wasn't involved in the business. She was used to her husband working long hours, and being away a lot." Ava looked thoughtful. "It's possible that Russ let her know. Remember that day she called us and requested a visit? As well as telling us about her affair with Russ, she also mentioned the fight between the two men. Gail said she was telling us this because she was concerned we'd get to hear about it and regard Paul as a prime suspect, but we probably wouldn't have known about either at all if she hadn't said anything. Maybe she was telling us *in case* we didn't find out?"

"Like she *wanted* us to suspect, and investigate him," Tom added, somewhat unnecessarily.

There was a silence as everyone appeared to consider the implications of this. Neal said, "Dana finding out about the affair could have been the trigger for Gail revealing her suspicions about Paul to Russ. She tells Russ, Russ confronts Paul . . ."

"Gail must have been terrified that Paul would find out that she was the one who alerted Russ. And if things aren't bad enough, Dana is murdered too and we find drugs in the house," Ava added.

"You lot certainly have a mess on your hands," Blunt said. "Most murders on my patch tend to be drugs and gang related these days." Neal wasn't sure if his tone was envious or grateful. "Any chance we can speak to this Fin character sometime soon?"

"I've sent a patrol car to pick Fin up from the hospital," Neal said. "Should be on his way."

"Good." Blunt retrieved a pack of cigarettes from his pocket and excused himself.

* * *

Val had returned from the hospital exhausted, having stayed with Ruth until Cam's condition started to improve. Even then she'd been reluctant to leave, but Ruth had persuaded her and Lizzie to go.

Lizzie dropped Val home at around four in the morning and she went straight to bed. She awoke five hours later, feeling refreshed. She phoned Ruth and learned that Fin was with her. He must have left Cambridge in the middle of the night to arrive so early.

Val tried calling her sister to tell her not to set out for the hospital too soon. To her annoyance, there was no answer, so she left a message, hoping that Lizzie had not gone already. Ruth and Fin deserved some time alone together with their son.

Val suppressed a pang of jealousy. Ever since Will's death, she'd felt that Lizzie had inveigled her way deeper and deeper into Ruth's life. She seemed to have latched onto Ruth as a surrogate for Will.

Val had tried talking to Russ about it, but he clammed up at any mention of Will. Maybe he couldn't contemplate losing a child in that way. And then Lizzie had lost Craig too. In the face of Lizzie's loss, Val's resentment had seemed selfish and petty. Nevertheless, her sense of being usurped by her sister still stung.

She'd even overheard Lizzie remark to Stephen that Ruth had 'two mothers,' and this hurt her. She had concealed her feelings expertly, as she always did. All through her childhood, people had compared her unfavourably to Lizzie, her parents in particular. Val, who'd eschewed cuddles and been stridently independent practically from birth, had seemed cold to them after the affectionate Lizzie.

The sisters' different temperaments had led to the two being treated differently too. Whenever she and her sister discussed their childhood, it seemed to Val that Lizzie had grown up in a different family, gone to a different school. It hadn't been until Val moved away from Stromford and out of her older sister's shadow that she'd felt like a person in her own right.

Perhaps she should have resisted Lizzie's annexation of Ruth more determinedly. But Ruth, too, had been deeply affected by the deaths of Will and her uncle. Almost overnight, she changed from being a rebellious but manageable teenager to a broody, unconfident young woman. Val had been at a loss as to how to deal with her. But aunt and niece seemed to form a bond of solidarity, from which Val felt excluded.

Val took a shower and went downstairs in search of breakfast. After the emergency with Cam the previous evening, she hadn't felt much like eating, and now she was hungry. Would someone give Ruth a slice of toast? Then she remembered that Fin was with her. He could always pop out to get her a snack.

Val stirred her porridge and rotated her stiff neck. She gazed out at her garden, and the red-brick wall beyond. Until Russ's murder, that wall had made Val feel safe. It was solid and lasting, yet it had also seen other families come and go and the old hall slide into ruin. Now it seemed like her own family might disintegrate within its bounds.

Tears blurred Val's eyes. She looked over at the big oak table and spotted one of Cam's toys, a technicolour blue furry creature from that surreal children's TV programme that her grandson so adored. She felt a rush of tenderness for her family.

Val took her bowl and perched on a stool at the kitchen island. From there she could watch the birds alight on the feeders dangling from the gnarled branches of the rowan tree. Russ had fed the birds religiously, and she had resolved to carry on. Their antics lightened her mood. Maybe the police would catch whoever had enacted this terrible act of violence. Maybe one day, she, Ruth, Fin and Cam could be a happy family together. Maybe all would be well.

As she watched a flurry of sparrows splashing in the bird bath, a movement at the far end of the garden caught her eye. A man dropped heavily from the top of the garden wall and landed awkwardly among the shrubs at its base. He was dressed in baggy trousers and a loose-fitting jacket, with the hood pulled around his face like a monk's cowl.

Val dropped her spoon into the steaming porridge and watched the man lope across her lawn, turning his head to glance around him as he went.

Val clutched at her throat. Then, in a panic, she slipped from the stool and crouched under the lip of the island. She waited, hunkered on the kitchen floor, knees pressed painfully against the hard granite tiles, desperately trying to think what to do next.

Where was her mobile phone? She couldn't remember. The landline was on the worktop opposite the island, out of reach. She didn't dare move until she knew that the man wasn't going to force entry through the French doors. They had been burgled once, and those doors had been the point of entry. Val shuddered, remembering the shattered glass. She'd felt violated, even though they'd been away on holiday when it happened.

Several minutes passed. Val's mind raced. What if the man came into the kitchen? Even if he didn't spot her, he was sure to see the half-eaten, still-steaming bowl of porridge. Perhaps he was already in the house? Should she make a dash for the phone?

There was a sound from the front of the house. And now she could hear him. He was inside, moving around the hallway. Kicking doors open. Coming closer.

The door to the kitchen was flung wide open. Val let out a gasp. She shrank back against the island's supporting column. The stool she'd been sitting on was slightly askew. Would he notice? Betrayed by an abandoned bowl of porridge and a lack of symmetry! She was on the verge of hysteria.

She could see his legs on the opposite side of the island. She heard him roar. The bowl of porridge went flying off the island, and clattered against the door of Val's beloved range. Shards of porcelain skittered across the floor, and blobs of porridge slid slowly down the range door.

"Fin! Where are you, you bastard?"

Val had only a moment to register surprise at the familiar name before the man appeared on her side of the island and hauled her roughly to her feet.

* * *

Gail Cornish drove very slowly up the tree-lined drive to the Marshes' house. She was apprehensive about seeing Val, and wasn't sure if she'd be able to keep from breaking down when she saw Russ's study. Gail had never found Val to be warm or approachable. Their husbands were friends and business partners, and it should have been easy for them to be friends. But though they'd been thrust together on numerous social occasions over the years, they'd never become close.

Of course, relations between all four of them had been strained after the affair between her and Russ. It was difficult for Gail to look Val in the eye, let alone be a proper friend.

Gail wondered if Val's demeanour would have softened now that she was a grieving widow. She had heard that Ruth was home, with her son, Cam. Maybe playing the role of grandmother would have smoothed the edges.

Val's car, a blue Citroen, was parked on the drive outside the garage. Another car was parked close by. Gail recognised the red Fiesta that Russ and Val had given Ruth for her eighteenth birthday. So Ruth was at home. Gail wondered how she was coping with her father's sudden death.

She parked beside the Citroen and made her way across the gravel to the front door. How could Val live in such an isolated spot? Kingfisher Lodge was private enough, but it had amenities such as the spa and shops and restaurants right on the doorstep.

And that wall! Gail had always thought it looked a mess. Her taste evidently differed entirely from Val's. Still, the interior was high spec enough, even if it wasn't all clean lines like Kingfisher Lodge.

Gail raised her hand to ring the doorbell and noticed that the door was slightly ajar. Odd. Perhaps living in the depths of the country made people careless about security. She stepped forward and pushed the door open. Calling Val's name, then Ruth's, she stepped over the threshold and into the hallway. The doors to all the rooms leading off the hall were standing open. Her eyes were inevitably drawn to the study, and she could make out the corner of the desk where Russ had been found. She shivered.

"Val! Ruth! Is anyone home?" Her voice seemed to reverberate in the eerie silence that followed. *Something's not right*, she thought, and shivered again. She stood in the hall, considering what to do. Perhaps she should drive into the village? Val and Ruth might have popped out to the shop to buy supplies for the baby. Yet both cars were here, so they couldn't have.

What Gail really wanted to do was turn and walk away. She could always drop by another time. But she remained standing in the hall, unable to shake the feeling that something was very wrong. Maybe no one had heard her call. She raised her voice and tried again.

"Is anyone home?"

She thought she heard a muffled sound coming from the kitchen. Someone was at home, then. She stepped forward.

Gail went to the kitchen door and stood, just inside the doorway, staring in disbelief at the scene before her. It took her a few moments to process what she was seeing. Val, bound and gagged, and tied to a chair, looked up at her with wide pleading eyes. The muffled sounds were Val's voice behind the tape plastered over her mouth.

With a start, Gail went to help Val. She peeled away the tape.

"Police," Val rasped. "Hospital."

Gail nodded, and immediately started to dial for the police and an ambulance, as Val fainted against her restraints.

Chapter Eighteen

After the uniformed officer took Fin back to the station for questioning, PJ lingered on at the hospital. She didn't need to, but some of Fin's anxiety had rubbed off on her.

"Ruth and Cam are perfectly safe here," she'd told him when he asked her to stay with them. "Even if this Darren did come to Stromford, how would he even know where to find them? This is the last place he'd think to look."

After he left, Ruth was the one to be anxious. "Is Fin going to be arrested? He couldn't have shot Liam Sharp. He's been in Stromford since yesterday evening. Hector Cornish can vouch for that, can't he?" PJ did her best to soothe her.

And there was another reason. PJ was simply reluctant to return to the nick and face her colleagues. Her conversation with Steve still weighed heavily on her mind — and heart. They'd been so happy these past few months. *Just shows you shouldn't take anything for granted.*

Ruth was crying again, this time about Lizzie. Rocking slightly, she clasped a teddy bear to her chest. It was the one Lizzie had brought for Cam. "Aunt Lizzie will probably never speak to me again. And I don't blame her."

PJ made no comment. She didn't know Lizzie Hamilton well enough to predict how she would react once she'd had time to absorb what she'd heard. At the time, she had blamed Russ Marsh for the tragedy, and had nothing more to do with him. Since her son's death, Lizzie had all but appropriated Ruth as a surrogate daughter. She must be grieving all over again.

Poor, brave Will. PJ hoped it would be some consolation to Lizzie to learn that her son had not started the fire, and that he had died a hero.

It was teatime on the wards. PJ heard the dishes clatter in the corridor outside, along with movement and the sound of cheery voices. The curtains to Ruth and Cam's room were drawn, so they couldn't see the ward outside, but the door was ajar, and PJ breathed in the aroma of macaroni cheese.

Ruth dabbed at her eyes. "I'm not hungry."

"I'm starving," PJ said. "Do you mind if I have yours?"

Ruth gave a disinterested shrug. But when the porter opened the door, he presented Ruth with a plate of salad that she must have ordered earlier in the day. PJ eyed it with some disappointment. She'd have preferred the macaroni cheese. She sat, munching on lettuce leaves, while Ruth, all cried out now, dozed in the chair and Cam slumbered on.

The porter collected her plate and a hush settled over the ward beyond the door. Visiting time was still some way off. PJ felt her eyelids begin to droop.

She roused herself. For one reason or another, she seemed to have spent most the past night and day at the hospital. Maybe it was time she left. She was about to get to her feet when the door flew open, and a young man slipped into the room. He closed the door behind him.

PJ felt a stab of alarm. "Are you looking for someone?" she asked. She didn't like the look of this character — young, male, with his hood pulled up around his face. Never a good sign. Nor did she like the way he stood with his back to the door, leaning against it. She liked it even less when he grabbed a chair and thrust it under the door handle.

"Hey! What do you think you're doing?" PJ was fully alert now.

"Shut up," he said. "Where's Fin?" He looked about the room.

"He's not here."

"I can see that. Where is he?"

Ruth had started awake, and was eyeing the man fearfully. "Who are you? What do you want with Fin?"

PJ was certain that, like her, Ruth had guessed who their visitor was.

"That his kid?" the man asked, nodding at Cam, now stirring in his cot.

"I'm a police officer," PJ said. "You're Darren Sharp. I know you've suffered a recent trauma. Why don't you calm down and we can talk?"

"Why don't you go fuck yourself, you stupid mare? Or better still, tell me where I can find Fin O'Shea."

Darren slid his hand inside his jacket and brought out a gun, which he pointed at PJ. Ruth gasped. PJ was suddenly acutely aware of her duty as a police officer. It was up to her to handle this situation, and to protect Ruth and Cam. "I know you're upset about what happened to your brother, Darren," she said, "but Fin wasn't responsible for that."

Darren turned the gun on Ruth. "You're Fin's partner."

"Please don't hurt us," Ruth pleaded. "Why won't you listen to what the detective said? Fin had nothing to do with your brother's murder."

Ignoring Ruth's plea, Darren continued to waver between pointing the gun at her and pointing it at PJ. After a moment he ordered PJ to push her chair next to Ruth's, and sit down. *At least he won't need to keep jiggling the gun around*, PJ thought. A steady gun was slightly less menacing than one that was in perpetual motion.

"He's been here," Darren said, catching sight of Fin's Cambridge University scarf hanging over the end of Cam's bed.

"That's not his scarf. It belongs to Ruth. She went to Cambridge too." Even as she spoke, PJ knew her fib was feeble.

"Shut up. I've seen Fin wearing that recently." Darren picked up the scarf and PJ could see what he was looking at. A patch of brown. Dried blood. Like the stains she had seen on Fin's sleeve earlier. Why hadn't she quizzed him about that?

"He'll be back to see you and his kid," Darren said, looking at Ruth. "I can wait."

"He's not coming back," PJ said. "He's at the station, being questioned by the police."

The news seemed to confuse Darren. He rubbed his forehead with the back of the hand holding the gun, and then leant against the wall. His jacket flapped open, offering a glimpse of his shirt. It was drenched in blood.

"Oh!" PJ exclaimed. "You're hurt. You got shot too." Darren pulled his jacket around him. PJ looked at the moisture on his brow. He was sweating, feverish.

"Call your colleagues," Darren said. "Tell them I want Fin O'Shea brought here, to this room." His eyes locked on PJ's. "Tell them if they don't bring him within the hour, I'm going to shoot his girlfriend, then his kid."

As if on cue, Cam woke up and let out a wail.

***

"PJ's been a while at the hospital." Scarcely were the words out of Ava's mouth when her phone rang. "Talk of the devil," she said. Tom looked up from his PC and grinned.

"Ava, I'm with Ruth and her son. At the hospital. Darren Sharp's here. He's got a gun and he's threatening to kill Ruth and Cam if Fin isn't brought here within the hour."

Ava wasn't sure what shocked her more — PJ's words, or how steady her voice was. She picked up the first thing she had to hand, a pen, and launched it at Tom to attract his attention.

"Ouch. What was that for?" Tom glared at her.

Ava put her phone on speaker. "Ava? Did you hear me?" PJ's voice was less steady this time.

"Sorry, Peej. I caught, 'Ruth and Cam,' then you broke up a bit. Can you repeat that?"

"I said, Darren Sharp's here, at the hospital. He has a gun. He wants Fin brought to the hospital or he says he'll kill Ruth and Cam. You have one hour to get Fin here."

Tom jolted to his feet. Ava realised that she was shaking. "PJ . . ." Ava had no idea what she was going to say next, but then a man's voice took over.

"You heard her. Clock's ticking." The call ended.

Tom spoke first. "I'll get Neal." Ava nodded, too shocked to say anything. Tom went off at a run. Ava stumbled backwards into her chair, sick to her stomach. What had PJ got herself into? Poor, sweet PJ. She'd only just been promoted to detective constable. She wasn't ready for this.

Footsteps reverberated in the corridor outside. "Ava!" It was Neal, jerking her out of her state of panic. The sight of Neal, in panic mode himself, rallied her. He was barking out orders into his phone, calling for an armed response vehicle, for the hospital to be alerted, the area in the vicinity of the room where PJ and the others were being held to be evacuated. A hostage negotiator, for fuck's sake!

Blunt materialised, along with Fin. Had Fin been told about the threat to Ruth? To his son? One look at his face provided the answer.

"Ava, you're with me," Neal said. "Tom, take Blunt and Fin with you." He nodded at Fin. "Make damn sure he does as he's told. On no account is he to get out of the car."

The journey to the hospital seemed to take for ever. Ava sat tense and fearful, her racing mind churning out an endless stream of scenarios, none of which ended well. Beside her, Neal gripped the wheel, his knuckles white, tight-lipped and silent.

Ava needed to act. But this was a hostage situation. It required calm, restraint. Neither were qualities that Ava possessed. *But PJ does*, she told herself. *If anyone can stay composed in a situation like this, it's PJ.*

As if reading her mind, Neal said, "Ava, we need to keep our heads in there. I know it's PJ, but we won't help her if we act on impulse and rush in at the wrong moment."

He knew how reckless Ava could be. *Not this time*, she told herself, *there's too much at stake.* She nodded. "I hear you, sir."

Ava turned her head and stared out of the window. Shops, houses, people, all flashed by in a monochrome blur. Only the sky, purple and overcast, hinted at some colour in the world. Ava felt as if she was in a film.

* * *

They had arrived. "No sign of the ARV," Neal said.

They'd received radio communication moments ago, to say that it was on its way. Neal parked near the out patients' entrance, the nearest access point to the children's wards. A couple of patrol cars had beaten them to it, and uniformed officers were already securing the area.

"Shit. This is going to be all over the news in no time," Ava said.

Tom pulled up behind them. "Tom," Neal said, "stay here and guard Fin. Cuff him if he gives you any grief. Do not bring him inside unless I say so. I'll be in radio contact. And inform me as soon as the armed officers arrive."

Tom looked disappointed, and Ava felt for him. She had half expected him to exclude her too at this point. She was determined to do nothing to undermine his confidence in her.

"Ready?" Neal looked at Ava, at Blunt and the two uniforms who were to go with them.

"Yes, sir."

"Then let's resolve this speedily and get everyone out safe and sound." As rallying cries go, it wasn't much of one.

They were making their way along eerily deserted corridors to the children's ward. "This is it," Ava said, pointing down a corridor with cheerful yellow walls decorated with cartoon characters and pictures of balloons and butterflies. It all seemed incongruous in their present situation.

They pushed through a set of double doors and into the ward. Neal put a finger to his lips and they advanced silently..

And now they were standing outside the room. All was quiet inside, and its curtained window revealed no hint of the drama playing out within. Ava glanced at her watch. Half an hour since PJ's momentous call.

The whole ward was deserted. There were gaping spaces where some of the beds had been wheeled away, other beds empty, their covers cast aside, belongings strewn all over. Signs of a hasty exodus. The staff had reacted with lightning efficiency.

Ava wondered if Neal had a plan. He hadn't said. Was he merely acting on his wits, there being no time for anything else? Signalling to the others to keep back, Neal approached the door.

"PJ. It's DI Neal. Are you alright?"

"Yes, sir."

"Ruth? Cam?"

"They're okay too."

For now. Ava longed to add some words of reassurance to her friend.

"Darren? Can you hear me?" Neal said.

"You took your time."

"We're here now. My name is DI Jim Neal. I want to help."

"Have you brought Fin?"

"He's outside. In the car park. I'm not bringing him in here."

Don't rattle him, Ava chided in her head. Before Darren could respond, Neal spoke again.

"I know you think Fin was responsible for your brother's murder. You're grieving, Darren. Grief can distort the way we think. It keeps us from seeing the truth." He paused. "Fin had nothing to do with Liam's murder. We believe someone ordered a hit on your brother."

Neal's police radio crackled. It was Tom. Armed assistance had arrived. Almost simultaneously, the double doors to the ward were edged open, and two heavily suited, armed officers crept in. Somehow the sight of them moving cautiously down the corridor wasn't as reassuring as it should have been.

"That's bollocks." Darren's voice sounded rasping, laboured. He was injured, she remembered. There could be blood loss. He could be weak. Ava didn't dare hope.

"It's . . . complicated," Neal was saying now. "There are things you don't know about. Things we can talk about if you surrender your gun to DC Jenkins and come outside."

No response. The armed officers were taking up position. At a signal from Neal, they would storm the door and bring an end to this nightmare. It could all be over in a couple of seconds. But at what cost? Anything could happen in a couple of seconds. Startled by their entry, all Darren had to do was squeeze the trigger. Someone would die. *Oh, Peej, don't let it be you.* Ava shut her eyes, and tried not to cry.

Neal was talking again. "Darren. The people in that room with you have nothing to do with all this. I know you don't really want to hurt anyone."

Ava glanced at Blunt and saw him frown. Had Neal just made an error of judgement? Maybe Blunt should be doing the talking. He was more familiar with Darren's world, after all.

An ominous silence followed Neal's words. What the hell was going on in there? Was the time for talking over? Ava tensed, and willed herself to stay put.

A series of loud wails rent the air and everyone jumped. It was Cam, crying at the top of his lungs.

Ava glared at Neal, willing him to make use of the distraction. What was he waiting for? Why didn't he give the order?

And then he did.

* * *

At first there was only noise and confusion, and an agony of fearful anticipation. At Neal's signal, the armed officers kicked the door, which splintered from its frame, and stormed the room, yelling, "Armed police! Let's see your hands!"

Instinctively, Ava covered her ears, waiting for the crack of gunfire, but it didn't come. Instead of shots, calls of "Clear!" and "Suspect disarmed," rang out from inside the room.

Ava was on the move in an instant, racing forward to see what had happened, if PJ was safe. Her eyes swept the room. There, face down on the floor, lay Darren Sharp, one officer cuffing his hands behind his back, while the other trained his gun on him. In the far corner, cradling a still wailing Cam, Ruth Marsh crouched, wide-eyed and visibly shaking. And here, right next to Ava now, was PJ, telling her that she was alright, no need to panic. It struck Ava as almost comical that PJ should be the one offering reassurance. How very like her.

Still, the repeated assertions of "I'm okay, I'm okay, I'm okay" sounded a little like shock. Blunt disappeared and returned with two blankets, which he wrapped around Ruth and Cam, and around PJ.

Tom Knight materialised in the doorway, accompanied by a near-hysterical Fin.

The armed police hauled Darren to his feet and led him away, ashen-faced and barely conscious.

"What happened?" Ava asked PJ. "Are you okay to talk?"

They all moved outside, leaving Ruth, Fin and Cam together for a moment. Blunt took out his cigarettes and excused himself. Neal, Tom, Ava and PJ sat down at the abandoned nurses' station.

"Take your time, PJ," Neal said.

"Fin was picked up to be taken to his interview with you and DI Blunt," PJ began. "I think he foresaw something like this happening. He was reluctant to go, and asked me to sit with Ruth and Cam until he got back. I thought I'd just stay for a little while, and then make my way back to the station. I was just about to leave when Darren showed up. That's more or less when I phoned you, Ava."

"How did he seem?" Neal asked.

"His frame of mind? He seemed a bit crazy. Definitely agitated. I didn't realise he was wounded at first. Then I saw the blood, and I realised he must be feverish. He must have lost a lot of blood. His shirt was soaked through, even though I think he'd bandaged himself up a bit. He was in pain too, I could tell. I think that's why he behaved the way he did, why everything was so . . . so . . . sort of . . . urgent."

Ava rolled her eyes. "Don't make excuses for him, Peej. He would have killed you all and not given a shit."

PJ looked sad. "I hate to agree, but you're probably right. I saw the look in Darren's eyes when the DI said that thing about him not really wanting to hurt anyone. Whether because of the fever . . . or . . . or . . . I don't know what . . . I sensed he'd pull that trigger."

"It's alright, PJ," Neal said, sounding almost angry. "Carry on."

PJ looked embarrassed, and she sounded more hesitant. "I, um . . . know what you were trying to do, talking to him, but I don't think . . . I mean . . . he wasn't, um, listening to you. Everything you said only seemed to make him more agitated. He just wanted you to bring Fin. I don't think he could think past that in the state he was in."

If Neal was disappointed that his intervention had made no difference, he didn't show it. Ava was aware that in this job it was never okay to act recklessly. Still, she couldn't help feeling a bit annoyed at Neal for not giving the signal to break down the door sooner. Perhaps she'd see it differently later on. For now, she was grateful that there'd been a successful outcome.

Tom said helpfully, "I bet he was doped up too. No one could predict what he'd do in there."

"So, just before Cam started crying," PJ went on, "Darren seemed to be having difficulty breathing. And he was shaking. Shuddering, really. I thought he was going to pass out. He was leaning against the wall, like it was all that was holding him up. He was still agitated but I think he was starting to lose his grip. And not just metaphorically."

They all stared at her, not understanding. "He dropped the gun," she explained. "Cam's sudden outburst startled him, and he literally let go of it. And then the door exploded." PJ gave a strange half-smile. "There was no need for all the drama in the end. Bit of an anticlimax really."

"That's one way of putting it," Ava said.

Blunt had reappeared and caught the end of PJ's account. He was eager to question Fin over the shooting on his patch.

"Give him a bit longer," Neal said. "His partner and his son could have died in there."

"Do you want me to call Steve?" Ava asked PJ.

"No." PJ almost snapped.

"Well, let's go up to the canteen. Get you a cup of something hot and sweet."

"I'd rather go somewhere else," PJ said. "If you don't mind. I've had enough of this place for the time being. And I could do with something a bit stronger than a cup of tea."

Twenty minutes later, PJ and Ava were sitting in a pub, some distance from the hospital. On duty or not, Ava felt her friend deserved a stiff drink after everything she'd been through.

"What's up?" Ava asked. "Have you and Steve had bad news?"

To her surprise, PJ gave a sardonic laugh. "Depends how you look at it. It's not bad news for Steve. Pretty good news for him, actually." Her tone was increasingly bitter. "So good, in fact, that he's decided he's got a lot of other things he wants to do with his life instead of settling down with me."

"Oh, Peej. I'm so sorry. He got the all-clear, then?"

PJ nodded. "Clean bill of health. Apparently the experience has taught him that he should" — she made air quotes — "'live for the day.' He wants to 'embrace life with open arms, get out there and experience everything.' Because 'you never know what's round the next corner.' I think he swallowed a cliché generator."

Ava squeezed her friend's arm. "I'm sorry," she said again.

"Well, don't be," PJ said, suddenly cheerful. "You know what? I've just had my own brush with mortality. And guess what it's made me realise?"

"What?" Ava asked, confident she knew the answer. PJ squeezed her arm in return.

"This," she said. "This is what's important. Friends, family. People you love and who love you."

"Oh, PJ, I think you've known that all along," Ava said, and smiled.

Chapter Nineteen

Neal sat facing Fin in the interview room, with Blunt beside him. After a nod from Neal, Blunt got the proceedings underway.

"First off," Blunt said, "I'd just like to say how glad I am that your partner and son are okay. None of us wants to think about what might have happened . . ." He paused. "Which prompts me to ask, what was it all about, son? You've been involved with these characters before, haven't you? Remember DS Bob Fletcher? He knew you back in the day." Fin nodded. "Now, why the hell would you want to get mixed up with that lot again?"

A lot of it they knew already, from Hector, but they needed to hear the story from Fin himself. As Fin went over the details, what emerged most strongly was his love for his partner. He'd been willing to risk everything he'd achieved so that Ruth could keep her secret.

Fin echoed PJ when he said that he had tried to make Ruth accept that she hadn't murdered her cousin. "In her mind, she really believes that she deserved to go to prison. If only her father hadn't sworn her to secrecy, and if Lizzie hadn't latched onto her the way she did, Ruth might have spoken to someone and got some help. Instead, she bottled it all up and, over the years, it's taken its toll on her mental well-being."

Blunt nodded, but he was more concerned with hearing about the events leading up to the shooting on his patch. "So when Hector stole the coke from him, Liam sent Darren to you."

"I'd vouched for Hector, so Liam would have held me responsible for his behaviour. And he would have taken it as an insult. That's the kind of twisted thinking you get in his world."

Blunt nodded. "But you managed to get Hector a reprieve."

"Yes."

"And how did Hector intend to repay Liam?"

"Last time I saw him, he told me his father was taking care of it."

"And that was, when, early this morning?"

Fin nodded.

Blunt looked at Neal. Only hours before Liam had been fatally wounded and his brother injured. If Paul Cornish had had anything to do with the shooting, he must have acted fast. Still, all he had to do was pick up the phone. There would have been nothing to connect the incident with his family. That Liam had survived the shooting long enough to mention Hector and Fin was a stroke of bad luck that Paul couldn't have foreseen, and a gift the police hadn't dared hope for.

"And Hector didn't elaborate when he said his father had 'taken care' of it?"

"No. I imagine that, like me, he thought his dad had arranged to repay Liam." Fin stared at them. "You think Paul Cornish had something to do with it? Like a hit or something?"

"It's one theory," Blunt said. "Of course, Liam Sharp had other enemies. An organised gang is gradually taking control of his patch. Liam was small time, but he was doing good enough trade to piss off the serious dealers that wanted to move in."

And there was the problem, Neal thought. 'Respectable' businessman versus lawless, territorial drug gangs. Didn't need to be a genius to predict who would come out looking dirtier. Just then his phone rang. It was Ava.

"Sir. Just had a report come through. Val Marsh was attacked in her home earlier today. From the description of the intruder, I think it might have been Darren Sharp, before he turned up at the hospital. Gail Cornish raised the alarm after finding Val tied up and gagged."

"Why didn't we learn about this sooner?"

"Don't know, sir. Possibly the attending officer didn't make the connection with the case we're investigating. Val Marsh was in shock when they arrived, maybe she wasn't able to tell them much. She and Gail Cornish are at the hospital now."

Neal sighed deeply. Blunt raised an eyebrow.

"Ava, can you and PJ go back to the hospital and take statements from them?"

"On it, sir."

* * *

After overhearing Ruth's confession, Lizzie Hamilton stumbled out of the hospital, not knowing where to go or what to do. In the short stay car park, she stood outside her car, fumbling with her keys, uncertain whether she was capable of driving. In the end, she walked away, continuing along the road leading to the top end of town. Tears blurred her eyes and memories flooded her mind. She thought of Will, of Craig, and all the years since their deaths that she'd spent hating Russ Marsh for putting work before her son.

All those dinner parties she'd endured, all those social occasions — the birthdays, Christmases, family events. At all of these, she'd suffered Russ's presence for the sake of remaining close to Val. And above all, close to Ruth.

Val had been right. She had indeed latched onto Ruth as a substitute for Will. Lizzie clearly remembered the moment it had happened, at Will's funeral, when she'd looked along the row of family members and witnessed Ruth, overcome with grief, her shoulders shaking under her father's comforting arm.

She had been somewhat surprised at Ruth being so upset. She and Will had got on well as far as it went, but Lizzie wouldn't have said they were particularly close. Lizzie's heart had gone out to her niece in that moment, and ever since she'd felt they had a special bond.

Special bond! Thinking of it now made Lizzie sick to her stomach. What she had taken for grief on Ruth's part had been guilt, fear even. Now, as Lizzie grasped its true significance, the memory was sullied for ever.

Russ was still to blame, she thought. Ruth's revelation did not completely exonerate him. Lizzie still felt nothing but relief at the thought of her brother-in-law lying slumped over his desk, his head blasted to smithereens. In her opinion, justice had been done.

Stromford Cathedral loomed up in front of her, its thousand years of history reminding her that, in the long run, everything passes. When she met Stephen Hamilton, she'd believed that given time, her grief over Will would transmute into acceptance. Ruth's confession had sent her hurtling back, through grief and pain, to her worst nightmare.

Lizzie looked up at the spires of the cathedral piercing the sky. Just months ago, a man had been pushed to his death from up there. It had saddened her at the time, the thought of him falling through empty space towards certain death. Now she envied him. To fall, weightless, into oblivion seemed a kinder fate than to have to live the rest of her life with this burden of sadness. Slowly, with measured steps, Lizzie began walking towards the heavy timbered doorway of the west entrance.

* * *

"They're saying we can see your daughter now."

Gail had left Val in the waiting area while she went to ask at reception if there was any more news about Ruth. Val had come round in the ambulance, and begun babbling about her attacker, a man with a gun who was looking for Ruth's partner, Fin. In the middle of his tirade, the phone had rung and Ruth's voice had piped up on the answerphone. She'd mentioned Fin and the hospital, and on hearing this, the gunman had dashed off, leaving Val tied up and unable to raise the alarm.

By the time Gail and Val arrived at the hospital, something was evidently going off. There were police cars everywhere, and one of the paramedics said he'd seen a couple of armed police officers enter the building. Both women had feared the worst.

No one seemed to know what was going on. The most they could glean was that the police were responding to a serious incident on the children's ward. That had been enough to tip Val into hysterics. There were rumours that the ward had been evacuated, of a possible hostage situation.

Now, after a long, anxious wait, they'd been given the go-ahead to see Ruth and Cam. "Are you okay to walk, or shall I fetch one of those wheelchairs?" Gail asked. Val stood up, looking indignant. Once the shock of her ordeal had passed, she hadn't required any treatment.

Together they made their way along the tunnel-like corridors to the children's ward, where a police officer posted at the door was initially reluctant to let them in. Luckily, the nurse who'd accompanied them reassured him that Val was the mother of one of the hostages, and they were admitted.

There was still a police presence on the ward. Ruth and Cam had been transferred to another room, where another officer was posted sentry. Gail waited outside while Val and Ruth shared an emotional reunion. She listened in from the corridor, and got the gist of the story. When she heard Ruth mention Hector's name, she slipped inside and stood, unnoticed, behind the open door. She couldn't believe what she was hearing. What was this? Hector involved with an East End drug dealer? Hector blackmailing Ruth and her partner over the death of Ruth's cousin?

And yet. Gail had had her suspicions when the police found those drugs in Dana's room. Dana could never have afforded that much cocaine on what she was earning as a skivvy in the Cornish household. The likeliest explanation was that the drugs belonged to Hector.

Paul had been to see Hector at the penthouse a couple of nights ago and had returned in a filthy mood. Whatever they'd discussed, Gail hadn't been informed of it.

"I've just had a text from Fin," Gail heard Ruth say. "The police think someone ordered a hit on Darren and his brother. Can you believe that?"

Ruth's words struck home. The mobile phone she'd been holding slid from her hand and clattered on the floor.

Val looked up, confused. "Gail?" She'd thought Gail had gone. "What's wrong? You look . . . Oh! Did you overhear what Ruth was saying about Hector?"

"Yes," Gail said, flustered. As she bent to retrieve her phone, she felt a sudden crushing pain in her chest. A tingling sensation ran up and down her left arm, from her shoulder to her fingertips. It was difficult to breathe. Gail clutched at her chest and sank to the floor.

"Mum?" Ruth turned to Val, panicking. "Is she having a heart attack?"

Val knelt on the floor by Gail's side and called for Ruth to get help. Suddenly Gail was afraid that she might be running out of time to put things right. Her right hand fastened itself on Val's arm. The pain was more intense now, and it was hard to speak. "Paul . . . killed Russ . . . and . . . Dana," she rasped. "He's . . . been . . . laundering money for a man called . . . Leavitt . . . Russ . . . knew."

Had she said enough? She didn't think she could speak any more. Not if she wanted to breathe. She let go of Val's arm. Val took her hand. Gail wanted to tell her that she was sorry about the affair with Russ, but she really couldn't utter a word. And besides, it wasn't true. She hoped Val would understand.

"Thank goodness," she heard Val exclaim, as the room was suddenly invaded by medics. "I think she's having a heart attack."

* * *

"Bloody hell, what's happening now?" Ava said, seeing the commotion outside Ruth's room. A crash cart blocked the doorway, and a number of doctors and nurses were kneeling around someone lying on the floor.

"Stand back!" shouted one of the medics.

Ava saw Val and Ruth Marsh, standing at a distance, Ruth cradling Cam in her arms.

The last thing Ava wanted to do was get in the way, but she edged nearer until she was able to see the face of the person the medics were working on.

"It's Gail Cornish," she whispered to PJ, stepping back again. "Looks like a heart attack or something."

PJ shook her head. "These families . . ."

Across the room, Val Marsh was signalling frantically to Ava and PJ. There was obviously something urgent she needed to tell them, but it would have to wait until the entrance was clear.

After what seemed an eternity — in reality no more than a few minutes — Gail was wheeled off on a stretcher, an oxygen mask over her grey face. Val immediately rushed over to them.

Ava and PJ listened to Val tell them what Gail had said as she lay in the throes of her attack. "I'm sure she believed she was dying," Val said. "She seemed like she was sort of confessing, in case she never got another chance."

Ava glanced at Ruth. Seemed like deathbed confessions were the thing these days. She nodded to Val. "Right."

Inside, Ava was boiling over with excitement and anxiety. How much did Gail know? Did she have proof? *Oh shit, don't let her die*, Ava thought, and immediately felt guilty. A glance at PJ's face told her that she was equally conflicted. This could be a lucky break. But it would be a big fat nothing if Gail Cornish died before she could tell them.

Val Marsh looked stricken. "Do you think it's true? That Paul killed Russ? And . . . and that girl, Dana Schell?"

"Gail might have been confused," Ava said. "We need to question her, when . . ."

"Or if," Val added.

"You said that you weren't aware of any animosity lately between your husband and Paul Cornish?"

"No, but Russ said he was worried about some aspect of the business."

"Did you ask if he'd spoken with Paul about it? Or did he give any clue that he might be taking it up with Paul?"

"Not in so many words, but they were partners. I assumed he would as a matter of course."

Ruth helped her mother to a chair. She looked at PJ and shook her head. "This day. I can't wait for it to be over."

"You can say that again," said PJ.

* * *

Neal had stepped outside the interview room to take Ava's latest call. Now he was back inside with Fin and DI Blunt.

"There's been a bit of a development," he said. "Gail Cornish has had a heart attack. Before losing consciousness, she told Val Marsh and her daughter that Paul killed both Russ Marsh and Dana Schell."

Blunt stared at him. "Shit! Did she say anything to substantiate her claim? Is she going to survive?"

Neal could forgive Blunt's lack of concern for Gail Cornish's welfare. He'd been thinking along exactly the same lines. "Don't know. To both questions," he answered.

"Can I go back to the hospital?" Fin pleaded. "Ruth needs me."

"For now," Neal said. Fin's lies about Dana Schell had wasted a lot of police time. He'd also facilitated the buying and selling of a class A drug, but Neal appreciated that he'd done so under duress. He hadn't yet decided whether to charge Fin with anything. Well, a bit of uncertainty about his future wouldn't hurt the guy.

"I'll get Tom Knight to drive you there. That way he can keep an eye on you in case you get yourself into any more trouble."

Chapter Twenty

Joel Agard had been the doctor treating Darren Sharp when he'd been rushed to A&E after he collapsed following being taken into custody for holding PJ, Ruth Marsh and Cam hostage. Ava had just finished speaking with him.

"Any luck?" PJ asked.

"His condition is stable. They'll allow us to talk to him for a bit, though Joel says he's pretty doped up."

"The chief will be pleased," PJ said. "He's been like a bear with a sore head since yesterday."

"Yeah, well, I think the frustration's getting to us all," Ava said.

Until now, both Darren Sharp and Gail Cornish had been considered medically unfit for questioning. Frustrating indeed.

"And Gail Cornish?"

"They're saying she needs surgery, a bypass operation. Apparently she's desperate to talk to us. Joel says she shouldn't be upset, but on balance, he reckons it will be more stressful for her if she's not allowed to. Paul was with her until the early hours of the morning. That alone must have stressed her out."

Gail wasn't the only one to be suffering from stress. She must have had good reason for accusing her husband of murder, but until she could be questioned, the police's hands were tied. If only they could arrest Paul and bring him in, but they had no grounds for doing so, and every hour that passed gave him more time to cover his tracks.

Of course, Paul knew nothing of Gail's accusation. But by now he must be aware that the hit on Liam and Darren Sharp had gone badly wrong, and that would surely panic him. Ava had been on tenterhooks all night. From her colleagues' drawn faces when they arrived for work that morning, she guessed that none of them had slept a wink either.

"I'll let Neal know," Ava said.

Neal looked up from his computer and beckoned her into his office. On hearing her news, he immediately snatched up his jacket. "Let's go."

"Go get 'em," PJ said, as Ava passed by her desk. Tom wasn't around. Unable to bear the inaction, he'd gone to the forensics lab to chase the results on both cases.

"Cam was discharged from the hospital last night," Ava told Neal as they travelled to the hospital. The child's recovery was the one positive note in a day that looked to be as calamitous as the one before it.

"Here we are again," Ava sighed as she parked in the hospital car park. "Who first?"

"Gail Cornish, I think."

Ava had learned from Joel that Gail was not out of danger. Apparently she had a congenital heart condition, for which she had been receiving treatment. Without surgery, there was considerable risk of a more serious heart attack. Neal had no doubt borne this in mind, but Ava suspected he also wanted to give her a chance to unburden herself.

Hooked up to monitoring equipment and dressed only in a loose hospital gown, Gail bore little resemblance to the woman Ava and Neal had first met in the grand surroundings of Kingfisher Lodge. When she saw her grey, pinched face Ava wondered whether they should be disturbing her at all. But the nurse who had shown them to the bedside gave them a nod of encouragement. She said she would remain close by, to monitor her patient.

Ava fetched two orange plastic chairs. Neal sat nearest to Gail. "Mrs Cornish, I know you're not feeling your best, but we've been told that you are anxious to speak with us about the serious accusation you made against your husband last night."

Gail nodded. She lay, sunk back against the pillows, and made no attempt to rise. She wouldn't have had the strength. The nurse approached the bed and offered her a sip of water. It seemed to revive her a bit.

"Yes," she said, in a low, hoarse whisper. "I thought I was going to die. I still might. I didn't want to die without . . . the truth being told."

Ava wondered at Neal's patient calm, and her own. Like her, he must be churning up inside, desperate to shake the words out of Gail Cornish so that they could get down to business. Ava thought back to the day before. She'd had to hold herself back then too, when PJ and the others were in danger. When she'd made the decision to become a police officer, she had envisioned a life full of action, not this constant need for restraint.

"Take your time, Mrs Cornish. Tell us why you believe your husband is guilty of murdering Russ Marsh and Dana Schell."

"You can only live for so long with someone without knowing what they truly are," Gail began. *Just get to the point*, Ava thought. But Gail seemed determined to set some sort of context.

"It took a while, but there came a point when I began to suspect the kind of person Paul really was." Her voice shook. "It wasn't anything specific, you understand. That's important. To me, at any rate." Gail's eyes sought Neal's. He gave her an encouraging nod.

"It crept up on me slowly. To think I didn't see it for so long . . ." Her voice trailed off and she signalled for more water. She took a couple of sips. "Thank you. I suppose it was because we were leading such busy lives. We were in London for a few years, and then we moved to Stromford. Paul was busy all the time, first in the City, and then building up the business with Russ. I carried on working part-time until the twins came along. I was so . . . occupied. At home, and then socially as well. Paul and I were always out."

"When did you first suspect that Paul was a sociopath?" Neal asked. Ava was glad he'd been so blunt. The word was out there now. Gail didn't need to skirt around it.

"After the twins were born."

Ava did the maths. Rupert and Quentin were nearly eighteen. So Gail had been married for approximately six years when she realised she'd married a monster.

"I knew he had a ruthless streak. You don't thrive in the City without that." She sighed. "There are always exceptions, of course."

"Russ Marsh?" Ava said.

"Yes," Gail said, tears in her eyes.

"Mrs Cornish?" The nurse looked anxious. "Are you sure you want to continue?"

"Yes, I'm alright." She managed a weak smile, and turned back to Neal and Ava. "I'm sorry. You don't need to hear all this. I just want to say one more thing. I did love Paul. I can see now that he was a controlling bully, but I never felt it at the time. I was completely under the spell of his charm, just like everyone else. I did what I was told without even realising it. Or, stranger still, I believed it was what I wanted too."

"Sociopaths can be very manipulative," Neal said. "Their charisma is part of their power."

"Yes. That's how it was. I wanted to please him, make him happy. And even after I began to suspect what kind of man he truly was, that didn't change. I still admired him. It was only after I began seeing Russ that I understood . . . how different things could be."

Ava willed Gail to speed up, get to the heart of the matter.

"Dana found out that I was still seeing Russ. She was trying to blackmail him over it. She sent him texts, even went round to his house and spoke to him about it."

"Yes, we recovered both their phones," Ava said. "We saw the messages."

Gail looked surprised. "I was terrified of Paul finding out. He was furious when he found out the first time it happened. Russ and I were careless that time and I knew Paul suspected, so I confessed and told him it had been just one night. It was a stupid mistake that I wasn't going to repeat. He made a big show of forgiving us, but he never did. Even though he had affairs all the time, he couldn't bear the thought that his wife and friend had betrayed him. His family life was important to him, you see. He liked to think of himself as the perfect husband and father, and of course, it was useful for him to be seen that way. Good for business. It made people trust him."

"Gail, what did you know about your husband's business practices? Did Russ ever mention that he suspected Paul of corruption?"

"I knew that Paul could be ruthless, but I didn't know how far he was prepared to go. And, yes, it was Russ who found out." Gail's eyes darted around the room, as if Paul were about to appear suddenly. There must have been a change in her vital signs, for the nurse stepped forward again, and asked if Gail needed to rest. "No, no, no," Gail protested, fervently.

Ava realised she'd been holding her breath. She let it go.

"Russ told me he'd been concerned about what Paul was up to for some time. Paul had a lot of side projects that Russ wasn't involved with. One day, Russ saw some financial transactions on Paul's computer that made him suspicious. The amounts of money involved . . . He started making discreet enquiries. Russ suspected that Paul might be involved in money laundering."

"Did he have any proof?" Neal asked.

"He hired a private investigator," Gail said.

Ava didn't know why she felt so astonished. It was what Russ Marsh did, after all. He'd hired a PI to spy on his own daughter, hadn't he?

"And?" Neal prompted.

"He took pictures. Of Paul, meeting with people the PI recognised. In particular, a man called Tony Leavitt. He said these people were known drug dealers who'd been on the police's radar before. Can you believe it? Paul got himself so worked up over Hector being involved with drugs, yet he was deeply mired in that world himself."

"And this was what your husband and Russ really fought over that night when Russ advised Paul to watch his back?" Neal said. "It wasn't about Russ lending Hector money at all."

"I think so. I told Russ to go to the police. But he was under Paul's spell too. He said he wanted to give him a chance to explain himself."

"You gave your husband an alibi. Did you lie when you told us he was at home with you all evening?" Neal said.

"Yes. He said he'd been working at his office, but that the police would never believe him because of the fight, and because he and Russ were business partners. He asked me to lie for him. I was going to tell you but I was afraid. I needed time to think. I called and asked to speak to the police. When the two of you came around, my courage deserted me. There were the children to consider . . . These people Paul's involved with are ruthless, aren't they? They come after your family. Look at Ruth Marsh. I did try to alert you. I hoped that telling you about the fight and linking it to the business might make you look in the right direction."

Neal nodded. Ava suspected he was suppressing his anger. She was angry too. All that wasted time and energy. Not to mention resources. They could have offered Gail and her children protection.

"And Dana? How do you know it was Paul that killed her?"

"I had to do the housework myself after . . . after Dana died. I was collecting the laundry. I picked up one of Paul's jumpers, a cashmere one. A lovely shade of blue. There was a snag in the wool. I found a fragment of a false nail caught in the sleeve. Dana had been to have her nails done the night she died . . ." Gail's voice tailed off. She looked exhausted and her eyelids began to droop.

"Did you keep it?" Ava spoke over Neal, unable to contain her excitement any longer. "Mrs Cornish?"

The nurse intervened. "Her meds are kicking in, they're making her drowsy."

Ava stood up. She had another strong urge to shake Gail Cornish. Then Gail said, faintly, but just loud enough to be heard. "Yes. It's in my jewellery box."

And then she was asleep.

* * *

Neal instructed PJ to obtain a warrant to search Kingfisher Lodge. Next, he made a phone call and requested that Paul Cornish be brought in for questioning. He also contacted Val Marsh and asked for details of the private investigator Russ had hired to look into Fin O'Shea's background.

"Now for Darren Sharp." Neal and Ava strode down the corridors to the side ward where Darren was being treated. A police guard stood at the door, and Darren was handcuffed to his bed. A nurse warned them that the patient was heavily medicated and would drift in and out of sleep.

Ava found it hard to look at him. Despite his pathetic appearance — his ashen face and defeated look, the expanse of gauze across the wound on his stomach — she couldn't summon much pity for the man who had held her friend hostage, and threatened to kill Ruth Marsh and an innocent child.

This time Neal fetched the chairs and Ava took the lead.

"You're in a lot of trouble, Darren," she began.

Darren, who had only glanced at Ava and Neal when they entered the room, now acted as if they weren't there. He knew they were police even before they showed him their ID.

Neal spoke more gently. "I understand you've been informed that your brother, Liam, died of his injuries. I'm sorry for your loss, Darren."

That got a reaction. Darren swallowed hard and coughed a little. His eyes filled with tears. In spite of herself, Ava felt a glimmer of pity.

"Fin O'Shea had nothing to do with what happened to your brother," Ava said.

"No, but that cheating prick he brought to our house did." Darren looked straight ahead.

"Hector Cornish," she said. "Yeah, well, it wasn't him either. Look, Darren, we're pretty sure you and your brother were the targets of a hit. We have an idea how it came about but we can't prove it. I know you cared about your brother and that you want justice for him. You help us out here, and that might become a possibility. How did you get away? Did you see the shooter?"

"Did more than see him. I shot the fucker," Darren said. His words were slurred from the medication, but there was an unmistakeable hint of pride in his voice.

"How badly injured was he?" she asked.

He almost smiled. "Got him in the arm. He dropped his gun. I got to it first, and he ran. There was a driver waiting for him."

"Where is the gun now? What did you do with it?"

Darren shrugged. "It's safe." No doubt he'd been intending to sell it at some later date.

Ava stared at him. "Come on, Darren. Tell us where it is. You want us to find him, don't you?"

Darren's eyes began to roll back in their sockets. Ava shook his arm.

"What the . . . ?" He started awake. "I jacked a car. Drove up here. Gun's in the boot."

"Where's the car now, Darren?" Darren waved his arm. "Here."

"Here? In the hospital car park?" Darren nodded, and yawned.

Neal stood up and went to the other side of the room. He whipped out his radio and spoke into it quietly. If the car was in the car park, they'd find it soon enough.

Darren made an effort to rouse himself. "Liam?" he said, for the first time looking straight at Ava. "He wasn't dead when I left him."

"No. He survived the attack. But not for long. He spoke to the police before he died."

"Wh-what did he say?" Ava thought for a moment. Blunt had told them Liam had been rambling and incoherent. He'd mentioned Fin and Hector, probably because Darren had just got back from Stromford and informed him of the deal he'd made with Fin. She knew what Darren was fishing for. She could easily make something up. She glanced at Neal, still speaking softly into his radio, and then back at Darren, his eyes pleading for some words of comfort.

"Nothing," she said at last. "Nothing about you."

It was the truth, after all.

Chapter Twenty-one

Ava arrived just in time for the morning briefing. She sat down next to PJ, who was by Tom and Lesley Curran. Lesley had joined them for the meeting to give a report on the case that she and her team were slowly building against Paul Cornish.

"Good morning," Neal said. Like all of them, he was looking more rested than he had for days. Ava flashed him a smile. She was feeling better disposed towards him since Maggie Neal's call the previous evening. Maggie had put her in the picture about the reason for Myrna's recent visit. Neal smiled too. But he was smiling at everyone. There was a lot for everyone to smile about this morning.

Paul had been arrested and charged with the murders of Russ Marsh and Dana Schell. Gail had withdrawn her support for his alibi on the evening of Paul's murder, and he had failed to supply an appropriate alibi for the time of Dana's murder. Moreover, the forensic case against him was building.

The fragment of false nail which Gail Cornish had found clinging to Paul's jumper had been retrieved from her jewellery box. Traces of Paul's DNA were on it. Dana had tried to grab at his face in her dying moments, and clutched at his jumper, tearing off a section of her new nail. But they had more than that.

"Just to bring everyone up to speed," Neal said. "The gun used to kill Liam Sharp and injure Darren was retrieved from the stolen car. There were traces of the shooter's blood on it."

He paused, appearing to bask in his colleagues' approving nods.

"DI Blunt commented that murders committed by a hitman are hard to prove. Apprehending that hitman is even harder, and yet we've done that very thing, in a matter of days. Ironically, Darren Sharp was our unwitting accomplice. We were able to identify the man from police records. We'd expected him to disappear, but Darren's bullet hit an artery and he couldn't stop the bleeding. His driver dropped him at the nearest A&E, where he immediately set off alarm bells. By his own account, he regarded time in prison as being preferable to dying from loss of blood. Anyway, to cut to the chase, he's given us a truckload of information in the hope of obtaining a reduced sentence and police protection. We now have the means to go after not only Paul Cornish, but also the Nottingham-based drug gang he was laundering money for."

Neal glanced at Lesley, who smiled broadly. She said, "My colleagues in finance are going to have a field day thanks to your investigation."

"What I still don't understand is why Paul Cornish didn't just pay Liam the money Hector owed," PJ said. "It would have been far easier."

"Power. Ego. People like Cornish have their own moral code, not unlike that of Darren Sharp and his brother. They do things because they can," Tom said. "Believe me, people involved in the drugs business don't have room in their heads for pangs of conscience."

"I understand why he killed Russ Marsh. He had to ensure Russ didn't blow the whistle on his corruption, but why Dana Schell?" Lesley asked.

Neal attempted to provide an answer. "Dana tried to blackmail Russ over his affair with Gail. We suspect she tried it on with Paul too. She most likely told him she'd tell Gail she'd been having sex with him in return for gifts and money. Paul's pride wouldn't have allowed him to stand for that. It's also likely that Dana told Paul that Hector was dealing drugs, and wanted to be paid to keep her mouth shut about that too. Hector was already a liability to Paul. If he were prevented from taking up his position in the City because of a drugs scandal, Paul's name would also be tainted. It would be bad for business. But more than any of that, we think Paul saw the messages on Russ's mobile, and misunderstood. It's likely he thought Dana had somehow found him out in something incriminating, and was offering to give Russ information in exchange for money. It was Paul that deleted the texts on Russ's phone."

"Why didn't Paul just get rid of Dana's phone? I mean, I know he threw it into the bushes, but it was easy enough for us to find it," Lesley said.

"We think he was disturbed. When we appealed for witnesses, a couple came forward, who'd been cutting through the wood at around that time. He probably panicked, and didn't want to be found with it on his person."

Neal looked around. "Good work, everyone."

Ava noticed that PJ was looking a bit troubled. "Okay, PJ?" she asked.

"I was just thinking about Lizzie Hamilton and the Marshes."

"Ah," Ava said. She knew that Stephen Hamilton had contacted Neal the morning after the hostage incident at the hospital. Lizzie had not come home, and Stephen had been out of his mind with worry.

A little later, Neal had spoken with Laurence Brand, a suspect on a case that he and Ava had investigated some months ago. Laurence's wife worked in the café at the cathedral. He had been making his way over to meet her when he came across a woman sitting on the wall, near the west front. He would have walked on, but something about her made him pause. She was hunched over, shuddering violently.

Laurence had persuaded Lizzie Hamilton, for that is who it was, to accompany him to the café to warm up. She confessed she had been sitting outside all night. Inside, she'd told him she'd contemplated taking her own life the night before.

She'd allowed Laurence to call Stephen Hamilton.

"Lizzie's had so much tragedy to deal with in her life," PJ said.

"If you ask me, that whole family needs to go into therapy," Ava added.

"It's worse than you know," PJ said. Everyone looked at her. PJ gave a sigh. "I went round to see Val and Ruth Marsh yesterday. Remember that first time you and the DI interviewed the sisters, the morning Val discovered Russ's body?" Ava nodded, wondering what was coming next. "You sensed a tension between them. I remember reading something in your notes, Ava, about the strange sort of interplay between them. How one of them seemed dominant, then the other?"

"Yes. That was weird. They both strike me as strong women, but in each other's company they seem to be unsure of themselves."

"Well, there's a lot of history . . ."

"Are we talking about abuse?" Neal said.

That was perceptive of him, Ava thought, as PJ nodded.

"Which sister?" Tom asked.

"Val, of course," PJ said. "It was infrequent. It started when their father lost his job and began drinking. Val was fifteen. That's why she left home. Lizzie refused to believe Val at the time."

"And does she now?" Ava was appalled.

"Val thinks she does. Lizzie said something to Val about understanding why Ruth never told her about her part in Will's tragedy. She said Ruth was struck speechless by her guilt, or words to that effect. She told her sister that's how she felt about Val's accusation against their father. Speechless. Lizzie had always been the favourite. Maybe she wondered why her father hadn't chosen her. Maybe that's why he didn't choose her. Either way, Lizzie felt guilty for not protecting her younger sister. But she couldn't bring herself to talk about it."

"Let's hope they get the help they need and can start to rebuild their lives," Ava said. "This case. I think we all need a drink later, to put it to bed."

"I'll second that," Tom said.

Lesley Curran gave him a dismissive look. "Count me out. I've got a ton of work to do."

Ava saw PJ and Tom exchange a meaningful look. She'd have to ask PJ what it meant.

"So, PJ," she heard Tom say. "I hear you're into laser tag?"

"For pity's sake, Tom. Don't you think PJ's seen enough of guns to last her a lifetime?" Ava said.

"On the contrary," PJ said. "I can think of nothing I'd rather do to get this case out of my system."

"That's settled, then. I'll book a slot. This evening, six thirty. That okay with you two?" Tom asked, looking from Neal to Ava.

Neal gave a doubtful nod.

"Can't wait," Ava said. She put her two fingers together like a gun and pointed them at Neal.

As they all moved away, PJ whispered in Ava's ear, "You got him. Straight in the heart."

THE END

My thanks to Graham Bartlett, author and police procedural advisor, for his help in clarifying some legal questions.

Thank you for reading this book. If you enjoyed it please leave feedback on Amazon, and if there is anything we missed or you have a question about then please get in touch. The author and publishing team appreciate your feedback and time reading this book.

Our email is office@joffebooks.com

www.joffebooks.com

ALSO BY JANICE FROST

DEAD SECRET
DARK SECRET
HER HUSBAND'S SECRET
THEIR FATAL SECRETS
DIRTY SECRETS

Printed in Poland
by Amazon Fulfillment
Poland Sp. z o.o., Wrocław

53004907R00153